THE LOST CHILDHOOD

By Graham Greene

THE
LOST CHILDHOOD

and other essays

by

GRAHAM GREENE

1951

EYRE & SPOTTISWOODE
London

This book is printed in Great Britain for
Eyre & Spottiswoode (Publishers) Ltd.,
15 Bedford Street, London, W.C.2, by
Butler & Tanner Ltd., Frome and London

ACKNOWLEDGEMENTS

ACKNOWLEDGEMENTS are due to the following publishers for permission to reprint essays contained in this volume:

Messrs. Chatto & Windus in whose *The English Novelists* edited by Derek Verschoyle the essay 'Henry James: The Private Universe' first appeared; Messrs. Elkin Matthews in whose *Contemporary Essays, 1933* edited by Sylva Norman 'Henry James: The Religious Aspect' first appeared; Oxford University Press for whose edition in the World's Classics the introduction to *The Portrait of a Lady* was first written; Messrs. Hamish Hamilton who printed 'The Young Dickens' as an introduction to *Oliver Twist*; Messrs. Cassells in whose volume *From Anne to Victoria* edited by Bonamy Dobrée, the essay on Fielding and Sterne first appeared; Messrs. John Lane for whom 'The Burden of Childhood' was written as an introduction to Saki's stories; Messrs. Faber & Faber in whose volume *Tribute to Walter de la Mare* the essay on Walter de la Mare's short stories first appeared; Messrs. Hutchinson and Mr. Leonard Russell, compiler of *The Saturday Book* in which 'The Revolver in the Corner Cupboard' was first published.

Acknowledgements are also made to editors of the following periodicals: –

The New Statesman, The Spectator, Time & Tide, The London Mercury, Night and Day, France Libre, Horizon, The Month.

CONTENTS

Part One: PERSONAL PROLOGUE

Part Two: NOVELS AND NOVELISTS

Part Three: SOME CHARACTERS

CONTENTS

Part Four: PERSONAL POSTSCRIPT

THE LOST CHILDHOOD

Part One
PERSONAL PROLOGUE

THE LOST CHILDHOOD

PERHAPS it is only in childhood that books have any deep influence on our lives. In later life we admire, we are entertained, we may modify some views we already hold, but we are more likely to find in books merely a confirmation of what is in our minds already: as in a love affair it is our own features that we see reflected flatteringly back.

But in childhood all books are books of divination, telling us about the future, and like the fortune teller who sees a long journey in the cards or death by water they influence the future. I suppose that is why books excited us so much. What do we ever get nowadays from reading to equal the excitement and the revelation in those first fourteen years? Of course I should be interested to hear that a new novel by Mr. E. M. Forster was going to appear this spring, but I could never compare that mild expectation of civilized pleasure with the missed heartbeat, the appalled glee I felt when I found on a library shelf a novel by Rider Haggard, Percy Westerman, Captain Brereton or Stanley Weyman which I had not read before. No, it is in those early years that I would look for the crisis, the moment when life took a new slant in its journey towards death.

I remember distinctly the suddenness with which a key turned in a lock and I found I could read – not just the sentences in a reading book with the syllables coupled like railway carriages, but a real book. It was paper-covered with the picture of a boy, bound and gagged, dangling at the end of a rope inside a well with the water rising above his waist – an adventure of Dixon Brett, detective. All a long summer holiday I kept my secret, as I believed: I did not want anybody to know that I could read. I suppose I half consciously realized even then that this was the dangerous moment. I was safe so long as I could not read – the wheels had not begun to turn, but now the future stood around on bookshelves everywhere waiting for the child to choose – the life of a chartered accountant perhaps, a colonial civil servant, a planter in China, a steady job in a bank, happiness and misery, eventually one particular form of death, for surely we choose our death much as we choose our job. It grows out of our acts and our evasions, out of our fears and out of our moments of courage. I suppose my mother must have discovered my secret, for on the journey home I was presented for the train with another real book, a copy of Ballantyne's

Coral Island with only a single picture to look at, a coloured frontispiece. But I would admit nothing. All the long journey I stared at the one picture and never opened the book.

But there on the shelves at home (so many shelves for we were a large family) the books waited – one book in particular, but before I reach that one down let me take a few others at random from the shelf. Each was a crystal in which the child dreamed that he saw life moving. Here in a cover stamped dramatically in several colours was Captain Gilson's *The Pirate Aeroplane*. I must have read that book six times at least – the story of a lost civilization in the Sahara and of a villainous Yankee pirate with an aeroplane like a box kite and bombs the size of tennis balls who held the golden city to ransom. It was saved by the hero, a young subaltern who crept up to the pirate camp to put the aeroplane out of action. He was captured and watched his enemies dig his grave. He was to be shot at dawn, and to pass the time and keep his mind from uncomfortable thoughts the amiable Yankee pirate played cards with him – the mild nursery game of Kuhn Kan. The memory of that nocturnal game on the edge of life haunted me for years, until I set it to rest at last in one of my own novels with a game of poker played in remotely similar circumstances.

And here is *Sophy of Kravonia* by Anthony Hope – the story of a kitchen-maid who became a queen. One of the first films I ever saw, about 1911, was made from that book, and I can hear still the rumble of the Queen's guns crossing the high Kravonian pass beaten hollowly out on a single piano. Then there was Stanley Weyman's *The Story of Francis Cludde*, and above all other books at that time of my life *King Solomon's Mines*.

This book did not perhaps provide the crisis, but it certainly influenced the future. If it had not been for that romantic tale of Allan Quatermain, Sir Henry Curtis, Captain Good, and, above all, the ancient witch Gagool, would I at nineteen have studied the appointments list of the Colonial Office and very nearly picked on the Nigerian Navy for a career? And later, when surely I ought to have known better, the odd African fixation remained. In 1935 I found myself sick with fever on a camp bed in a Liberian native's hut with a candle going out in an empty whisky bottle and a rat moving in the shadows. Wasn't it the incurable fascination of Gagool with her bare yellow skull, the wrinkled scalp that moved and contracted like the hood of a cobra, that led me to work all through 1942 in a little stuffy office in Freetown, Sierra Leone? There is not much in common between the land of the Kukuanas, behind the desert and the mountain range of Sheba's Breast, and a tin-roofed house on a bit of swamp where the vultures moved like domestic turkeys and the pi-dogs kept me awake on moonlight nights with their wailing, and the white women yellowed by atebrin drove by to the club; but the two belonged at any rate to the same continent, and, however distantly, to the same region of the imagination – the region of uncertainty, of not knowing the way about. Once I came a little nearer to Gagool and her witch-hunters, one night in Zigita on the Liberian side of the French Guinea border, when my servants sat in their shuttered hut with their hands over their eyes and someone beat a drum and a whole town stayed behind closed doors while the big bush devil – whom it would mean blindness to see – moved between the huts.

But *King Solomon's Mines* could not finally satisfy. It was not the right answer. The key did not quite fit. Gagool I could recognize – didn't she wait for me in dreams every night in the passage by the linen cupboard, near the nursery door? and she continues to wait, when the mind is sick or tired, though now she is dressed in the theological garments of Despair and speaks in Spenser's accents:

> The longer life, I wote the greater sin,
> The greater sin, the greater punishment.

Yes, Gagool has remained a permanent part of the imagination, but Quatermain and Curtis – weren't they, even when I was only ten years old, a little too good to be true? They were men of such unyielding integrity (they would only admit to a fault in order to show how it might be overcome) that the wavering personality of a child could not rest for long against those monumental shoulders. A child, after all, knows most of the game – it is only an attitude to it that he lacks. He is quite well aware of cowardice, shame, deception, disappointment. Sir Henry Curtis perched upon a rock bleeding from a dozen wounds but fighting on with the remnant of the Greys against the hordes of Twala was too heroic. These men were like Platonic ideas: they were not life as one had already begun to know it.

But when – perhaps I was fourteen by that time – I took Miss Marjorie Bowen's *The Viper of Milan* from the library shelf, the future for better or worse really struck. From that moment I began to write. All the other possible futures slid away: the potential civil servant, the don, the clerk had to look for other incarnations. Imitation after imitation of Miss Bowen's magnificent novel went into exercise books – stories of sixteenth-century Italy or twelfth-century England marked with enormous brutality and a despairing romanticism. It was as if I had been supplied once and for all with a subject.

Why? On the surface *The Viper of Milan* is only the story of a war between Gian Galeazzo Visconti, Duke of Milan, and Mastino della Scala, Duke of Verona, told with zest and cunning and an amazing pictorial sense. Why did it creep in and colour and explain the terrible living world of the stone stairs and the never quiet dormitory? It was no good in that real world to dream that one would ever be a Sir Henry Curtis, but della Scala who at last turned from an honesty that never paid and betrayed his friends and died dishonoured and a failure even at treachery – it was easier for a child to escape behind his mask. As for Visconti, with his beauty, his patience and his genius for evil, I had watched him pass by many a time in his black Sunday suit smelling of mothballs. His name was Carter. He exercised terror from a distance like a snowcloud over the young fields. Goodness has only once found a perfect incarnation in a human body and never will again, but evil can always find a home there. Human nature is not black and white but black and grey. I read all that in *The Viper of Milan* and I looked round and I saw that it was so.

There was another theme I found there. At the end of *The Viper of Milan* – you will remember if you have once read it – comes the great scene of complete success – della Scala is dead, Ferrara, Verona, Novara, Mantua have all fallen, the messengers pour in with news of fresh victories, the whole world outside is cracking up, and Visconti sits and jokes in the wine light. I was not on the classical side or I would have discovered, I suppose, in Greek literature instead of in Miss Bowen's novel the sense of doom that lies over success – the feeling that the pendulum is about to swing. That too made sense; one looked around and saw the doomed everywhere – the champion runner who one day would sag over the tape; the head of the school who would atone, poor devil, during forty dreary undistinguished years; the scholar . . . and when success began to touch oneself too, however mildly, one could only pray that failure would not be held off for too long.

One had lived for fourteen years in a wild jungle country without a map, but now the paths had been traced and naturally one had to follow them. But I think it was Miss Bowen's apparent zest that made me want to write. One could not read her without believing that to write was to live and to enjoy, and before one had discovered one's mistake it was too late – the first book one does enjoy. Anyway she had given me my pattern – religion might later explain it to me in other terms, but the pattern was already there – perfect evil walking the world where perfect good can never walk again, and only the pendulum ensures that after all in the end justice is done. Man is never satisfied, and often I have wished that my hand had not moved further than *King Solomon's Mines*, and that the future I had taken down from the nursery shelf had been a district office in Sierra Leone and twelve tours of malarial duty and a finishing dose of blackwater fever when the danger of retirement approached. What is the good of wishing? The books are always there, the moment of crisis waits, and now our children in their turn are taking down the future and opening the pages. In his poem 'Germinal' A.E. wrote:

> In ancient shadows and twilights
> Where childhood had strayed,
> The world's great sorrows were born
> And its heroes were made.
> In the lost boyhood of Judas
> Christ was betrayed.

Part Two

NOVELS AND NOVELISTS

HENRY JAMES: THE PRIVATE UNIVERSE

THE TECHNICAL qualities of Henry James's novels have been so often and so satisfactorily explored, notably by Mr. Percy Lubbock, that perhaps I may be forgiven for ignoring James as the fully conscious craftsman in order to try to track the instinctive, the poetic writer back to the source of his fantasies. In all writers there occurs a moment of crystallization when the dominant theme is plainly expressed, when the private universe becomes visible even to the least sensitive reader. Such a crystallization is Hardy's often-quoted phrase: 'The President of the Immortals . . . had ended his sport with Tess', or that passage in his preface to *Jude the Obscure*, when he writes of 'the fret and fever, derision and disaster, that may press in the wake of the strongest passion known to humanity'. It is less easy to find such a crystallization in the works of James, whose chief aim was always to dramatize, who was more than usually careful to exclude the personal statement, but I think we may take the sentence in the scenario of *The Ivory Tower*, in which James speaks of 'the black and merciless things that are behind great possessions' as an expression of the ruling fantasy which drove him to write: a sense of evil religious in its intensity.

'Art itself', Conrad wrote, 'may be defined as a single-minded attempt to render the highest kind of justice to the visible universe', and no definition in his own prefaces better describes the object Henry James so passionately pursued, if the word visible does not exclude the private vision. If there are times when we feel, in *The Sacred Fount*, even in the exquisite *Golden Bowl*, that the judge is taking too much into consideration, that he could have passed his sentence on less evidence, we have always to admit as the long record of human corruption unrolls that he has never allowed us to lose sight of the main case; and because his mind is bent on rendering even evil 'the highest kind of justice', the symmetry of his thought lends the whole body of his work the importance of a system.

No writer has left a series of novels more of one moral piece. The differences between James's first works and his last are only differences of art as Conrad defined it. In his early work perhaps he rendered a little less than the highest kind of justice; the progress from *The American* to

The Golden Bowl is a progress from a rather crude and inexperienced symbolization of truth to truth itself: a progress from evil represented rather obviously in terms of murder to evil *in propria persona*, walking down Bond Street, charming, cultured, sensitive – evil to be distinguished from good chiefly in the complete egotism of its outlook. They are complete anarchists, these later Jamesian characters, they form the immoral background to that extraordinary period of haphazard violence which anticipated the first world war: the attempt on Greenwich Observatory, the siege of Sidney Street. They lent the tone which made possible the cruder manifestations presented by Conrad in *The Secret Agent*. Merton Densher, who planned to marry the dying Milly Theale for her money, plotting with his mistress who was her best friend; Prince Amerigo, who betrayed his wife with her friend, her father's wife; Horton, who swindled his friend Gray of his money: the last twist (it is always the friend, the intimate who betrays) is given to these studies of moral corruption. They represent an attitude which had been James's from very far back; they are not the slow painful fruit of experience. The attitude never varied from the time of *The American* onwards. Mme de Bellegarde, who murdered her husband and sold her daughter, is only the first crude presentation of a woman gradually subtilized, by way of Mme Merle in *The Portrait of a Lady*, into the incomparable figures of evil, Kate Croy and Charlotte Stant.

This point is of importance. James has been too often regarded as a novelist of superficial experience, as a painter of social types, who was cut off by exile from the deepest roots of experience (as if there were something superior in the Sussex or Shropshire of the localized talent to James's international scene). But James was not in that sense an exile; he could have dispensed with the international scene as easily as he dispensed with all the world of Wall Street finance. For the roots were not in Venice, Paris, London; they were in himself. Densher, the Prince, just as much as the redhaired valet Quint and the adulterous governess, were rooted in his own character. They were there when he wrote *The American* in 1876; all he needed afterwards to perfect his work to his own impeccable standard was technical subtlety and that other subtlety which comes from superficial observation, the ability to construct convincing masks for his own personality.

I do not use superficial in any disparaging sense. If his practice pieces, from *The Europeans* to *The Tragic Muse*, didn't engage his full powers, and were certainly not the vehicle for his most urgent fantasies, they were examples of sharp observation, the fruits of a direct objective experience, unsurpassed in their kind. He never again proved himself capable of drawing a portrait so directly, with such command of relevant detail. We know Charlotte Stant, of course, more thoroughly than we know Miss Birdseye in *The Bostonians*, but she emerges gradually through that long book, we don't 'see' her with the immediacy that we see Miss Birdseye:

> She was a little old lady with an enormous head; that was the first thing Ransom noticed – the vast, fair, protuberant, candid, ungarnished brow, surmounting a pair of weak, kind, tired-looking eyes. . . . The long practice of philanthropy had not given accent to her features; it had rubbed out their transitions, their meanings. . . . In her large countenance her dim little smile scarcely showed. It was a mere sketch of a smile, a kind of instalment, or payment on account; it seemed to say that she would smile more if she had time, but that you could see, without this, that she was gentle and easy to beguile. . . . She looked as if she had spent her life on platforms, in audiences, in conventions, in phalansteries, in seances; in her faded face there was a kind of reflexion of ugly lecture-lamps.

No writer's apprentice work contains so wide and brilliant a range of portraits from this very early Miss Birdseye to Mrs. Brookenham in *The Awkward Age*:

> Mrs. Brookenham was, in her forty-first year, still charmingly pretty, and the nearest approach she made at this moment to meeting her son's description of her was by looking beautifully desperate. She had about her the pure light of youth – would always have it; her head, her figure, her flexibility, her flickering colour, her lovely, silly eyes, her natural, quavering tone, all played together towards this effect by some trick that had never yet been exposed. It was at the same time remarkable that – at least in the bosom of her family – she rarely wore an appearance of gaiety less qualified than at the present juncture; she suggested for the most part the luxury, the novelty of woe, the excitement of strange sorrows and the cultivation of fine indifferencies. This was her special sign – an innocence dimly tragic. It gave immense effect to her other resources. . . .

The Awkward Age stands formidably between the two halves of James's achievement. It marks his decision to develop finally from *The American* rather than from *The Europeans*. It is the surrender of experience to fantasy. He hadn't found his method, but he had definitely found his theme. One may regret, in some moods, that his more superficial books had so few successors (English literature has too little that is light, lucid and witty), but one cannot be surprised that he discarded many of them from the collected edition while retaining so crude a fiction as *The American*, discarded even the delicate, feline *Washington Square*, perhaps the only novel in which a man has successfully invaded the feminine field and produced work comparable to Jane Austen's.

How could he have done otherwise if he was to be faithful to his deeper personal fantasy? He wrote of 'poor Flaubert' that

> he stopped too short. He hovered for ever at the public door, in the outer court, the splendour of which very properly beguiled him, and in which he seems still to stand as upright as a sentinel and as shapely as a statue. But that immobility and even that erectness were paid too dear. The shining arms were meant to carry further, the outer doors were meant to open. He should at least have listened at the chamber of the soul. This would have floated him on a deeper tide; above all it would have calmed his nerves.

His early novels, except *The American*, certainly belonged to the outer court. They had served their purpose, he had improved his masks, he was never to be more witty; but when he emerged from them again to take up his main study of corruption in *The Wings of the Dove* he had amazingly advanced: instead of murder, the more agonizing mental violence; instead of Mme de Bellegarde, Kate Croy; instead of the melodramatic heroine Mme de Cintré, the deeply felt, subjective study of Milly Theale.

For to render the highest justice to corruption you must retain your innocence: you have to be conscious all the time within yourself of treachery to something valuable. If Peter Quint is to be rooted in you, so must the child his ghost corrupts; if Osmond, Isabel Archer too. These centres of innocence, these objects of treachery, are nearly always women: the lovely daring Isabel Archer, who goes out in her high-handed wealthy way to meet life and falls to Osmond; Nanda, the young girl 'coming out', who is hemmed in by a vicious social set; Milly Theale, sick to death just at the time when life has most to offer, surrendering to Merton Densher and Kate Croy (apart from Quint and the Governess the most driven and 'damned' of all James's characters); Maggie Verver, the unsophisticated 'good' young American who encounters her particular corruption in the Prince and Charlotte Stant; the child Maisie tossed about among grown-up adulteries. These are the points of purity in the dark picture.

The attitude of mind which dictated these situations was a permanent one. Henry James had a marvellous facility for covering up his tracks (can we be blamed if we assume he had a reason?). In his magnificent prefaces he describes the geneses of his stories, where they were written, the method he adopted, the problems he faced: he seems, like the conjurer with rolled sleeves, to show everything. But you have to go further back than the anecdote at the dinner-table to trace the origin of such urgent fantasies. In this exploration his prefaces, even his autobiographies, offer very little help. Certainly they give his model for goodness; he is less careful to obliterate *that* trail back into youth (if one can speak of care in connexion with a design which was probably only half-conscious if it was conscious at all). His cousin, Mary Temple, was the model, a model in her deadly sickness and her high courage, above all in her hungry grip on life, for Milly Theale in particular.

> She had [James wrote of her] beyond any equally young creature I have known a sense for verity of character and play of life in others, for their acting out of their force or their weakness, whatever either might be, at no matter what cost to herself. . . . Life claimed her and used her and beset her — made her range in her groping: her naturally immature and unlighted way from end to end of the scale. . . . She was absolutely afraid of nothing she might come to by living with enough sincerity and enough wonder; and I think it is because one was to see her launched on that adventure in such bedimmed, such almost tragically compromised conditions that one is caught by her title to the heroic and pathetic mask.

Mary Temple then, whatever mask she wore, was always the point of purity, but again one must seek further if one is to trace the source of James's passionate distrust in human nature, his sense of evil. Mary Temple was experience, but that other sense, one feels, was born in him, was his inheritance.

It cannot but seem odd how little in his volumes of reminiscence, *A Small Boy and Others* and *Notes of a Son and Brother*, Henry James really touches the subject of his family. His style is at its most complex: the beauty of the books is very like the beauty of Turner's later pictures: they are all air and light: you have to look a long while into their glow before you discern the most tenuous outline of their subjects. Certainly of the two main figures, Henry James, Senior, and William James, you learn nothing of what must have been to them of painful importance: their sense of daemonic possession.

James was to draw the figure of Peter Quint with his little red whiskers and his white damned face, he was to show Densher and Kate writhing in their hopeless infernal sundering success; evil was overwhelmingly part of his visible universe; but the sense (we get no indication of it in his reminiscences) was a family sense. He shared it with his father and brother and sister. One may find the dark source of his deepest fantasy concealed in a family life which for sensitive boys must have been almost ideally free from compulsions, a tolerant cultured life led between Concord and Geneva. For nearly two years his father was intermittently attacked by a sense of 'perfectly insane and abject terror' (his own words); a damned shape seemed to squat beside him raying out 'a fetid influence'. Henry James's sister, Alice, was a prey to suicidal tendencies, and William James suffered in much the same way as his father.

> I went one evening into a dressing-room in the twilight to procure some article that was there; when suddenly there fell upon me without any warning, just as if it came out of the darkness, a horrible fear of my own existence. Simultaneously there arose in my mind the image of an epileptic patient whom I had seen in the asylum, a black-haired youth with greenish skin, entirely idiotic, who used to sit all day on one of the benches, or rather shelves against the wall, with his knees drawn up against his chin, and the coarse grey undershirt, which was his only garment, drawn over them enclosing his entire figure. . . . This image and my fear entered into a species of combination with each other. *That shape am I*, I felt potentially. Nothing that I possess can defend me against that fate, if the hour for it should strike for me as it struck for him. There was such a horror of him, and such a perception of my own merely momentary discrepancy from him, that it was as if something hitherto solid within my breast gave way entirely, and I became a mass of quivering fear. After this the universe was changed for me altogether. I awoke morning after morning with a horrible dread at the pit of my stomach, and with a sense of the insecurity of life, that I never knew before. . . . It gradually faded, but for months I was unable to go out into the dark alone.

This epileptic idiot, this urge towards death, the damned shape, are a more important background to Henry James's novels than Grosvenor House and late Victorian society. It is true that the moral anarchy of the age gave him his material, but he would not have treated it with such intensity if it had not corresponded with his private fantasy. They were materialists, his characters, but you cannot read far in Henry James's novels without realizing that their creator was not a materialist. If ever a man's imagination was clouded by the Pit, it was James's. When he touches this nerve, the fear of spiritual evil, he treats the reader with less than his usual frankness :'a fairy-tale pure and simple', something seasonable for Christmas, is a disingenuous description of *The Turn of the Screw*. One cannot avoid a conviction that here he touched and recoiled from an important inhibition.

It was just because the visible universe which he was so careful to treat with the highest kind of justice was determined for him at an early age that his family background is of such interest. There are two other odd gaps in his autobiographies; his two brothers, Wilky and Bob, play in them an infinitesimal part. To Miss Burr, the editor of Alice James's Journal, we owe most of our knowledge of these almost commonplace, almost low-brow members of a family intellectual even to excess. To Wilky 'the act of reading was inhuman and repugnant'; he wrote from his brigade, 'Tell Harry that I am waiting anxiously for his "next". I can find a large sale for any blood-and-thunder tale among the darks.' From his brigade: that was the point. It was the two failures, Wilky and Bob, who at eighteen and seventeen represented the family on the battlefields of the Civil War. William's eyesight was always bad, and Henry escaped because of an accident, the exact nature of which has always remained a mystery. One is glad, of course, that he escaped the obvious effects of war: Wilky was ruined physically, Bob nervously; both drifted in the manner of war-time heroes from farming in Florida to petty business careers in Milwaukee; and it is not improbable that the presence of these ruined heroes helped to keep Henry James out of America.

It is possible that through Wilky and Bob we can trace the source of James's main fantasy, the idea of treachery which was always attached to his sense of evil? James had not, so far as we know, been betrayed, like Monteith, like Gray, like Milly Theale and Maggie Verver and Isabel Archer, by his best friend, and it would have taken surely a very deep betrayal to explain an impulse which dictated *The American* in 1876 and *The Golden Bowl* in 1905, which attached itself to the family sense of supernatural evil and produced his great gallery of the damned. It takes some form of self-betrayal to dip so deep, and one need not go, like some of his modern critics, to a 'castration complex' to find the reason. There are psychological clues which point to James having evaded military service with insufficient excuse. A civil war is not a continental squabble; its motives are usually deeper, represent less superficial beliefs on the part of the ordinary combatant, and the James family at Concord were at the very spot where the motives of the North sounded at their noblest. His accident has an air of mystery about it (that is why some of his critics have imagined a literal castration), and one needs some explanation of his almost hysterical participation in the Great War on the side of a civilization about which he had no illusions, over whose corruption he had swapped amusing anecdotes with Alice. It will be remembered that in his magnificent study of treachery, *A Round of Visits*, Monteith's betrayer, like all the others, was a very near friend. 'To live thus with his un-removed, undestroyed, engaging, treacherous face, had been, as our traveller desired, to live with all of the felt pang.' His unremoved face, the felt pang: it is not hard to believe that James suffered from a long subconscious uneasiness about a personal failure.

This, then, was his visible universe: visible indeed if it faced him daily in his glass: the treachery of friends, the meanest kind of lies, 'the black and merciless things', as he wrote in the scenario of *The Ivory Tower*, 'that are behind great possessions'. But it is perhaps the measure of his greatness, of the wideness and justice of his view, that critics of an older generation, Mr. Desmond MacCarthy among them, have seen him primarily as a friendly, rather covetous follower of the 'best' society. The sense of evil never obsessed him, as it obsessed Dostoievsky; he never ceased to be primarily an artist, unlike those driven geniuses, Lawrence and Tolstoy, and he could always throw off from the superfluity of his talent such exquisite amiable fragments as *Daisy Miller* and *The Pension Beaurepas*: satire so gentle, even while so witty, that it has the quality of nostalgia, a looking back towards a way of life simple and unreflecting, with a kind of innocence even in its greed. 'Common she might be,' he wrote of Daisy Miller, 'yet what provision was made by that epithet for her queer little native grace.' It is in these diversions, these lovely little marginalia, that the Marxist critic, just as much as Mr. MacCarthy, finds his material. He was a social critic only when he was not a religious one. No writer was more conscious that he was at the end of a period, at the end of the society he knew. It was a revolution he quite explicitly foresaw; he spoke of

> the class, as I seemed to see it, that had had the longest and happiest innings in history . . . and for whom the future wasn't going to be, by most signs, anything like so bland and benedictory as the past. . . . I cannot say how vivid I felt the drama so preparing might become – that of the lapse of immemorial protection, that of the finally complete exposure of the immemorially protected.

But the Marxists, just as much as the older critics, are dwelling on the marginalia. Wealth may have been almost invariably connected with the treacheries he described, but so was passion. When he was floating on his fullest tide, 'listening' as he put it, 'at the chamber of the soul', the evil of capitalist society is an altogether inadequate explanation of his theme. It was not the desire for money alone which united Densher and Kate, and the author of *The Spoils of Poynton* would no more have condemned passion than the author of *The Ambassadors* would have condemned private wealth. His lot and his experience happened to lie among the great possessions, but 'the black and merciless things' were no more intrinsically part of a capitalist than of a socialist system: they belonged to human nature. They amounted really to this: an egotism so complete that you could believe that something inhuman, supernatural, was working there through the poor devils it had chosen.

In *The Jolly Corner* Bridon, the cultured American expatriate, returned to his New York home and found it haunted. He hunted the ghost down. It was afraid of him (the origin of that twist is known to us. In *A Small Boy* James has described the childish dream he built his story on). He drove it to bay in its evening dress under the skylight in the hall, discovered in the 'evil, odious, blatant, vulgar' features the reflection of himself. This was what he would have been if he had stayed and joined the Wall Street racket and prospered. It is easy to take the mere social criticism implied, but I have yet to find socialist or conservative who can feel any pity for the evil *he* denounces, and the final beauty of James's stories lies in their pity: 'The poetry is in the pity.' His egotists, poor souls, are as pitiable as Lucifer. The woman Bridon loved had also seen the ghost; he had not appeared less blatant, less vulgar to her with his ruined sight and maimed hand and million a year, but the emotion she chiefly felt was pity.

'He has been unhappy, he has been ravaged,' she said.
'And haven't I been unhappy? Am not I – you've only to look at me! – ravaged?'
'Ah, I don't say I like him *better*,' she granted after a thought. 'But he's grim, he's worn – and things have happened to him. He doesn't make shift, for sight, with your charming monocle.'

James wasn't a prophet, he hadn't a didactic purpose; he wished only to render the highest kind of justice, and you cannot render the highest kind of justice if you hate. He was a realist: he had to show the triumphs of egotism; he was a realist: he had to show that a damned soul has its chains. Milly Theale, Maggie Verver, these 'good' people had their escapes, they were lucky in that they loved, could sacrifice themselves like Wilky and Bob, they were never quite alone on the bench of desolation. But the egotists had no escape, there was no tenderness in their passion and their pursuit of money was often no more than an interest, a hobby: they were, inescapably, themselves. Kate and Merton Densher get the money for which they'd schemed; they don't get each other. Charlotte Stant and the Prince satisfy their passion at the expense of a lifetime of separation.

This is not 'poetic justice'; it was not as a moralist that James designed his stories, but as a realist. His family background, his personal failure, determined his view of the visible universe when he first began to write, and there was nothing in the society of his time to make him reconsider his view. He had always been strictly just to the truth as he saw it, and all that his deepening experience had done for him was to alter a murder to an adultery, but while in *The American* he had not pitied the murderer, in *The Golden Bowl* he had certainly learned to pity the adulterers. There was no victory for human beings, that was his conclusion; you were punished in your own way, whether you were of God's or the Devil's party. James believed in the supernatural, but he saw evil as an equal force with good. Humanity was cannon fodder in a war too balanced ever to be concluded. If he had been guilty himself of the supreme egotism of preserving his own existence, he left the material, in his profound unsparing analysis, for rendering even egotism the highest kind of justice, of giving the devil his due.

> It brought Spencer Brydon to his feet. 'You "like" that horror –?'
> 'I *could* have liked him. And to me,' she said, 'he was no horror, I had accepted him.'

'I had accepted him.' James, who had never taken a great interest in his father's Swedenborgianism, had gathered enough to strengthen his own older more traditional heresy. For his father believed, in his own words, that 'the evil or hellish element in our nature, even when out of divine order . . . is yet not only no less vigorous than the latter, but on the contrary much more vigorous, sagacious and productive of eminent earthly uses' (so one might describe the acquisition of Milly Theale's money). The difference, of course, was greater than the resemblance. The son was not an optimist, he didn't share his father's hopes of the hellish element, he only pitied those who were immersed in it; and it is in the final justice of his pity, the completeness of an analysis which enabled him to pity the most shabby, the most corrupt, of his human actors, that he ranks with the greatest of creative writers. He is as solitary in the history of the novel as Shakespeare in the history of poetry.

HENRY JAMES: THE RELIGIOUS ASPECT

IT IS possible for an author's friends to know him too well. His books are hidden behind the façade of his public life, and his friends remember his conversations when they have forgotten his characters. It is a situation which by its irony appealed to Henry James. At the time of his own siege of London, he took note of Robert Browning, the veteran victor seen at every dinner table.

> I have never ceased to ask myself [James wrote], in this particular loud, sound, normal hearty presence, all so assertive and so whole, all bristling with prompt responses and expected opinions and usual views . . . I never ceased, I say, to ask myself what lodgement, on such premises, the rich proud genius one adored could ever have contrived, what domestic commerce the subtlety that was its prime ornament and the world's wonder have enjoyed, under what shelter the obscurity that was its luckless drawback and the world's despair have flourished.

It is a double irony that James himself should have so disappeared behind the public life. There are times when those who met him at Grosvenor House, those who dined with him at Chelsea, even the favoured few who visited him at Rye, seem, while they have remembered his presence (that great bald brow, those soothing and reassuring gestures) and the curiosity of his conversation (the voice ponderously refining and refining on his meaning), to have forgotten his books. This, at any rate, is a possible explanation of Mr. MacCarthy's statement in a delightful and deceptive essay on *The World of Henry James*: 'The universe and religion are as completely excluded from his books as if he had been an eighteenth-century writer. The sky above his people, the earth beneath them, contain no mysteries for them', and in the same essay that the religious sense 'is singularly absent from his work'.

It would indeed be singular if the religious sense were absent. Consider the father, the son of a Presbyterian and intended for the ministry, who travelling in England was possessed (during a nervous disorder) by the teaching of Swedenborg and devoted the rest of his life to writing theological books which no one read. His inspiration was the same as William Blake's and it was not less strong because its expression was chilled within the icy limits of Boston. It is difficult to believe that a child brought up by Henry James senior did not inherit a few of his father's perplexities if not his beliefs. Certainly he inherited a suspicion of organized religion, although that suspicion conflicted with his deepest instinct, his passion for Europe and tradition.

It is a platitude that in all his novels one is aware of James's deep love of age; not one generation had tended the lawns of his country houses, but centuries of taste had smoothed the grass and weathered the stone, 'the warm, weary brickwork'. This love of age and tradition, even without his love of Italy, was enough to draw him towards the Catholic Church as, in his own words, 'the most impressive convention in all history'. As early as 1869, in a letter from Rome, he noted its aesthetic appeal.

> In St. Peter's I stayed some time. It's even beyond its reputation. It was filled with foreign ecclesiastics – great armies encamped in prayer on the marble plains of its pavement – an inexhaustible physiognomical study. To crown my day, on my way home, I met his Holiness in person – driving in prodigious purple state – sitting dim within the shadows of his coach with two uplifted benedictory fingers – like some dusky Hindoo idol in the depths of its shrine. . . . From the high tribune of a great chapel of St. Peter's I have heard in the Papal choir a strange old man sing in a shrill unpleasant soprano. I've seen troops of little tortured neophytes clad in scarlet, marching and counter-marching and ducking and flopping, like poor little raw recruits for the heavenly host.

But no one can long fail to discover how superficial is the purely aesthetic appeal of Catholicism; it is more accidental than the closeness of turf. The pageantry may be well done and excite the cultured visitor or it may be ill done and repel him. The Catholic Church has never hesitated to indulge in the lowest forms of popular 'art'; it has never used beauty for the sake of beauty. Any little junk shop of statues and holy pictures beside a cathedral is an example of what I mean. 'The Catholic Church, as churches go to-day,' James wrote in *A Little Tour in France*, 'is certainly the most spectacular; but it must feel that it has a great fund of impressiveness to draw upon when it opens such sordid little shops of sanctity as this.' If it had been true that Henry James had no religious sense and that Catholicism spoke only to his aesthetic sense, Catholicism and Henry James at this point would finally have parted company; or if his religious sense had been sufficiently vague and 'numinous', he would then surely have approached the Anglican Church to discover whether he could find there satisfaction for the sense of awe and reverence, whether he could build within it his system of 'make-believe'. If the Anglican Church did not offer to his love of age so unbroken a tradition, it offered to an Englishman or an American a purer literary appeal.

Crashaw's style, if it occasionally has the beauty of those 'marble plains', is more often the poetical equivalent of the shop for holy statues; it has neither the purity nor the emotional integrity of Herbert's and Vaughan's; nor as literature can the Douai Bible be compared with the Authorized Version. And yet the Anglican Church never gained the least hold on James's interest, while the Catholic Church seems to have retained its appeal to the end. He never even felt the possibility of choice; it was membership of the Catholic Church or nothing. Rowland Mallet wondered 'whether it be that one tacitly concedes to the Roman Church the monopoly of a guarantee of immortality, so that if one is indisposed to bargain with her for the precious gift one must do without it altogether'.

In James's first novel, *Roderick Hudson*, published in 1875, six years after his first sight of the high tribune and the tortured neophytes, the hero 'pushed into St. Peter's, in whose vast clear element the hardest particles of thought ever infallibly entered into solution. From a heartache to a Roman rain there were few contrarieties the great church did not help him to forget.' The same emotion was later expressed in novel after novel. In times of mental weariness, at moments of crisis, his characters inevitably find their way into some dim nave, to some lit altar; Merton Densher, haunted by his own treachery, enters the Brompton Oratory, 'on the edge of a splendid service – the flocking crowd told of it – which glittered and resounded, from distant depths, in the blaze of altar lights and the swell of organ and choir. It didn't match his own day, but it was much less of a discord than some other things actual and possible.'

It is a rather lukewarm tribute to a religious system, but Strether in *The Ambassadors*, published in 1903, enters Notre-Dame for a more significant purpose.

> He was aware of having no errand in such a place but the desire not to be, for the hour, in certain other places; a sense of safety, of simplification, which each time he yielded to it he amused himself by thinking of as a private concession to cowardice. The great church had no altar for his worship, no direct voice for his soul; but it was none the less soothing even to sanctity; for he could feel while there what he couldn't elsewhere, that he was a plain tired man taking the holiday he had earned. He was tired, but he wasn't plain – that was the pity and the trouble of it; he was able, however, to drop his problem at the door very much as if it had been the copper piece that he deposited, on the threshold, in the receptacle of the inveterate blind beggar. He trod the long dim nave, sat in the splendid choir, paused before the clustered chapels of the east end, and the mighty monument laid upon him its spell. . . . This form of sacrifice did at any rate for the occasion as well as another; it made him quite sufficiently understand how, within the precinct,

c

for the real refugee, the things of the world could fall into abeyance. That was the cowardice, probably – to dodge them, to beg the question, not to deal with it in the hard outer light; but his own oblivions were too brief, too vain, to hurt anyone but himself, and he had a vague and fanciful kindness for certain persons whom he met, figures of mystery and anxiety, and whom, with observation for his pastime, he ranked with those who were fleeing from justice. Justice was outside, in the hard light, and injustice too; but one was as absent as the other from the air of the long aisles and the brightness of the many altars.

It is worth noting, in connexion with Mr. MacCarthy's criticism, that this was not Strether's first visit to Notre-Dame:

he had lately made the pilgrimage more than once by himself – had quite stolen off, taking an unnoticed chance and making no point of speaking of the adventure when restored to his friends.

In 1875, Rowland Mallet found in St. Peter's relief for most contrarieties 'from a heartache to a Roman rain'; in 1903 Strether found in Notre-Dame 'a sense of safety, of simplification'; the difference is remarkably small, and almost equally small the difference between Strether's feelings and those of the 'real refugee', whom he watches 'from a respectable distance, remarking some note of behaviour, of penitence, of prostration, of the absolved, relieved state'. Strether wondered whether the attitude of a woman who sat without praying 'were some congruous fruit of absolution, of "indulgence". He knew but dimly what indulgence, in such a place, might mean; yet he had, as with a soft sweep, a vision of how it might indeed add to the zest of active rights.' It would have been a more astonishing avowal if Strether's knowledge had been less dim, and it must be admitted that the vagueness of James's knowledge, which led him sometimes ludicrously astray, may have contributed to the emotional appeal.

But it would be unfair to attribute this constant intrusion of the Catholic Church merely to the unreasoning emotions. There were dogmas in Catholic teaching, avoided by the Anglican Church, which attracted James, and one of these dealt with prayers for the dead.

Mr. MacCarthy mentions James's horror of 'the brutality and rushing confusion of the world, where the dead are forgotten', and James himself, trying to trace the genesis of that beautiful and ridiculous story *The Altar of the Dead*, came to the conclusion that the idea embodied in it 'had always, or from ever so far back, been there'. This is not to say that he was conscious of how fully Catholic teaching might have satisfied his desire not merely to commemorate but to share life with the dead.

Commemoration – there is as much acreage of marble monuments in the London churches as any man can need; James wanted something more living, something symbolized in his mind, in the story to which I refer, by candles on an altar. It was not exactly prayer, but how close it was to prayer, how near James was to believing that the dead have need of prayer, may be seen in the case of George Stransom.

He had not had more losses than most men, but he had counted his losses more; he hadn't seen death more closely, but had in a manner felt it more deeply. He had formed little by little the habit of numbering his Dead: it had come to him early in life that there was something one had to do for them. They were there in their simplified intensified essence, their conscious absence and expressive patience, as personally there as if they had only been stricken dumb. When all sense of them failed, all sound of them ceased, it was as if their purgatory were really still on earth: they asked so little that they got, poor things, even less, and died again, died every day, of the hard usage of life. They had no organized service, no reserved place, no honour, no shelter, no safety.

The Altar of the Dead I have called ridiculous as well as beautiful, and it is ridiculous because James never understood that his desire to help the dead was not a personal passion, that it did not require secret subjective rites. Haunted by this idea of the neglected dead, 'the general black truth that London was a terrible place to die in', by the phrase of his foreign friend, as they watched a funeral train 'bound merrily by' on its way to Kensal Green, 'Mourir à Londres, c'est être bien mort', James was literally driven into a church. Stransom leaves the grey foggy afternoon for 'a temple of the old persuasion, and there had evidently been a function – perhaps a service for the dead; the high altar was still a blaze of candles. This was an exhibition he always liked, and he dropped into a seat with relief. More than it had ever yet come home to him it struck him as good there should be churches.' This one might expect to be the end of Stransom's search. He had only to kneel, to pray, to remember. But again the subjective beauty of the story is caricatured by the objective action. Stransom buys an altar for one of the chapels: 'the altar and the sacred shell that half encircled it, consecrated to an ostensible and customary worship, were to be splendidly maintained; all that Stransom reserved to himself was the number of his lights and the free enjoyment of his intentions.' Surely no one so near in spirit, at any rate in this one particular, to the Catholic Church was ever so ignorant of its rules. How was it that a writer as careful as James to secure the fullest authenticity for his subjects could mar in this way one of his most important stories? It cannot be said that he had not the time to study Catholicism: there was no limit to the time which James would devote to anything remotely connected with his art. Was it perhaps that the son of the old Swedenborgian was afraid of capture? A friend of James once spoke to him of a lady who had been converted to Catholicism. James was silent for a long while; then he remarked that he envied her.

The second point which may have attracted James to the Church was its treatment of supernatural evil. The Anglican Church had almost relinquished Hell. It smoked and burned on Sundays only in obscure provincial pulpits, but no day passed in a Catholic Church without prayers for deliverance from evil spirits 'wandering through the world for the ruin of souls'. This savage elementary belief found an echo in James's sophisticated mind, to which the evil of the world was very present. He faced it in his work with a religious intensity. The man was sensitive, a lover of privacy, but it is absurd for Mr. MacCarthy to picture the writer 'flying with frightened eyes and stopped ears from that City of Destruction till the terrified bang of his sanctuary door leaves him palpitating but safe'.

If he fled from London to Rye, it was the better to turn at bay. This imaginary world, which according to Mr. MacCarthy he created, peopled with 'beings who had leisure and the finest faculties for comprehending and appreciating each other, where the reward of goodness was the recognition of its beauty', comes not from James's imagination but from Mr. MacCarthy's; the world of Henry James's novels is a world of treachery and deceit, of Gilbert Osmond and Mme Merle, of Kate Croy and Merton Densher, of Catherine Stant and the Prince, of Bloodgood, of Mme de Vionnet; a realist's world in which Osmond is victorious, Isabel Archer defeated, Densher gains his end and Milly Theale dies disillusioned. The novels are only saved from the deepest cynicism by the religious sense; the struggle between the beautiful and the treacherous is lent, as in Hardy's novels, the importance of the supernatural, human nature is not despicable in Osmond or Densher, for they are both capable of damnation. 'It is true to say', Mr. Eliot has written in an essay on Baudelaire, 'that the glory of man is his capacity for salvation; it is also true to say that his glory is his capacity for damnation. The worst that can be said of most of our malefactors, from statesmen to thieves, is that they are not men enough to be damned.' This worst cannot be said of James's characters: both Densher and the Prince have on their faces the flush of the flames.

One remembers in this context the poor damned ghost of Brydon's other self, Brydon, the American expatriate and cultured failure, who returns after many years and in his New York house becomes aware of another presence, the self he might have been, unhappy and ravaged with a million a year and ruined sight and crippled hand. Through the great house he hunts the ghost, until it turns at bay under the fanlight in the entrance hall.

> Rigid and conscious, spectral yet human, a man of his own substance and stature waited there to measure himself with his power to dismay. This only could it be – this only till he recognized, with his advance, that what made the face dim was the pair of raised hands that covered it and in which, so far from being offered in defiance, it was buried as for dark deprecation. So Brydon, before him, took him in; with every fact of him now, in the higher light, hard and acute – his planted stillness, his vivid truth, his grizzled bent head and white masking hands, his queer actuality of evening dress, of dangling double eyeglass, of gleaming silk lappet and white linen, of pearl button and gold watchguard and polished shoe. . . . He could but gape at his other self in this other anguish, gape as a proof that *he*, standing there for the achieved, the enjoyed, the triumphant life, couldn't be faced in his triumph. Wasn't the proof in the splendid covering hands, strong and completely spread? – so spread and so intentional that, in spite of a special verity that surpassed every other, the fact that one of these hands had lost two fingers which were reduced to stumps, as if accidentally shot away, the face was effectually guarded and saved.

When the hands drop they disclose a face of horror, evil, odious, blatant, vulgar, and as the ghost advances, Brydon falls back 'as under the hot breath and the roused passion of a life larger than his own, a rage of personality before which his own collapsed'.

The story has been quoted by an American critic as an example of the fascination and repulsion James felt for his country. The idea that he should have stayed and faced his native scene never left him; he never ceased to wonder whether he had not cut himself off from the source of deepest inspiration. This the story reveals on one level of consciousness; on a deeper level it is not too fanciful to see in it an expression of faith in man's ability to damn himself. A rage of personality – it is a quality of the religious sense, a spiritual quality which the materialist writer can never convey, not even Dickens, by the most adept use of exaggeration.

It is tempting to reinforce this point – James's belief in supernatural evil – with *The Turn of the Screw*. Here in the two evil spirits – Peter Quint, the dead valet, with his ginger hair and his little whiskers and his air of an actor and 'his white face of damnation', and Miss Jessel 'dark as midnight in her black dress, her haggard beauty and her unutterable woe' – is the explicit breath of Hell. They declare themselves in every attitude and glance, with everything but voice, to be suffering the torments of the damned, the torments which they intend the two children to share. It is tempting to point to the scene of Miles's confession, which frees him from the possession of Peter Quint. But James himself has uttered too clear a warning. The story is, in his own words, 'a fairy-tale pure and simple', something seasonable for Christmas, 'a piece of ingenuity pure and simple, of cold artistic calculation, an amusette to catch those not easily caught . . . the jaded, the disillusioned, the fastidious'. So a valuable ally must be relinquished, not without a mental reservation that no one by mere calculation could have made the situation so 'reek with the air of Evil' and amazement that such a story should have been thought seasonable for Christmas.

Hell and Purgatory, James came very close to a direct statement of his belief in both of these. What personal experience of treachery and death stood between the actor of *Washington Square* and *The Bostonians* and the author of *The Wings of a Dove* and *The Golden Bowl* is not known. The younger author might have developed into the gentle, urbane social critic of Mr. MacCarthy's imagination, the latter writer is only just prevented from being as explicitly religious as Dostoievsky by the fact that neither a philosophy nor a creed ever emerged from his religious sense. His religion was always a mirror of his experience. Experience taught him to believe in supernatural evil, but not in supernatural good. Milly Theale is all human; her courage has not the supernatural support which holds Kate Croy and Catherine Stant in a strong coil. The rage of personality is all the devil's. The good and the beautiful meet betrayal with patience and forgiveness, but without sublimity, and their death is at best a guarantee of no more pain. Ralph Touchett dying at Gardencourt only offers himself the consolation that pain is passing. 'I don't know why we should suffer so much. Perhaps I shall find out.'

It would be wrong to leave the impression that James's religious sense ever brought him nearer than hailing distance to an organized system, even to a system organized by himself. The organizing ability exhausted itself in his father and elder brother. James never tried to state a philosophy and this reluctance to trespass outside his art may have led Mr. MacCarthy astray. But no one, with the example of Hardy before them, can deny that James was right. The novelist depends preponderantly on his personal experience, the philosopher on correlating the experience of others, and the novelist's philosophy will always be a little lop-sided. There is much in common between the pessimism of Hardy and of James; both had a stronger belief in supernatural evil than in supernatural good, and if James had, like Hardy, tried to systematize his ideas, his novels too would have lurched with the same one-sided gait. They retain their beautiful symmetry at a price, the price which Turgenev paid and Dostoievsky refused to pay, the price of refraining from adding to the novelist's distinction that of a philosopher or a religious teacher of the second rank.

THE PORTRAIT OF A LADY

THE CONCEPTION of a certain young lady affronting her destiny' – that is how Henry James described the subject of this book, for which he felt, next to *The Ambassadors*, the greatest personal tenderness. In his wonderful preface (for no other book in the collected edition of his works did he write a preface so rich in revelations and memories) he compares *The Portrait of a Lady* several times to a building, and it is as a great, leisurely built cathedral that one thinks of it, with immense smooth pillars, side-chapels, and aisles, and a dark crypt where Ralph Touchett lies in marble like a crusader with his feet crossed to show that he has seen the Holy Land; sometimes, indeed, it may seem to us too ample a shrine for one portrait until we remember that this master-craftsman always has his reasons: those huge pillars are required to bear the weight of Time (that dark backward and abysm that is the novelist's abiding problem): the succession of side-chapels are all designed to cast their particular light upon the high altar: no vista is without its ambiguous purpose. The whole building, indeed, is a triumph of architectural planning: the prentice hand which had already produced some works – *Roderick Hudson* and *The American* – impressive if clumsy, and others – *The Europeans* and *Washington Square* – graceful if slight, had at last learnt the whole secret of planning for permanence. And the subject? 'A certain young woman affronting her destiny.' Does it perhaps still, at first thought, seem a little inadequate?

The answer, of course, is that it all depends on the destiny, and about the destiny Henry James has in his preface nothing to tell us. He is always something of a conjurer in these prefaces: he seems ready to disclose everything – the source of his story: the technique of its writing: even the room in which he settles down to work and the noises of the street outside. Sometimes he blinds the reader with a bold sleight of hand, calling, for example, *The Turn of the Screw* 'a fairy-tale pure and simple'. We must always remain on our guard while reading these prefaces, for at a certain level no writer has really disclosed less.

The plot in the case of this novel is far from being an original one: it is as if James, looking round for the events which were to bring his young woman, Isabel Archer, into play, had taken the first to hand: a fortune-hunter, the fortune-hunter's unscrupulous mistress, and a young American heiress caught in the meshes of a loveless marriage. (He was to use almost identically the same plot but with deeper implications and more elaborate undertones in *The Wings of the Dove*.) We can almost see the young James laying down some popular three-decker of the period in his Roman or Venetian lodgings and wondering. 'What could I do with even that story?' For a plot after all is only the machinery – the machinery which will show the young woman (what young woman?) affronting her destiny (but what destiny?). In his preface, apparently so revealing, James has no answer to these questions. Nor is there anything there which will help us to guess what element it was in the melodramatic plot that attracted the young writer at this moment when he came first into his full powers as a novelist, and again years later when as an old man he set to work to crown his career with the three poetic masterpieces, *The Wings of the Dove*, *The Ambassadors*, and *The Golden Bowl*.

The first question is the least important and we have the answer in Isabel Archer's relationship to Milly Theale in *The Wings of the Dove*: it is not only their predicament which is the same, or nearly so (Milly's fortune-hunter, Merton Densher, was enriched by the later James with a conscience, a depth of character, a dignity in his corruption that Gilbert Osmond lacks: indeed in the later book it is the fortune-hunter who steals the tragedy, for Milly dies and it is the living whom we pity): the two women are identical. Milly Theale, if it had not been for her fatal sickness, would have affronted the same destiny and met the same fate as Isabel Archer: the courage, the generosity, the confidence, and inexperience belong to the same character, and James has disclosed to us the source of the later portrait – his young and much-loved cousin Mary Temple who died of tuberculosis at twenty-four. This girl of infinite potentiality, whose gay sad troubled letters can be read in *Notes of a Son and Brother*, haunted his memory like a legend; it was as if her image stood for everything that had been graceful, charming, happy in youth – 'the whole world of the old New York, that of the earlier dancing years' – everything that was to be betrayed by life. We have only to compare these pages of his autobiography, full of air and space and light, in which the figures of the son and brother, the Albany uncles, the beloved cousin, move like the pastoral figures in a Poussin landscape, with his description of America when he revisited the States in his middle age, to see how far he had travelled, how life had closed in. In his fiction he travelled even farther. In his magnificent last short story, *The Jolly Corner*, Brydon, the returned expatriate, finds his old New York house haunted by the ghost of himself, the self he would have become if he had remained in America. The vision is pursued by the unwitting Brydon from room to room until finally it is brought to bay under the fanlight in the hall and presents a face 'evil, odious, blatant, vulgar'. At that moment one remembers what James also remembered: 'the springtime of '65 as it breathed through Denton streets', the summer twilight sailing back from Newport, Mary Temple.

> In none of the company was the note so clear as in this rarest, though at the same time symptomatically or ominously palest, flower of the stem; who was natural at more points and about more things, with a greater sense of freedom and ease and reach of horizon than any of the others dreamed of. They had that way, delightfully, with the small, after all, and the common matters – while she had it with those too, but with the great and rare ones over and above; so that she was to remain for us the very figure and image of a felt interest in life, an interest as magnanimously farspread, or as familiarly and exquisitely fixed, as her splendid shifting sensibility, moral, personal, nervous, and having at once such noble flights and such touchingly discouraged drops, such graces of indifference and inconsequence, might at any moment determine. She was really to remain, for our appreciation, the supreme case of a taste for life as life, as personal living; of an endlessly active and yet somehow a careless, an illusionless, a sublimely forewarned curiosity about it: something that made her, slim and fair and quick, all straightness and charming tossed head, with long light and yet almost sliding steps and a large light postponing, renouncing laugh, the very muse or amateur priestess of rash speculation.

Even if we had not James's own word for it, we could never doubt that here is the source: the fork of his imagination was struck and went on sounding. Mary Temple, of course, never affronted her destiny: she was betrayed quite simply by her body, and James uses words of her that he could as well have used of Milly Theale dying in her Venetian palace – 'death at the last was dreadful to her; she would have given anything to live', but isn't it significant that whenever an imaginary future is conceived for this brave spontaneous young woman it always ends in betrayal? Milly Theale escapes from her betrayal simply by dying; Isabel Archer, tied for life to Gilbert Osmond – that precious vulgarian, cold as a fishmonger's slab – is deserted even by her creator. For how are we to understand the ambiguity of the closing pages when Isabel's friend, Henrietta Stackpole, tries to comfort the faithful and despairing 'follower' (this word surely best describes Caspar Goodwood's relationship to Isabel)?

'Look here, Mr. Goodwood,' she said, 'just you wait!'

On which he looked up at her – but only to guess, from her face, with a revulsion, that she simply meant he was young. She stood shining at him with that cheap comfort, and it added, on the spot, thirty years to his life. She walked him away with her, however, as if she had given him now the key to patience.

It is as if James, too, were handing his more casual readers the key to patience, while at the same time asserting between the lines that there is no way out of the inevitable betrayal except the way that Milly Theale and Mary Temple took involuntarily. There is no possibility of a happy ending: this is surely what James always tells us, not with the despairing larger-than-life gesture of a romantic novelist but with a kind of bitter precision. He presents us with a theorem, but it is we who have to work out the meaning of x and discover that x equals no-way-out. It is part of the permanent fascination of his style that he never does all the work for us, and there will always be careless mathematicians prepared to argue the meaning of that other ambiguous ending, when Merton Densher, having gained a fortune with Milly Theale's death, is left alone with his mistress, Kate Croy, who had planned it all, just as Mme Merle had planned Isabel's betrayal.

> He heard her out in stillness, watching her face but not moving. Then he only said: 'I'll marry you, mind you, in an hour.'
> 'As we were?'
> 'As we were.'
> But she turned to the door, and her headshake was now the end. 'We shall never be again as we were!'

Some of James's critics have preferred to ignore the real destiny of his characters, and they can produce many of his false revealing statements to support them; he has been multitudinously discussed as a social novelist primarily concerned with the international scene, with the impact of the Old World on the New. It is true the innocent figure is nearly always American (Roderick Hudson, Newman, Isabel and Milly, Maggie Verver and her father), but the corrupted characters – the vehicles for a sense of evil unsurpassed by the theological novelists of our day, M. Mauriac or M. Bernanos – are also American: Mme Merle, Gilbert Osmond, Kate Croy, Merton Densher, Charlotte Stant. His characters are mainly American, simply because James himself was American.

No, it was only on the superficial level of plot, one feels, that James was interested in the American visitor; what deeply interested him, what was indeed his ruling passion, was the idea of treachery, the 'Judas complex'. In a very early novel which he never reprinted, *Watch and Ward*, James dealt with the blackmailer, the man enabled to betray because of his intimate knowledge. As he proceeded in his career he shed the more obvious melodramatic trappings of betrayal, and in *The Portrait of a Lady*, melodrama is at the point of vanishing. What was to follow was only to be the turning of the screw. Isabel Archer was betrayed by little more than an acquaintance; Milly Theale by her dearest friend; until we reach the complicated culmination of treacheries in *The Golden Bowl*. But how many turns and twists of betrayal we could follow, had we space and time, between *Watch and Ward* and that grand climax!

This then is the destiny that not only the young women affront – you must betray or, more fortunately perhaps, you must be betrayed. A few – James himself, Ralph Touchett in this novel, Mrs. Assingham in *The Golden Bowl* – will simply sadly watch. We shall never know what it was at the very start of life that so deeply impressed on the young James's mind this sense of treachery; but when we remember how patiently and faithfully throughout his life he drew the portrait of one young woman who died, one wonders whether it was just simply a death that opened his eyes to the inherent disappointment of existence, the betrayal of hope. The eyes once open, the material need never fail him. He could sit there, an ageing honoured man in Lamb House, Rye, and hear the footsteps of the traitors and their victims going endlessly by on the pavement. It is of James himself that we think when we read in *The Portrait of a Lady* of Ralph Touchett's melancholy vigil in the big house in Winchester Square:

> The square was still, the house was still; when he raised one of the windows of the dining-room to let in the air he heard the slow creak of the boots of a lone constable. His own step, in the empty place, seemed loud and sonorous; some of the carpets had been raised, and whenever he moved he roused a melancholy echo. He sat down in one of the armchairs; the big dark dining table twinkled here and there in the small candle-light; the pictures on the wall, all of them very brown, looked vague and incoherent. There was a ghostly presence as of dinners long since digested, of table-talk that had lost its actuality. This hint of the supernatural perhaps had something to do with the fact that his imagination took a flight and that he remained in his chair a long time beyond the hour at which he should have been in bed; doing nothing not even reading the evening paper. I say he did nothing, and I maintain the phrase in the face of the fact that he thought at these moments of Isabel.

THE PLAYS OF HENRY JAMES

THERE had always been – let us face it – a suspicion of vulgarity about the Old Master. Just as the tiny colloquialism was sometimes hidden unnoticeably away in the intricate convolutions of his sentences, so one was sometimes fleetingly aware of small clouds – difficult to detach in the bland wide sunlit air of his later world – of something closely akin to the vulgar. Was it sometimes his aesthetic approach to the human problem, his use of the word 'beautiful' in connexion with an emotional situation? Was it sometimes a touch of aesthetic exclusiveness as in the reference to Poynton and its treasures, 'there were places much grander and richer, but no such complete work of art, nothing that would appeal so to those really informed'? Was it sometimes a hidden craving for the mere treasures themselves, for the cash value? We must do James justice. He would not have altered a sentence of a novel or a story for the sake of popularity or monetary reward, but the craving was there, disguised by references to financial problems that did not really exist – his private income was adequate, even comfortable. But if only, it surely occurred to him, there were some literary Tom Tiddler's ground he could enter as a stranger where he could not be compromised if observed in the act of stooping to pick up the gold and silver; in that case he was ready for a while to put integrity in the drawer and turn the key. Fate was kind to him: other artists have had the same intention and have been caught by success. James found neither cash nor credit on the stage and returned enriched by his failure.

Of course it would be wrong to suggest that the appeal of the theatre to James was purely commercial. He was challenged, as any artist, by a new method of expression; the pride and interest in attempting the difficult and the new possessed him. He wrote to his brother:

> I feel at last as if I had found my real form, which I am capable of carrying far, and for which the pale little art of fiction, as I have practised it, has been, for me, but a limited and restricted substitute. The strange thing is that I always, universally, knew *this* was my more characteristic form – but was kept away from it by a half-modest, half-exaggerated sense of the difficulty (that is, I mean the practical odiousness) of the conditions. But now that I have accepted them and met them, I see that one isn't at all, needfully, their victim, but is, from the moment one *is* anything, one's self, worth speaking

of, their *master*: and may use them, command them, squeeze them, lift them up and better them. As for the form *itself*, its honour and inspiration are (à defaut d'autres) in its difficulty. If it were easy to write a good play I couldn't and wouldn't think of it; but it is in fact damnably hard (to this truth the paucity of the article – in the English-speaking world – testifies), and that constitutes a solid respectability – guarantees one's *intellectual* self-respect.

But even in this mood is not the self-respect a little too underlined, the protest purposely loud to drown another note, which was to be repeated again and again? 'I am very impatient to get to work writing for the stage – a project I have long had. I am . . . certain I should succeed and it would be an open gate to money making,' and later he turned with some ignobility on Wilde, when *The Importance of Being Earnest* had followed his own catastrophic failure *Guy Domville* at the St. James's Theatre: 'There is nothing fortunately so dead as a dead play – unless it be sometimes a living one. Oscar Wilde's farce . . . is, I believe, a great success – and with his two roaring successes running now at once he must be raking in the profits.' The ring of the counter is in the phrase.

Until Mr. Edel published this huge volume* (over 800 pages, the greater part in double column) we had no idea how completely James had failed. The two volumes of *Theatricals* published in his lifetime were slight affairs. The theatre of his time was so bad, we had wondered whether it was not possible that his contemporaries had simply failed to recognize his genius as a playwright. We knew the sad story of the production of *Guy Domville*, the successful first act, the laughter in the second, the storm of catcalls at the close; we had heard how the critics had defended it, how the prose was praised by the young Bernard Shaw, and yet there existed, so far as one could discover, only a typewritten copy in the Lord Chamberlain's office. Yes, one had expectations and excitement. Now the picture has been filled in, and reading the deplorable results of 'the theatrical years' we need to bear always in mind James's recovery. This is unmistakably trash, but it is not the end of a great writer: out of the experience and failure with another technique came the three great novels *The Wings of the Dove*, *The Ambassadors*, *The Golden Bowl*. He was never so much of a dramatist as when he had ceased to have theatrical ambitions.

Mr. Edel has done a magnificent editorial work. Why should the word 'painstaking' carry implications of dullness? Here every pain has been taken and every pain has had its reward. Each play has a separate factual

* *The Complete Plays of Henry James*. Edited by Leon Edel.

preface of extreme readability: particularly fascinating is the long preface to *Guy Domville* which traces the disastrous first night almost hour by hour: the early afternoon when two unknown ladies sent a telegram from Sloane Street Post Office to George Alexander, 'With hearty wishes for a complete failure'; James sitting in the Haymarket listening to Wilde's epigrams and unaware of the applause at his own first curtain; the disastrous laughable hat in the second act; the first mutter from the gallery in the third, when Alexander began to deliver the speech, 'I am the last, my lord, of the Domvilles,' to be answered, 'It's a bloody good thing y'are'; the pandemonium at the close when this too sensitive author, who had anticipated failure but not this savage public execration, was flung helplessly into the turmoil from the peace of the night in St. James's Square and fled into the wings his face 'green with dismay'; the grim first night supper party which took place 'as arranged'.

It is easier now to understand the public than the critics who were perhaps influenced by horror of the Roman holiday. H. G. Wells found the play 'finely conceived and beautifully written': Shaw wrote, 'Line after line comes with such a delicate turn and fall that I unhesitatingly challenge any of our popular dramatists to write a scene in verse with half the beauty of Mr. James's prose. . . . *Guy Domville* is a story and not a mere situation hung out on a gallows of plot. And it is a story of fine sentiment and delicate manners, with an entirely worthy and touching ending.' To us today the story of *Guy Domville* seems singularly unconvincing, one more example of the not always fortunate fascination exercised on James by the Christian faith and by Catholicism in particular. It stands beside *The Altar of the Dead* and *The Great Good Place* as an example of how completely James could miss the point. Mr. Edel writes truly of James's interest in Catholicism being mainly an interest in a refuge and a retreat; when James wrote in that mood from the outside he conveyed a genuine and moving sense of nostalgia. But in *Guy Domville* he was rashly attempting to convey the sense of Catholicism from within: his characters are Catholics, his hero a young man brought up to become a priest. Domville is on the eve of leaving England to enter a seminary when he becomes heir to a fortune and estate (money again!) and is tempted temporarily by a mistaken sense of duty to his family to re-enter the world. The story is set in the eighteenth century, and the period falls like a dead hand over the prose. Unlike the hero of *The Sense of the Past* we never really go back. Can we believe in a young man who speaks of a girl as 'attached to our Holy Church'? There is really more truth to the religious life in the novels of Mrs. Humphrey Ward. Here for an example is *Guy Domville's* first reply to temptation,

> Break with all the past, and break with it this minute? – turn back from the threshold, take my hand from the plough? – The hour is too troubled, your news too strange, your summons too sudden!

Strangely enough the failure of *Guy Domville* was not the end. Now that he had given up any hopes of stage success, perhaps he felt a certain freedom in his relations with that 'insufferable little art'. The love affair was at an end and he need no longer try to please. 'The hard meagreness inherent in the theatrical form' could be ignored. One critic had observed of his early plays, 'We wish very much that Mr. James would write some farces to please himself, and not to please the stage,' and right at the close with *The Outcry* – a thin amusing story of how a picture was saved for the nation against the will of the owner, an individualistic peer who wanted to sell it for sheer cussedness to an American dealer – he very nearly succeeded in producing an actable comedy. A comedy, for the author of *The Turn of the Screw* and *The Wings of the Dove* strangely failed when he tried on the stage to express the horrors or tragedies of the human situation. 'You don't know – but we're abysses,' one of the characters cries in his creaking melodrama, *The Other House*, but it was just the sense of the abyss that he failed on those flat boards ever to convey. Turn to his ghost story of *Owen Wingrave*, the story of a young man who refused to continue the military tradition of his family and died bravely facing the supernatural in his own home ('Owen Wingrave, dressed as he had last seen him, lay dead on the spot on which his ancestor had been found. He was all the young soldier on the gained field') and compare the dignity of this story, which does indeed convey a sense of the abyss, with the complicated and unspeakable prattle of the stage adaptation.

> That proud old Sir Philip, and that wonderful Miss Wingrave, Deputy-Governor, herself, of the Family Fortress – that they with their immense Military Tradition, and with their particular responsibility to his gallant Father, the Soldier Son, the Soldier Brother sacrificed on an Egyptian battle-field, and whose example – as that of his dead Mother's, of so warlike a race too – it had been their religion to keep before him; that *they* should take his sudden startling action hard is a fact I indeed understand and appreciate. But – I maintain it to you – I should deny my own intelligence if I didn't find our young man, at our crisis, and certainly at *his*, more interesting, perhaps, than ever!

Unwillingly we have to condemn the Master for a fault we had previously never suspected the possibility of his possessing – incompetence.

THE LESSON OF THE MASTER

No writer has been the victim of more misleading criticism than Henry James, from the cruel caricature by Mr. Wells to the rather snappy sentimentalities of Mr. Van Wyck Brooks. Mr. MacCarthy, too, has contributed to the common idea of James as a man who withdrew shrinkingly from 'real life' into an ivory tower where he contented himself with beautifully portraying the surface of civilized society. A great deal of superficiality and intellectual dishonesty has gone to this misrepresentation: one remembers Mr. MacCarthy's astounding statement that the religious sense is almost entirely absent from James's work, and innumerable examples come to mind from Mr. Brooks's bright modish criticism of deviations from the truth. It is quite forgotten that the novel which lends its title, *The Ivory Tower*, to so many grudging appraisals has a subject as 'real', even gross, as it is religious: 'the black and merciless things that are behind great possessions'.

James needed to express his sense of the cruelties and deceptions beneath civilized relationships. He was a puritan with a nose for the Pit, as religious as Bunyan and as violent as Shakespeare. Life is violent and art has to reflect that violence: you can't avoid Hyacinth Harvey's suicide, Milly Theale's betrayal, the swindling of Gray. Those who complain that James's men and women never reach the point of a proposal forget that they often reach the point of suicide, adultery, even murder. Their complaint is the best evidence that James's method, described in his prefaces to the collected edition, was successful. The novel by its nature is dramatic, but it need not be melodramatic, and James's problem was to admit violence without becoming violent. He mustn't let violence lend the tone (that is melodrama): violence must draw its tone from all the rest of life; it must be subdued, and it must not, above all, be sudden and inexplicable. The violence he worked with was not accidental; it was corrupt; it came from the Pit, and therefore it had to be fully understood. Otherwise, the moral background would be lost. This, too, helped to determine his method, for fully to understand, unless the author indulged in tiresome explanation, in the 'platitude of statement' you had to be yourself inside the story, within a consciousness of unusual intelligence.

The prefaces represent the means to his end: and it is absurd to make out that the means ever became more important to him than the end. He never hesitated to break his own rules, but he broke them with a full consciousness of his responsibility, shivering a little with the temerity of his 'exquisite treacheries'; and it remains true today that no novelist can begin to write until he has taken those rules into consideration; you cannot be a protestant before you have studied the dogmas of the old faith. James's argument, as Mr. Blackmur has written, was 'that in art what is merely stated is not presented, what is not presented is not vivid, what is not vivid is not represented, and what is not represented is not art'. That is a dogma which no one will dispute. The long care which James gave to the technique of his art was all a gain for vividness, and the kind of ivory tower that he inhabited admitted life more truthfully than a hatter's castle. His rules were not cramping; they had as their object the liberation of his genius, and the extent of the liberation is best seen when we compare him to his great contemporary, Thomas Hardy. Hardy wrote as he pleased just as any popular novelist does, quite unaware of the particular problems of his art, and yet it is Hardy who gives the impression of being cramped, of being forced into melodramatic laocoon attitudes, so that we begin to appreciate his novels only for the passages where the poet subdues the novelist. In James the poet and the novelist were inseparable.

This is the chief importance of James's prefaces: that they have made future novelists conscious: that the planned effect has been substituted for the lucky stroke (and Hardy shows how seldom even genius can depend on the lucky stroke). But to the common reader they should have an almost equal value, for our enjoyment of a novel is increased when we can follow the method of the writer (if they are sometimes difficult reading it is only because James had to invent his terms; he was the first critic of the novel). There is an uneducated pleasure to be obtained from pictures and music; but few will dispute that a subtler pleasure is enjoyed by the educated. The numinous pleasure is not lost if we know a little of the way in which it has been transmitted; a fine stroke by a novelist should be at least as exciting as a fine stroke by a batsman. And there is no reason for sentimentalists to be afraid. We have watched James choose his point of view, work out his ironic antitheses, arrange his scenes, but the peculiar aptitude remains; even given the directions no one has equalled him.

THE YOUNG DICKENS

A CRITIC must try to avoid being a prisoner of his time, and if we are to appreciate *Oliver Twist* at its full value we must forget that long shelf-load of books, all the stifling importance of a great author, the scandals and the controversies of the private life; it would be well too if we could forget the Phiz and the Cruikshank illustrations that have frozen the excited, excitable world of Dickens into a hall of waxworks, where Mr. Mantalini's whiskers have always the same trim, where Mr. Pickwick perpetually turns up the tails of his coat, and in the Chamber of Horrors Fagin crouches over an undying fire. His illustrators, brilliant craftsmen though they were, did Dickens a disservice, for no character any more will walk for the first time into our memory as we ourselves imagine him, and *our* imagination after all has just as much claim to truth as Cruikshank's.

Nevertheless the effort to go back is well worth while. The journey is only a little more than a hundred years long, and at the other end of the road is a young author whose sole claim to renown in 1837 had been the publication of some journalistic sketches and a number of comic operas: *The Strange Gentleman, The Village Coquette, Is She His Wife?* I doubt whether any literary Cortez at that date would have yet stood them upon his shelves. Then suddenly with *The Pickwick Papers* came popularity and fame. Fame falls like a dead hand on an author's shoulder, and it is well for him when it falls only in later life. How many in Dickens's place would have withstood what James called 'the great corrupting contact of the public', the popularity founded, as it almost always is, on the weakness and not the strength of an author?

The young Dickens, at the age of twenty-five, had hit on a mine that paid him a tremendous dividend. Fielding and Smollett, tidied and refined for the new industrial bourgeoisie, had both salted it; Goldsmith had contributed sentimentality and Monk Lewis horror. The book was enormous, shapeless, familiar (that important recipe for popularity). What Henry James wrote of a long-forgotten French critic applies well to the young Dickens: 'He is homely, familiar and colloquial; he leans his elbows on his desk and does up his weekly budget into a parcel the reverse of compact. You can fancy him a grocer retailing tapioca and hominy full weight for the price; his style seems a sort of integument of brown paper.'

This is, of course, unfair to *The Pickwick Papers*. The driest critic could not have quite blinkered his eyes to those sudden wide illuminations of comic genius that flap across the waste of words like sheet lightning, but could he have foreseen the second novel, not a repetition of this great loose popular holdall, but a short melodrama, tight in construction, almost entirely lacking in broad comedy, and possessing only the sad twisted humour of the orphans' asylum?

> 'You'll make your fortune, Mr. Sowerberry,' said the beadle, as he thrust his thumb and forefinger into the proffered snuff-box of the undertaker: which was an ingenious little model of a patent coffin.

Such a development was as inconceivable as the gradual transformation of that thick boggy prose into the delicate and exact poetic cadences, the music of memory, that so influenced Proust.

We are too inclined to take Dickens as a whole and to treat his juvenilia with the same kindness or harshness as his later work. *Oliver Twist* is still juvenilia – magnificent juvenilia: it is the first step on the road that led from *Pickwick* to *Great Expectations*, and we can condone the faults of taste in the early book the more readily if we recognize the distance Dickens had to travel. These two typical didactic passages can act as the first two milestones at the opening of the journey, the first from *Pickwick*, the second from *Oliver Twist*.

> And numerous indeed are the hearts to which Christmas brings a brief season of happiness and enjoyment. How many families, whose members have been dispersed and scattered far and wide, in the restless struggles of life, are then reunited, and meet once again in that happy state of companionship and mutual goodwill, which is a source of such pure and unalloyed delight, and one so incompatible with the cares and sorrows of the world, that the religious belief of the most civilized nations, and the rude traditions of the roughest savages, alike number it among the first joys of a future condition of existence, provided for the blest and happy.

> The boy stirred and smiled in his sleep, as though these marks of pity and compassion had awakened some pleasant dream of a love and affection he had never known. Thus, a strain of gentle music, or the rippling of water in a silent place, or the odour of a flower, or the mention of a familiar word, will sometimes call up sudden dim remembrances of scenes that never were, in this life; which vanish like a breath; which some brief memory of a happier existence, long gone by, would seem to have awakened; which no voluntary exertion of the mind can ever recall.

The first is certainly brown paper: what it wraps has been chosen by the grocer to suit his clients' tastes, but cannot we detect already in the second passage the tone of Dickens's secret prose, that sense of a mind speaking to itself with no one there to listen, as we find it in *Great Expectations*?

> It was fine summer weather again, and, as I walked along, the times when I was a little helpless creature, and my sister did not spare me, vividly returned. But they returned with a gentle tone upon them that softened even the edge of Tickler. For now, the very breath of the beans and clover whispered to my heart that the day must come when it would be well for my memory that others walking in the sunshine should be softened as they thought of me.

It is a mistake to think of *Oliver Twist* as a realistic story: only late in his career did Dickens learn to write realistically of human beings; at the beginning he invented life and we no more believe in the temporal existence of Fagin or Bill Sykes than we believe in the existence of that Giant whom Jack slew as he bellowed his Fee Fi Fo Fum. There were real Fagins and Bill Sykes and real Bumbles in the England of his day, but he had not drawn them, as he was later to draw the convict Magwitch; these characters in *Oliver Twist* are simply parts of one huge invented scene, what Dickens in his own preface called 'the cold wet shelterless midnight streets of London'. How the phrase goes echoing on through the books of Dickens until we meet it again so many years later in 'the weary western streets of London on a cold dusty spring night' which were so melancholy to Pip. But Pip was to be as real as the weary streets, while Oliver was as unrealistic as the cold wet midnight of which he formed a part.

This is not to criticize the book so much as to describe it. For what an imagination this youth of twenty-six had that he could invent so monstrous and complete a legend! We are not lost with Oliver Twist round Saffron Hill: we are lost in the interstices of one young, angry, gloomy brain, and the oppressive images stand out along the track like the lit figures in a Ghost Train tunnel.

> Against the wall were ranged, in regular array, a long row of elm boards cut into the same shape, looking in the dim light, like high shouldered ghosts with their hands in their breeches pockets.

We have most of us seen those nineteenth-century prints where the bodies of naked women form the face of a character, the Diplomat, the Miser and the like. So the crouching figure of Fagin seems to form the mouth, Sykes with his bludgeon the jutting features and the sad lost Oliver the eyes of one man, as lost as Oliver.

Chesterton, in a fine imaginative passage, has described the mystery behind Dickens's plots, the sense that even the author was unaware of what was really going on, so that when the explanations come and we reach, huddled into the last pages of *Oliver Twist*, a naked complex narrative of illegitimacy and burnt wills and destroyed evidence, we simply do not believe. 'The secrecy is sensational; the secret is tame. The surface of the thing seems more awful than the core. It seems almost as if these grisly figures, Mrs. Chadband and Mrs. Clennan, Miss Havisham and Miss Flite, Nemo and Sally Brass, were keeping something back from the author as well as from the reader. When the book closes we do not know their real secret. They soothe the optimistic Dickens with something less terrible than the truth.'

What strikes the attention most in this closed Fagin universe are the different levels of unreality. If, as one is inclined to believe, the creative writer perceives his world once and for all in childhood and adolescence, and his whole career is an effort to illustrate his private world in terms of the great public world we all share, we can understand why Fagin and Sykes in their most extreme exaggerations move us more than the benevolence of Mr. Brownlow or the sweetness of Mrs. Maylie – they touch with fear as the others never really touch with love. It was not that the unhappy child, with his hurt pride and his sense of hopeless insecurity, had not encountered human goodness – he had simply failed to recognize it in those streets between Gadshill and Hungerford Market which had been as narrowly enclosed as Oliver Twist's. When Dickens at this early period tried to describe goodness he seems to have remembered the small stationers' shops on the way to the blacking factory with their coloured paper scraps of angels and virgins, or perhaps the face of some old gentleman who had spoken kindly to him outside Warren's factory. He has swum up towards goodness from the deepest world of his experience, and on this shallow level the conscious brain has taken a hand, trying to construct characters to represent virtue and, because his age demanded it, triumphant virtue, but all he can produce are powdered wigs and gleaming spectacles and a lot of bustle with bowls of broth and a pale angelic face. Compare the way in which we first meet evil with his introduction of goodness.

> The walls and ceiling of the room were perfectly black with age and dirt. There was a deal table before the fire: upon which were a candle, stuck in a

ginger-beer bottle, two or three pewter pots, a loaf and butter, and a plate. In a frying pan, which was on the fire, and which was secured to the mantel-shelf by a string, some sausages were cooking; and standing over them, with a toasting-fork in his hand, was a very old shrivelled Jew, whose villainous-looking and repulsive face was obscured by a quantity of matted red hair. He was dressed in a greasy flannel gown, with his throat bare . . . 'This is him, Fagin,' said Jack Dawkins: 'my friend Oliver Twist.' The Jew grinned; and, making a low obeisance to Oliver, took him by the hand, and hoped he should have the honour of his intimate acquaintance.

Fagin has always about him this quality of darkness and nightmare. He never appears on the daylight streets. Even when we see him last in the condemned cell, it is in the hours before the dawn. In the Fagin dark-ness Dickens's hand seldom fumbles. Hear him turning the screw of horror when Nancy speaks of the thoughts of death that have haunted her:

'Imagination,' said the gentleman, soothing her.
'No imagination,' replied the girl in a hoarse voice. 'I'll swear I saw "coffin" written in every page of the book in large black letters, – aye, and they carried one close to me, in the streets tonight.'
'There is nothing unusual in that,' said the gentleman; 'They have passed me often.'
'Real ones,' rejoined the girl. 'This was not.'

Now turn to the daylight world and our first sight of Rose:

The younger lady was in the lovely bloom and springtime of woman-hood; at that age, when, if ever angels be for God's good purposes enthroned in mortal forms, they may be, without impiety, supposed to abide in such as hers. She was not past seventeen. Cast in so slight and exquisite a mould; so mild and gentle; so pure and beautiful; that earth seemed not her element, nor its rough creatures her fit companions.

Or Mr. Brownlow as he first appeared to Oliver:

Now, the old gentleman came in as brisk as need be; but he had no sooner raised his spectacles on his forehead, and thrust his hands behind the skirts of his dressing-gown to take a good long look at Oliver, than his counten-ance underwent a very great variety of odd contortions. . . . The fact is, if the truth must be told that Mr. Brownlow's heart, being large enough for any six ordinary old gentlemen of humane disposition, forced a supply of tears into his eyes by some hydraulic process which we are not sufficiently philosophical to be in a condition to explain.

How can we really believe that these inadequate ghosts of goodness can triumph over Fagin, Monks and Sykes? And the answer, of course, is that they never could have triumphed without the elaborate machinery of the plot disclosed in the last pages. This world of Dickens is a world without God; and as a substitute for the power and the glory of the omnipotent and omniscient are a few sentimental references to heaven, angels, the sweet faces of the dead, and Oliver saying, 'Heaven is a long way off, and they are too happy there to come down to the bedside of a poor boy.' In this Manichaean world we can believe in evil-doing, but goodness wilts into philanthropy, kindness, and those strange vague sicknesses into which Dickens's young women so frequently fall and which seem in his eyes a kind of badge of virtue, as though there were a merit in death.

But how instinctively Dickens's genius recognized the flaw and made a virtue out of it. We cannot believe in the power of Mr. Baldwin, but nor did Dickens, and from his inability to believe in his own good characters springs the real tension of his novel. The boy Oliver may not lodge in our brain like David Copperfield, and though many of Mr. Bumble's phrases have become and deserve to have become familiar quotations we can feel he was manufactured: he never breathes like Mr. Dorrit; yet Oliver's predicament, the nightmare fight between the darkness where the demons walk and the sunlight where ineffective goodness makes its last stand in a condemned world, will remain part of our imaginations forever. We read of the defeat of Monks, and of Fagin screaming in the condemned cell, and of Sykes dangling from his self-made noose, but we don't believe. We have witnessed Oliver's temporary escapes too often and his inevitable recapture: *there* is the truth and the creative experience. We know that when Oliver leaves Mr. Brownlow's house to walk a few hundred yards to the bookseller, his friends will wait in vain for his return. All London outside the quiet, shady street in Pentonville belongs to his pursuers; and when he escapes again into the house of Mrs. Maylie in the fields beyond Shepperton, we know his security is false. The seasons may pass, but safety depends not on time but on daylight. As children we all knew that: how all day we could forget the dark and the journey to bed. It is with a sense of relief that at last in twilight we see the faces of the Jew and Monks peer into the cottage window between the sprays of jessamine. At that moment we realize how the whole world, and not London only, belongs to these two after dark. Dickens, dealing out his happy endings and his unreal retributions, can never ruin the validity and dignity of that moment. 'They had recognized him, and he them; and their look was as firmly impressed upon his memory, as if it had been deeply carved in stone, and set before him from his birth.'

'From his birth' – Dickens may have intended that phrase to refer to the complicated imbroglios of the plot that lie outside the novel, 'something less terrible than the truth'. As for the truth, is it too fantastic to imagine that in this novel, as in many of his later books, creeps in, unrecognized by the author, the eternal and alluring taint of the Manichee, with its simple and terrible explanation of our plight, how the world was made by Satan and not by God, lulling us with the music of despair?

FIELDING AND STERNE

All, all, of a piece throughout:
　　Thy Chase had a Beast in View;
　　Thy Wars brought nothing about;
　　Thy Lovers were all untrue.
'Tis well an Old Age is out,
　　And time to begin a New.

SO DRYDEN, looking back from the turn of the century on the muddle of hopes and disappointments, revolution and counter-revolution and revolution again. The age had been kept busily spinning, but to the poet in 1700 it seemed to have amounted to little: what Cromwell had overthrown, Charles had rebuilt: what James would have established, William had destroyed. But literature may thrive on political disturbance, if the disturbance goes deep enough and arouses a sufficiently passionate agreement or denial. One remembers Trotsky's account of the first meeting of the Soviet after the October days of 1917: 'Among their number were completely grey soldiers, shell-shocked as it were by the insurrection, and still hardly in control of their tongues. But they were just the ones who found the words which no orator could find. That was one of the most moving scenes of the revolution, now first feeling its power, feeling the unnumbered masses it has aroused, the colossal tasks, the pride in success, the joyful failing of the heart at the thought of the morrow which is to be still more beautiful than today.'

These terms can be transposed to fit the seventeenth century as they cannot to fit the eighteenth, the century to which Fielding was born in 1707 and Sterne six years later. Bunyan, Fox, the Quakers and Levellers, those were the grey, the shell-shocked soldiers who found the words which no official orator of the Established Church could find, and one cannot question among some of the poets who welcomed the return of Charles a genuine thankfulness for a morrow which they believed was to be still more beautiful. The great figure of Dryden comprises the whole of the late seventeenth-century scene: like some infinitely subtle meteorological instrument, he was open to every wind: he registered the triumph of Cromwell, the hopes of the Restoration, the Catholicism of James, the final disillusionment. When he died, in 1700, he left the new

58

age, the quieter, more rational age, curiously empty. Not until the romantics at the end of the century was politics again to be of importance to the creative, the recording mind, not until Newman and Hopkins orthodox religion. All that was left was the personal sensibility or the superficial social panorama, from the highwayman in the cart and the debtor in gaol to the lascivious lord at Vauxhall and the virtuous heroine bent over the admirable, unenthusiastic works of Bishop Burnet.

One cannot separate literature and life. If an age appears creatively, poetically, empty, it is fair to assume that life too had its emptiness, was carried on at a lower, less passionate level. I use the word poetry in the widest sense, in the sense that Henry James was a poet and Defoe was not. When Fielding published his first novel, *Joseph Andrewes*, in 1742, Swift was on the verge of death and Pope as well, Cowper was ten years old and Blake unborn. Dramatic poetry, which had survived Dryden's death only in such feeble hands as Addison's and Rowe's, was to all intents a finished form.

But fiction is one of the prime needs of human nature, and someone in that empty world had got to begin building again. One cannot in such a period expect the greatest literature: the old forms are seen to be old when the fine excitement is over, and all that the best minds can do is to construct new forms in which the poetic imagination may eventually find itself at home. Something in the eighteenth century had got to take the place of dramatic poetry (perhaps it is not too fanciful to see in the innumerable translations of Homer, Virgil, Lucan a popular hunger for the lost poetic fiction), and it was Fielding who for the first time since the Elizabethan age directed the poetic imagination into prose fiction. That he began as a parodist of Richardson may indicate that he recognized the inadequacy of *Pamela*, of the epistolary novel, to satisfy the hunger of the age.

In the previous century the distinction between prose fiction and poetic fiction had been a very simple one: one might almost say that prose fiction had been pornographic fiction, in the sense that it had been confined to a more or less flippant study of sexual relations (whether you take the plays of Wycherley, the prose comedies of Dryden, the novels of Aphra Behn, the huge picaresque novel of Richard Head and Francis Kirkman, the generalization remains true almost without exception), while poetic fiction had meant heroic drama, a distinction underlined in plays like *Marriage à la Mode* which contained both poetry and prose – the heroic and the pornographic. Nowhere during the Restoration period, except perhaps in Cowley's great comedy, does one find prose used in fiction as Webster and other Jacobean playwrights used it, as a medium of equal dignity and intensity to poetry, indeed as poetry with the rhythm of ordinary speech. It was from the traditional ideal of prose fiction that Defoe's novels were derived: *Moll Flanders* is only a more concise *English Rogue*, and it was left to Fielding, who had not himself the poetic mind (he declared roundly: 'I should have honoured and loved Homer more had he written a true history of his own times in humble prose'), to construct a fictional form which could attract the poetic imagination. *Tom Jones* was to prove the archetype not only of the picaresque novelists. James and Joyce owe as much to it as Dickens.

Today, when we have seen in the novels of Henry James the metaphysical poet working in the medium of prose fiction, in Lawrence's and Conrad's novels the romantic, we cannot easily realize the revolutionary nature of *Tom Jones* and *Amelia*. Sterne who came later – the first volumes of *Tristram Shandy* were published five years after Fielding's death – bears so much more the obvious marks of a revolutionary, simply because he remains, in essentials, a revolutionary still. Even today he continues magnificently to upset all our notions of what a novel's form should be; it is his least valuable qualities which have been passed on. His sensibility founded a whole school of Bages and Bancrofts and Blowers (I cannot remember who it was who wrote: 'Great G – d, unless I have greatly offended Thee, grant me the luxury, sometimes to slip a bit of silver, though no bigger than a shilling, into the clammy-cold hand of the decayed wife of a baronet,' but it was to the author of *The Sentimental Journey* that he owed his sensibility), while his whimsicality was inherited by the essayists, by Lamb in particular. But his form no one has ever tried to imitate, for what would be the good? An imitation could do nothing but recall the original. *Tristram Shandy* exists, a lovely sterile eccentricity, the last word in literary egotism. Even the fact that Sterne was – sometimes – a poet is less important to practitioners of his art than that Fielding – sometimes – tried to be one.

Sterne, the sly, uneasy, unhappily married cleric, the son of an elderly ensign who never had the means or the influence to buy promotion, had suffered so many humiliations from the world that he had to erect defences of sentiment and of small indecencies between him and it (he admired Rabelais, but how timidly, how 'naughtily', his chapter on Noses reflects the author of *The Heroic Deeds of Gargantua and Pantagruel*), so that he had nothing to offer us on our side of the barrier but his genius, his genius for expressing the personal emotions of the sly, the uneasy, the unhappily married. The appalling conceit of this genius, one protests, who claimed Posterity for his book without troubling himself a hang over the value of its contents: 'for what has this book done more than the Legation of Moses, or *The Tale of a Tub*, that it may not swim down the gutter of Time along with them?' The nearest that this shrinking sentimental man came to the ordinary run of life was Hall-Stevenson's pornographic circle, the nearest to passion his journals to Eliza who was safely separated from him by the Indian Ocean as well as by the difference in their years. There is nothing he can tell us about anyone, we feel, but himself, and that self has been so tidied and idealized that it would be unrecognizable, one imagines, to his wife.

Compare his position in the life of his time with that of Fielding, Fielding the rake, Fielding the country gentleman, Fielding the hack dramatist, and finally Fielding the Westminster magistrate who knew all the outcast side of life, from the thief and the cut-throat to the seedy genteel and the half-pay officer in the debtor's court, as no other man of his time. Compare the careful architecture of *Tom Jones*: the introductory essays which enable the author to put his point of view and to leave the characters to go their way untainted by the uncharacteristic moralizing of Defoe's; the introduction of parody in the same way and for the same purpose as Joyce's in *Ulysses*; the innumerable sub-plots which give the book the proportions of life, the personal story of Jones taking its place in the general orchestration; the movement back and forth in time as the characters meet each other and recount the past in much the same way as Conrad's, a craftsman's bluff by which we seem to get a glimpse of that 'dark backward and abysm' that challenges the ingenuity of every novelist. Compare all this careful architecture with the schoolboy squibs – the blank, the blackened and the marbled leaves, the asterisks – of *Tristram Shandy*. We cannot help but feel ungrateful when we think of the work that Fielding put into his books, the importance of his technical innovations, and realize that Sterne, who contributed nothing, can still give more pleasure because of what we call his genius, his skill at self-portraiture (even Uncle Toby is only another example of his colossal egotism: the only outside character he ever really drew – and all the time we are aware of the author preening himself at the tender insight of his admiration).

The man Sterne is unbearable, even the emotions he displayed with such amazing mastery were cheap emotions. Dryden is dead: the great days are over: Cavaliers and Roundheads have become Whigs and Tories: Cumberland has slaughtered the Stuart hopes at Culloden: the whole age cannot produce a respectable passion. So anyone must feel to whom the change, say, from the essays of Bacon and his true descendant Cowley to the essays of Lamb is a change for the worse in human dignity: a change from 'Revenge is a kind of wild justice' or 'It was the Funeral day of the late man who made himself to be called Protector' to 'I have no ear – Mistake me not, reader – nor imagine that I am by nature destitute of those exterior twin appendages or hanging ornaments . . .' or to the latest little weekly essay on 'Rising Early' or on 'Losing a Collar Stud'. The personal emotion, personal sensibility, the whim, in Sterne's day crept into our literature. It is impossible not to feel a faint disgust at this man, officially a man of God, who in *The Sentimental Journey* found in his own tearful reaction to the mad girl of Moulines the satisfactory conclusion: 'I am positive I have a soul; nor can all the books with which materialists have pester'd the world ever convince me of the contrary.'

It is a little galling to find the conceit of such a man justified. However much we hate the man, or hate rather his coy whimsical defences, he is more 'readable' than Fielding by virtue of that most musical style, the day-dream conversation of a man with a stutter in a world of his imagination where tongue and teeth have no problems to overcome, where no syllables are harsh, where mind speaks softly to mind with infinite subtlety of tone. 'The various accidents which befell a very worthy couple, after their uniting in the state of matrimony, will be the subject of the following history. The distresses which they waded through were some of them so exquisite, and the incidents which produced them so extraordinary that they seem to require not only the utmost malice, but the utmost invention which superstition hath ever attributed to Fortune.' So Fielding begins his most mature – if not his greatest – novel. How this book, one wants to protest, should appeal to the craftsman: the *tour de force* with which for half the long novel he unfolds the story of Booth and Amelia without abandoning the absolute unity of his scene, the prison where Booth is confined. It is quite as remarkable as the designed confusion of *Tristram Shandy*, but there is no answer to a reader who replies: 'I read to be entertained and how heavily this style of Fielding's weighs beside Sterne's impudent opening: "I wish either my father or my mother, or indeed both of them, as they were in duty both equally bound to it, had minded what they were about when they begot me . . ." '

No, one must surrender to Sterne most of the graces. What Fielding possessed, and Sterne did not, was something quite as new to the novel as Sterne's lightness and sensibility, moral seriousness. He was not a poet – and Sterne was at any rate a minor one – but this moral seriousness enabled him to construct a form which would later satisfy the requirements of major poets as Defoe's plain narrative could not. When we admire Tom Jones as being the first portrait of 'a whole man' (a description which perhaps fits only Bloom in later fiction), it is Fielding's seriousness to which we are paying tribute, his power of discriminating between immorality and vice. He had no high opinion of human nature: the small sensualities of Tom Jones, the incorrigible gambling propensities of Booth, his own direct statement, when he heard his poor dying body, ugly with the dropsy, mocked by the watermen at Rotherhithe ('it was a lively picture of that cruelty and inhumanity in the nature of men which I have often contemplated with concern, and which leads the mind into a train of very uncomfortable and melancholy thoughts'), prove it no more certainly than his quite incredible pictures of virtue, the rectitude of Mr. Allworthy, the heroic nature of the patient Amelia. Experience had supplied him with many a Booth and Tom Jones (indeed someone of the latter name appeared before him at Bow Street), but for examples of virtue he had to call on his imagination, and one cannot agree with Saintsbury who remarked quaintly and uncritically of his heroines: 'There is no more touching portrait in the whole of fiction than this heroic and immortal one of feminine goodness and forbearance.'

It is impossible to use these immoderate terms of Fielding without absurdity: to compare the kept woman, Miss Mathews, in *Amelia*, as Dobson did, with a character of Balzac's. He belonged to the wrong century for this kind of greatness. His heroic characters are derived from Dryden – unsuccessfully (the relation between Amelia and a character like Almeyda is obvious). But what puts us so supremely in his debt is this: that he had gathered up in his novels the two divided strands of Restoration fiction: he had combined on his own lower level the flippant prose fictions of the dramatists and the heroic drama of the poets.

On the lower, the unreligious level. His virtues are natural virtues, his despair a natural despair, endured with as much courage as Dryden's but without the supernatural reason.

> Brutus and Cato might discharge their Souls,
> And give them Furlo's for another World:
> But we like Centries are oblig'd to stand
> In Starless Nights, and wait th' appointed Hour.

So Dryden, and here more lovably perhaps, with purely natural virtue, Fielding faces death – death in the shape of a last hard piece of work for public order, undertaken in his final sickness with the intention of winning from government some pension for his wife and children: 'And though I disclaim all pretence to that Spartan or Roman patriotism which loved the public so well that it was always ready to become a voluntary sacrifice to the public good I do solemnly declare I have that love for my family.'

He hated iniquity and he certainly died in exile: his books do represent a moral struggle, but they completely lack the sense of supernatural evil or supernatural good. Mr. Eliot has suggested that 'with the disappearance of the idea of Original Sin, with the disappearance of the idea of intense moral struggle, the human beings presented to us both in poetry and in prose fiction . . . tend to become less and less real', and it is the intensity of the struggle which is lacking in Fielding. Evil is always a purely sexual matter: the struggle seems invariably to take the form of whether or not the 'noble lord' or Colonel James will succeed in raping or seducing Amelia, and the characters in this superficial struggle, carried out with quite as much ingenuity as Uncle Toby employed on his fortifications, do tend to become less and less real. How can one take seriously Mrs. Heartfree's five escapes from ravishment in twenty pages? One can only say in favour of this conception that it is at least expressed with more dignity than in *The Sentimental Journey* where Sterne himself has stolen the part of Pamela, of Amelia and Mrs. Heartfree, and asks us to be breathlessly concerned for *his* virtue ('The foot of the bed was within a yard and a half of the place where we were standing – I had still hold of her hands – and how it happened I can give no account, but I neither ask'd her – nor drew her – nor did I think of the bed –'). But the moral life in Fielding is apt to resemble one of those pictorial games of Snakes and Ladders. If the player's counter should happen to fall on a Masquerade or a ticket to Vauxhall Gardens, down it slides by way of the longest snake.

It would be ungrateful to end on this carping note. There had been picaresque novels before Fielding – from the days of Nashe to the days of Defoe – but the picaresque had not before in English been raised to an art, given the form, the arrangement, which separates art from mere realistic reporting however vivid. Fielding lifted life out of its setting and arranged it for the delight of all who love symmetry. He can afford to leave Sterne his graceful play with the emotions, his amusing little indecencies: the man who created Partridge had a distant kinship to the creator of Falstaff. 'Nothing,' Jones remarks, 'can be more likely to happen than death to men who go into battle. Perhaps we shall both fall in it – and what then?' 'What then?' replied Partridge; 'why then there is an end of us, is there not? When I am gone, all is over with me. What matters the cause to me, or who gets the victory, if I am killed? I shall never enjoy any advantage from it. What are all the ringing of bells, and bonfires, to one that is six foot under ground? there will be an end of poor Partridge.'

Fielding had tried to make the novel poetic, even though he himself had not the poetic mind, only a fair, a generous mind and a courageous mind, and the conventions which he established for the novel enabled it in a more passionate age to become a poetic art, to fill the gap in literature left when Dryden died and the seventeenth century was over. He was the best product of his age, the post-revolutionary age when politics for the first time ceased to represent any deep issues and religion excited only the shallowest feeling. His material was underpaid officers, highwaymen, debtors, noblemen who had nothing better to do than pursue sexual adventures, clergymen like Parson Adams whose virtues are as much pagan as Christian. 'At the moment when one writes,' to quote Mr. Eliot again, 'one is what one is, and the damage of a lifetime . . . cannot be repaired at the moment of composition.' We should not complain; rather we should be amazed at what so unpoetic a mind accomplished in such an age.

E

FROM FEATHERS TO IRON

STEVENSON'S reputation has suffered perhaps more from his early death than from any other cause. He was only forty-four when he died, and he left behind him what mainly amounts to a mass of juvenilia. Gay, bright and perennially attractive though much of this work may be, it has a spurious maturity which hides the fact that, like other men, he was developing. Indeed it was only in the last six years of his life – the Samoan years – that his fine dandified talent began to shed its disguising graces, the granite to show through. And how rich those last years were; *The Wrong Box*, *The Master of Ballantrae*, *The Island Nights' Entertainments*, *The Ebb Tide* and *Weir of Hermiston*. Could he have kept it up, Henry James wondered of the last unfinished book? and added with gracious pessimism, 'the reason for which he didn't reads itself back into his text as a kind of beautiful rash divination in him that he mightn't have to. Among prose fragments it stands quite alone, with the particular grace and sanctity of mutilation worn by the marble morsels of master-work in another art.'

Unfortunately Stevenson's reputation was not left in the hands of so cautious and subtle a critic. The early affected books of travel by canoe and donkey, the too personal letters full of 'rot about a fellow's behaviour', with a slang that rings falsely on the page like an obscenity in a parson's mouth, the immature musings on his craft ('Fiction is to the grown man what play is to the child'), the early ethical essays of *Virginibus Puerisque*, all these were thrust into the foreground by the appearance of collected edition after collected edition: his youthful thoughts still sprinkle the commercial calendars with quotations. His comparatively uneventful life (adventurous only to the sedate Civil Service minds of Colvin and Gosse) was magnified into a saga: early indiscretions were carefully obliterated from the record, until at last his friends had their reward – that pale hollow stuffed figure in a velvet jacket with a Lang moustache, kneeling by a chair of native wood, with the pokerwork mottoes just behind the head – 'to travel hopefully is a better thing than to arrive', etc., etc. Did it never occur to these industrious champions that as an adventurer, as a man of religion, as a traveller, as a friend of 'the coloured races' he must wither into insignificance beside that other Scotsman, with the name rather like his own but the letters reshuffled into a stronger pattern, Livingstone? If he is to survive for us today, it will not be as Tusitala or the rather absurd lover collapsing at Monterrey or the dandy of Davos, but as the tired disheartened writer of the last eight years, pegging desperately away at what he failed to recognize as his masterworks.

Miss Cooper in her short biography* has followed conventionally the well-worn tracks which James noticed had been laid carefully by the hero himself. 'Stevenson never covered his tracks,' James wrote. 'We follow them here, from year to year and from stage to stage, with the same charmed sense with which he has made us follow some hunted hero in the heather.' As an interpreter of his work she is incomparably less sensitive than Miss Janet Adam Smith who has already written to my mind the best possible book on Stevenson of this length. One cannot really dismiss *The Wrong Box* as '*a tour de force* sometimes enlivened by a faintly ghoulish humour, but with no breath of reality in the characters', and criticism such as this (Miss Cooper is dealing with *The Master of Ballantrae*) has too much of the common touch even for a popular series: 'The reader feels Henry's unhappiness, even when he finds it difficult to care very much about Henry, who is, it must be confessed, a dull dog.' Of *The Ebb Tide* the ignorant reader will learn only that it is 'a grim study of shady characters in the South Seas'.

However, here for those who want it (though insufficiently charted with dates) is the obvious trail: we can watch Stevenson scatter his scraps of paper across the clearings for his pursuers to spy. His immense correspondence was mainly written with an eye on his pursuers – he encouraged Colvin to arrange it for publication. Miss Emily Dickinson wrote with some lack of wisdom in one of her poems, 'I like a look of agony because I know it's true,' but we are never, before the last years, quite sure of the agony. Compare his Davos letters – 'Here a sheer hulk lies poor Tom Bowling and aspires, yes, C.B., with tears after the past' or doing his courageous act, 'I am better. I begin to hope that I may, if not outlive this wolverine on my shoulder, at least carry him bravely,' with the letters of his last year (for suffering like literature has its juvenilia – men mature and graduate in suffering):

> The truth is I am nearly useless at literature, and I will ask you to spare *St. Ives* when it goes to you. . . . No toil has been spared over the ungrateful canvas: and it *will not* come together, and I must live, and my family. Were

---

* *Robert Louis Stevenson*. By Lettice Cooper.

it not for my health, which made it impossible, I could not find it in my heart to forgive myself that I did not stick to an honest commonplace trade when I was young, which might have now supported me during these ill years. . . . It was a very little dose of inspiration, and a pretty little trick of style, long lost, improved by the most heroic industry. So far I have managed to please the journalists. But I am a fictitious article and have long known it.

A month before this he had written to his friend Baxter, admitting his life-long attempt to turn 'Bald Conduct' into an emotional religion and comparing with the dreariness of his own creed the new spirit of the anarchists in Europe, men who 'commit dastardly murders very basely, die like saints, and leave beautiful letters behind 'em . . . people whose conduct is inexplicable to me, and yet their spiritual life higher than that of most.' '*Si vieillesse pouvait*', he quoted, while Colvin supplied the asterisks. He was on the eve of *Weir*: the old trim surface was cracking up: the granite was coming painfully through. It is at that point, where the spade strikes the edge of the stone, that the biographer should begin to dig.

FRANÇOIS MAURIAC

AFTER the death of Henry James a disaster overtook the English novel: indeed long before his death one can picture that quiet, impressive, rather complacent figure, like the last survivor on a raft, gazing out over a sea scattered with wreckage. He even recorded his impressions in an article in *The Times Literary Supplement*, recorded his hope – but was it really hope or only a form of his unconquerable oriental politeness? – in such young novelists as Mr. Compton Mackenzie and Mr. David Herbert Lawrence, and we who have lived after the disaster can realize the futility of those hopes.

For with the death of James the religious sense was lost to the English novel, and with the religious sense went the sense of the importance of the human act. It was as if the world of fiction had lost a dimension: the characters of such distinguished writers as Mrs. Virginia Woolf and Mr. E. M. Forster wandered like cardboard symbols through a world that was paper-thin. Even in one of the most materialistic of our great novelists – in Trollope – we are aware of another world against which the actions of the characters are thrown into relief. The ungainly clergyman picking his black-booted way through the mud, handling so awkwardly his umbrella, speaking of his miserable income and stumbling through a proposal of marriage, exists in a way that Mrs. Woolf's Mr. Ramsay never does, because we are aware that he exists not only to the woman he is addressing but also in a God's eye. His unimportance in the world of the senses is only matched by his enormous importance in another world.

The novelist, perhaps unconsciously aware of his predicament, took refuge in the subjective novel. It was as if he thought that by mining into layers of personality hitherto untouched he could unearth the secret of 'importance', but in these mining operations he lost yet another dimension. The visible world for him ceased to exist as completely as the spiritual. Mrs. Dalloway walking down Regent Street was aware of the glitter of shop windows, the smooth passage of cars, the conversation of shoppers, but it was only a Regent Street seen by Mrs. Dalloway that was conveyed to the reader: a charming whimsical rather sentimental prose poem was what Regent Street had become: a current of air, a touch of scent, a sparkle of glass. But, we protest, Regent Street too has a right to exist; it is more

real than Mrs. Dalloway, and we look back with nostalgia towards
the chop houses, the mean courts, the still Sunday streets of Dickens.
Dickens's characters were of immortal importance, and the houses in
which they loved, the mews in which they damned themselves were lent
importance by their presence. They were given the right to exist as they
were, distorted if at all, only by their observer's eye – not further distorted
at a second remove by an imagined character.

M. Mauriac's first importance to an English reader, therefore, is that
he belongs to the company of the great traditional novelists: he is a writer
for whom the visible world has not ceased to exist, whose characters have
the solidity and importance of men with souls to save or lose, and a writer
who claims the traditional and essential right of a novelist, to comment,
to express his views. For how tired we have become of the dogmatic-
ally 'pure' novel, the tradition founded by Flaubert and reaching its
magnificent tortuous climax in England in the works of Henry James. One
is reminded of those puzzles in children's papers which take the form of a
maze. The child is encouraged to trace with his pencil a path to the centre
of the maze. But in the pure novel the reader begins at the centre and has
to find his way to the gate. He runs his pencil down avenues which must
surely go straight to the circumference, the world outside the maze, where
moral judgments and acts of supernatural importance can be found (even
the writing of a novel indeed can be regarded as a more important action,
expressing an intention of more vital importance, than the adultery of the
main character or the murder in chapter three), but the printed channels
slip and twist and slide, landing him back where he began, and he finds on
close examination that the designer of the maze has in fact overprinted the
only exit.

I am not denying the greatness of either Flaubert or James. The novel
was ceasing to be an aesthetic form and they recalled it to the artistic conscience. It was the later writers who by accepting the technical dogma
blindly made the novel the dull devitalized form (form it retained) that it
has become. The exclusion of the author can go too far. Even the author,
poor devil, has a right to exist, and M. Mauriac reaffirms that right. It is
true that the Flaubertian form is not so completely abandoned in this
novel* as in *Le Baiser au Lépreux*; the 'I' of the story plays a part in the
action; any commentary there is can be attributed by purists to this fictional 'I', but the pretence is thin – 'I' is dominated by I. Let me quote
two passages:

* *La Pharisienne.*

– Et puis, tellement beau, tu ne trouves pas?
Non, je ne le trouvais pas beau. Qu'est-ce que la beauté pour un enfant?
Sans doute, est-il surtout sensible à la force, à la puissance. Mais cette question dut me frapper puisque je me souviens encore, après toute une vie, de
cet endroit de l'allée où Michèle m'interrogea ainsi, à propos de Jean. Saurais-
je mieux définir aujourd'hui, ce que j'appelle beauté? saurais-je dire à quel
signe je la reconnais, qu'il s'agisse d'un visage de chair, d'un horizon, d'un
ciel, d'une couleur, d'une parole, d'un chant? A ce tresaillement charnel et
qui, pourtant, intéresse l'âme, à cette joie désespérée, à cette contemplation
sans issue et que ne recompense aucune etreinte . . .

Ce jour-là, j'ai vu pour la première fois à visage découvert, ma vieille
ennemie la solitude, avec qui je fais bon ménage aujourd'hui. Nous nous
connaissons: elle m'a asséné tous les coups imaginables, et il n'y a plus de
place où frapper. Je ne crois avoir évité aucun de ses pièges. Maintenant elle
a fini de me torturer. Nous tisonnons face à face, durant ces soirs d'hiver où
la chute d'une 'pigne'; un sanglot de nocturne ont autant d'intérêt pour mon
cœur qu'une voix humaine.

In such passages one is aware, as in Shakespeare's plays, of a sudden
tensing, a hush seems to fall on the spirit – this is something more important than the king, Lear, or the general, Othello, something which is un-
confined and unconditioned by plot. 'I' has ceased to speak, I is speaking.

One is never tempted to consider in detail M. Mauriac's plots. Who
can describe six months afterwards the order of events, say in *Ce Qui Etait
Perdu?* One remembers the simple outlines of *Le Baiser au Lépreux*, but
the less simple the events of the novel the more they disappear from the
mind, leaving in our memory only the characters whom we have known
so intimately that the events at the one period of their lives chosen by the
novelist can be forgotten without forgetting them. (The first lines of *La
Pharisienne* create completely the horrible Comte de Mirbel: ' "Approche
ici, garçon!" Je me retournai, croyant qu'il s'adressait à un de mes cama-
rades. Mais non, c'était bien moi qu'appelait l'ancien zouave pontifical,
souriant. La cicatrice de sa lèvre supérieure rendait le sourire hideux.')
M. Mauriac's characters exist with extraordinary physical completeness
(he has affinities here we feel to Dickens), but their particular acts are less
important than the force, whether God or Devil, that compels them, and
though M. Mauriac rises to extraordinary heights in his great 'scenes', as
when Jean de Mirbel, the boy whose soul is in such danger (a kind of
unhappy tortured Grand Meaulnes), is the silent witness outside the
country hotel of his beloved mother's vulgar adultery, the 'joins' of his
plot, the events which should make a plausible progression from one
scene to another, are often oddly lacking. Described as plots his novels

would sometimes seem to flicker like an early film. But who would attempt to describe them as plots? Wipe out the whole progression of events and we would be left still with the characters in a way I can compare with no other novelist. Take away Mrs. Dalloway's capability of self-expression and there is not merely no novel but no Mrs. Dalloway: take away the plot from Dickens and the characters who have lived so vividly from event to event would dissolve. But if the Comtesse de Mirbel had not committed adultery, if Jean's guardian, the evil Papal Zouave, had never lifted a hand against him: if the clumsy well-meaning saintly priest, the Abbé Calou, had never been put in charge of the boy: the characters, we feel, would have continued to exist in identically the same way. We are saved or damned by our thoughts, not by our actions.

The events of M. Mauriac's novels are used not to change characters (how little in truth are we changed by events: how romantic and false in comparison is such a book as Conrad's *Lord Jim*) but to reveal characters – reveal them gradually with an incomparable subtlety. His moral and religious insight is the reverse of the obvious: you will seldom find the easy false assumption, the stock figure in M. Mauriac. Take for example the poor pious usher M. Puybaraud. He is what we call in England a creeping Jesus, but M. Mauriac shows how in truth the creeping Jesus may creep towards Jesus. La Pharisienne herself under her layer of destructive egotism and false pity is disclosed sympathetically to the religious core. She learns through hypocrisy. The hypocrite cannot live insulated for ever against the beliefs she professes. There is irony but no satire in M. Mauriac's work.

I am conscious of having scattered too many names and comparisons in this short and superficial essay, but one name – the greatest – cannot be left out of any consideration of M. Mauriac's work, Pascal. This modern novelist, who allows himself the freedom to comment, comments, whether through his characters or in his own 'I', again and again in the very accents of Pascal.

'Les êtres ne changent pas, c'est là une vérité dont on ne doute plus à mon âge; mais ils retournent souvent à l'inclination que durant toute une vie ils se sont épuisés à combattre. Ce qui ne signifie point qu'ils finissent toujours par céder au pire d'eux-mêmes: Dieu est la bonne tentation à laquelle beaucoup d'hommes succombent à la fin.'

'Il y a des êtres qui tendent leurs toiles et peuvent jeûner longtemps avant qu'aucune proie s'y laisse prendre: la patience du vice est infinie.'

'Il ne faut pas essayer d'entrer dans la vie des êtres malgré eux: retiens cette leçon, mon petit. Il ne faut pas pousser la porte de cette seconde ni de cette troisième vie que Dieu seul connaît. Il ne faut jamais tourner la tête vers la ville secrète, vers la cité maudite des autres, si on ne veut pas être changé en statue de sel . . .'

'Notre-Seigneur exige que nous aimions nos ennemis; c'est plus facile souvent que de ne pas haïr ceux que nous aimons.'

If Pascal had been a novelist, we feel, this is the method and the tone he would have used.

THE BURDEN OF CHILDHOOD

THERE are certain writers, as different as Dickens from Kipling, who never shake off the burden of their childhood. The abandonment to the blacking factory in Dickens's case and in Kipling's to the cruel Aunt Rosa living in the sandy suburban road were never forgotten. All later experience seems to have been related to those months or years of unhappiness. Life which turns its cruel side to most of us at an age when we have begun to learn the arts of self-protection took these two writers by surprise during the defencelessness of early childhood. How differently they reacted. Dickens learnt sympathy, Kipling cruelty – Dickens developed a style so easy and natural that it seems capable of including the whole human race in its understanding: Kipling designed a machine, the cogwheels perfectly fashioned, for exclusion. The characters sometimes seem to rattle down a conveyor-belt like matchboxes.

There are great similarities in the early life of Kipling and Saki, and Saki's reaction to misery was nearer Kipling's than Dickens's. Kipling was born in India. H. H. Munro (I would like to drop that rather meaningless mask of the penname) in Burma. Family life for such children is always broken – the miseries recorded by Kipling and Munro must be experienced by many mute inglorious children born to the civil servant or the colonial officer in the East: the arrival of the cab at the strange relative's house, the unpacking of the boxes, the unfamiliar improvised nursery, the terrible departure of the parents, a four years' absence from affection that in child-time can be as long as a generation (at four one is a small child, at eight a boy). Kipling described the horror of that time in *Baa, Baa Black Sheep* – a story in spite of its sentimentality almost unbearable to read: Aunt Rosa's prayers, the beatings, the card with the word LIAR pinned upon the back, the growing and neglected blindness, until at last came the moment of rebellion.

> 'If you make me do that,' said Black Sheep very quietly, 'I shall burn this house down and perhaps I will kill you. I don't know whether I *can* kill you – you are so bony, but I will try.'
>
> No punishment followed this blasphemy, though Black Sheep held himself ready to work his way to Auntie Rosa's withered throat and grip there till he was beaten off.

In that last sentence we can hear something very like the tones of Munro's voice as we hear them in one of his finest stories *Sredni Vashtar*. Neither his Aunt Augusta nor his Aunt Charlotte with whom he was left near Barnstaple after his mother's death, while his father served in Burma, had the fiendish cruelty of Auntie Rosa, but Augusta ('a woman', Munro's sister wrote, 'of ungovernable temper, of fierce likes and dislikes, imperious, a moral coward, possessing no brains worth speaking of, and a primitive disposition') was quite capable of making a child's life miserable. Munro was not himself beaten, Augusta preferred his younger brother for that exercise, but we can measure the hatred he felt for her in his story of the small boy Conradin who prayed so successfully for vengeance to his tame ferret. ' "Whoever will break it to the poor child? I couldn't for the life of me!" exclaimed a shrill voice, and while they debated the matter among themselves Conradin made himself another piece of toast.' Unhappiness wonderfully aids the memory, and the best stories of Munro are all of childhood, its humour and its anarchy as well as its cruelty and unhappiness.

For Munro reacted to those years rather differently from Kipling. He, too, developed a style like a machine in self-protection, but what sparks this machine gave off. He did not protect himself like Kipling with manliness, knowingness, imaginary adventures of soldiers and Empire builders (though a certain nostalgia for such a life can be read into *The Unbearable Bassington*): he protected himself with epigrams as closely set as currants in an old-fashioned Dundee cake. As a young man trying to make a career with his father's help in the Burma Police, he wrote to his sister in 1893 complaining that she had made no effort to see *A Woman Of No Importance*. Reginald and Clovis are children of Wilde: the epigrams, the absurdities fly unremittingly back and forth, they dazzle and delight, but we are aware of a harsher, less kindly mind behind them than Wilde's. Clovis and Reginald are not creatures of fairy tale, they belong nearer to the visible world than Ernest Maltravers. While Ernest floats airily like a Rubens' cupid among the over-blue clouds, Clovis and Reginald belong to the Park, the tea-parties of Kensington and evenings at Covent Garden – they even sometimes date, like the suffragettes. They cannot quite disguise, in spite of the glint and the sparkle, the loneliness of the Barnstaple years – they are quick to hurt first, before they can be hurt, and the witty and devastating asides cut like Aunt Augusta's cane. How often these stories are stories of practical jokes. The victims with their weird names are sufficiently foolish to awaken no sympathy – they are the middle-aged, the people with power; it is right that they should suffer a temporary humiliation because the world is always on their side in the long run. Munro, like a chivalrous highwayman, only robs the rich: behind all these stories is an exacting sense of justice. In this they are to be distinguished from Kipling's stories in the same genre – *The Village That Voted The Earth Was Flat* and others where the joke is carried too far. With Kipling revenge rather than justice seems to be the motive (Aunt Rosa had established herself in the mind of her victim and corrupted it).

Perhaps I have gone a little too far in emphasizing the cruelty of Munro's work, for there are times when it seems to remind us only of the sunniness of the Edwardian scene, young men in boaters, the box at the Opera, long lazy afternoons in the Park, tea out of the thinnest porcelain with cucumber sandwiches, the easy irresponsible prattle.

Never be a pioneer. It's the Early Christian that gets the fattest lion.

There's Marion Mulciber, who *would* think she could ride down a hill on a bicycle; on that occasion she went to a hospital, now she's gone into a Sisterhood – lost all she had you know, and gave the rest to Heaven.

Her frocks are built in Paris, but she wears them with a strong English accent.

It requires a great deal of moral courage to leave in a marked manner in the middle of the second Act when your carriage is not ordered till twelve.

Sad to think that this sunniness and this prattle could not go on for ever, but the worst and cruellest practical joke was left to the end. Munro's witty, cynical hero, Comus Bassington, died incongruously of fever in a West African village, and in the early morning of November 13th, 1916, from a shallow crater near Beaumont Hamel, Munro was heard to shout 'Put out that bloody cigarette.' They were the unpredictable last words of Clovis and Reginald.

MAN MADE ANGRY

IT IS a waste of time criticizing Léon Bloy as a novelist: he hadn't the creative instinct – he was busy all the time being created himself, created by his own angers and hatreds and humiliations. Those who meet him first in this grotesque and ill-made novel* need go no further than the dedication to Brigand-Kaire, Ocean Captain, to feel the angry quality of his mind. 'God keep you safe from fire and steel and contemporary literature and the malevolence of the evil dead.' He was a religious man but without humility, a social reformer without disinterestedness, he hated the world as a saint might have done, but only because of what it did to him and not because of what it did to others. He never made the mistake by worldly standards of treating his enemies with tolerance – and in that he resembled the members of the literary cliques he most despised. Unlike his contemporary Péguy, he would never have risked damnation himself in order to save another soul, and though again and again we are surprised by sentences in his work of nobility or penetration, they are contradicted by the savage and selfish core of his intelligence. 'I must stop now, my beloved,' he wrote to his fiancée, 'to go and suffer for another day'; he had prayed for suffering, and yet he never ceased to complain that he had been granted more of it than most men; it made him at the same time boastful and bitter.

He wrote in another letter:

I am forty-three years old, and I have published some literary works of considerable importance. Even my enemies can see that I am a great artist. Also, I have suffered much for the truth, whereas I could have prostituted my pen, like so many others, and lived on the fat of the land. I have had plenty of opportunities, but I have not chosen to betray justice and I have preferred misery, obscurity and indescribable agony. It is obvious that these things ought to merit respect.

It is obvious too that these things would have been better claimed for him by others. It is the self-pity of this attitude, the luxurious bitterness that prevents Bloy from being more than an interesting eccentric of the Catholic religion. He reminds us – in our own literature – a little of Patmore, and sometimes of Corvo. He is near Patmore in his brand of

* *The Woman Who Was Poor.*

pious and uxorious sexuality which makes him describe the character of Clotilde, the heroine of his novel, as 'chaste as a Visitationist Sister's rosary', and near Corvo in the furious zest with which he takes sides against his characters: 'She bellowed, if the comparison may be permitted, like a cow that has been forgotten in a railway truck.' Indeed the hatred he feels for the characters he has himself created (surely in itself a mark of limited imagination) leads him to pile on the violence to a comic extent — 'a scandalous roar of cachinnation . . . like a bellowing of cattle from some goitred valley colonized by murderers.'

No, one reads this novel of Bloy not for his characters, who are painted only deformity-deep, nor for his story, but for the occasional flashes of his poetic sense, for images like, 'upright souls are reserved for rectilinear torments'; for passages with a nervous nightmare vision which reminds us of Rilke:

> A little middleclass township, with a pretension to the possession of gardens, such as are to be found in the quarters colonized by eccentrics, where murderous landlords hold out the bait of horticulture to trap those condemned to die.

We read him with pleasure to just the extent that we share the hatred of life which prevented him from being a novelist or a mystic of the first order (he might have taken as his motto Gauguin's great phrase — 'Life being what it is, one dreams of revenge') and because of a certain indestructible honesty and self-knowledge which in the long run always enabled him to turn his fury on himself, as when in one of his letters he recognizes the presence of 'that bitch literature' penetrating 'even the most *naif* stirrings of my heart'.

EVERY creative writer worth our consideration, every writer who can be called in the wide eighteenth-century use of the term a poet, is a victim: a man given over to an obsession. Was it not the obsessive fear of treachery which dictated not only James's plots but also his elaborate conceits (behind the barbed network of his style he could feel really secure himself), and was it not another obsession, a terrible pity for human beings, which drove Hardy to write novels that are like desperate acts of rebellion in a lost cause? What obsession then do we find in Mr. de la Mare – one of the few living writers who can survive in this company?

The obsession is perhaps most easily detected in the symbols an author uses, and it would not be far from the truth – odd as it may seem on the face of it – to say that the dominant symbol in Mr. de la Mare's short stories is the railway station or the railway journey: sometimes the small country railway station, all but deserted except by a couple of travellers chance met and an aged porter, at dusk or bathed in the quiet meditative light of a harvest afternoon: sometimes the waiting room of a great junction with its dying dusty fire and its garrulous occupant. But if not the dominant symbol at least this symbol – or rather group of symbols – occurs almost as frequently as do the ghosts of his poems – the ghosts that listen to the mother as she reads to her children, the lamenting ghosts that rattle the door like wind or moisten the glass like rain. Prose is a more intractible medium than verse. In prose we must be gently lured outside the boundaries of our experience. The symbol must in a favourable sense of the word be prosaic.

One hasty glance around him showed that he was the sole traveller to alight on the frosted timbers of the obscure little station. A faint rosiness in the west foretold the decline of the still wintry day. The firs that flanked the dreary passenger-shed of the platform stood burdened already with the blackness of coming night. (*The Tree*)

When murky winter dusk begins to settle over the railway station at Crewe its first-class waiting-room grows steadily more stagnant. Particularly if one is alone in it. The long grimed windows do little more than sift the failing light that slopes in on them from the glass roof outside and is too feeble to penetrate into the recesses beyond. And the grained massive black-leathered furniture becomes less and less inviting. It appears to have been made for a scene of extreme and diabolical violence that one may hope will never occur. One can hardly at any rate imagine it to have been designed by a really *good* man! (*Crewe*)

. . . at this instant the sad neutral winter landscape, already scarcely perceptible beneath a thin grey skin of frozen snow and a steadily descending veil of tiny flakes from the heavens above it, was suddenly blotted out. The train lights had come on, and the small cabin in which the two of them sat together had become a cage of radiance. How Lavinia hated too much light. (*A Froward Child*)

She was standing at the open window, looking out, but not as if she had ever entirely desisted from looking in – an oval face with highish cheek-bones, and eyes and mouth from which a remote smile was now vanishing as softly and secretly as a bird enters and vanishes into its nest. (*A Nest of Singing Birds*)

The noonday express with a wildly soaring crescendo of lamentation came sweeping in sheer magnificence of onset round the curve, soared through the little green empty station – its windows a long broken faceless glint of sunlit glass – and that too vanished. Vanished! A swirl of dust and an unutterable stillness followed after it. The skin of a banana on the plat-form was the only proof that it had come and gone. Its shattering clamour had left for contrast an almost helpless sense of peace. 'Yes, yes!' we all seemed to be whispering – from the Cedar of Lebanon to the little hyssop in the wall – 'here we all are; and still, thank heaven, safe. *Safe!*' (*Ding Dong Bell*)

It is surely impossible not to feel ourselves in the presence of an obsession – the same obsession that haunts the melancholy subtle cadences of Mr. de la Mare's poetry. Such trite phrases as 'ships that pass', 'travellers through life', 'journey's end' are the way in which for centuries the common man has taken a sidelong glance at the common fate (to be here, and there, and gone) – and looked away again. But every once in a while, perhaps only once or twice in a century, a man finds he cannot so easily dismiss with a regulation phrase what meets his eyes: the eyes linger: the obsession is born – in an Emily Brontë, a Beddoes, a James Thomson, in Mr. de la Mare.

'*Mors*. And what does *Mors* mean?' enquired that oddly indolent voice in the quiet. 'Was it his name, or his initials, or is it a charm?' 'It means – well, sleep,' I said. 'Or nightmare, or dawn, or nothing, or – it might mean everything.' I confess, though, that to my ear it had the sound at that moment of an enormous breaker, bursting on the shore of some unspeakably remote island; and we two marooned. (*Ding Dong Bell*)

One thing, it will be noticed in all these stories, *Mors* does not mean – it does not mean Hell – or Heaven. That obsession with death that fills Mr. de la Mare's poetry with the whisper of ghosts, that expresses itself over and over again in the short story in the form of *revenants*, has never led him to accept – or even to speculate on – the Christian answer. Christianity when it is figured in these stories is like a dead religion of which we see only the enormous stone memorials. Churches do occur – in *All Hallows, The Trumpet, Strangers and Pilgrims*, but they are empty haunted buildings.

> At this moment of the afternoon the great church almost cheated one into the belief that it was possessed of a life of its own. It lay, as I say, couched in its natural hollow, basking under the dark dome of the heavens like some half-fossilized monster that might at any moment stir and awaken out of the swoon to which the wand of the enchanter had committed it. (*All Hallows*)

What an odd world, to those of us with traditional Christian beliefs, is this world of Mr. de la Mare's: the world where the terrible Seaton's Aunt absorbs the living as a spider does and remains alive herself in the company of the dead. 'I don't look to flesh and blood for my company. When you've got to be my age, Mr. Smithers (which God forbid), you'll find life a very different affair from what you seem to think it is now. You won't seek company then, I'll be bound. It's thrust on you'; the world of the recluse Mr. Bloom, that spiritualist who had pressed on too far ignoring the advice that the poet would have given him.

> Bethink thee: every enticing league thou wend
> Beyond the mark where life its bound hath set
> Will lead thee at length where human pathways end
> And the dark enemy spreads his maddening net.

How wrong, however, it would be to give the impression that Mr. de la Mare is just another, however accomplished, writer of ghost stories, yet what is it that divides this world of Mr. Kempe and Mr. Bloom and Seaton's Aunt, the dubious fellow-passenger with Lavinia in the train, the stranger in Crewe waiting room from the world of the late M. R. James's creation – told by the antiquary? M. R. James with admirable skill invented ghosts to make the flesh creep; astutely he used the image which would best convey horror; he was concerned with truth only in the sense that his stories must ring true – while they were being read. But Mr. de la Mare is concerned, like his own Mr. Bloom, to find out: his stories are true in the sense that the author believes – and conveys his belief – that

F

this is the real world, but only in so far as he has yet discovered it. They are tentative. His use of prose reminds us frequently of a blind man trying to describe an object from the touch only – 'this thing is circular, or nearly circular, oddly dinted, too hard to be a ball: it might be, yes it might be, a human skull'. At any moment we expect a complete discovery, but the discovery is delayed. We, as well as the author, are this side of Lethe. When I was a child I used to be horrified by Carroll's poem *The Hunting of the Snark*. The danger that the snark might prove to be a boojum haunted me from the first page, and sometimes reading Mr. de la Mare's stories, I fear that the author in his strange fumbling at the invisible curtain may suddenly come on the inescapable boojum truth, and just as quickly vanish away.

For how they continually seek their snark, his characters – in railway trains, in deserted churches, even in the bars of village inns. Listen to them speaking, and see how all the time they ignore what is at least a fact – that an answer to their questions has been proposed: how intent they are to find an alternative, personal explanation: how they hover and debate and touch and withdraw, while the boojum waits.

> There's Free Will, for example; there's Moral Responsibility; and such little riddles as where we all come from and where we are going to, why, we don't even know what we are – in ourselves, I mean. And how many of us have tried to find out? (*Mr. Kempe*)

> 'The points as I take it, sir, are these. First,' he laid forefinger on forefinger, 'the number of those gone as compared with ourselves who are still waiting. Next, there being no warrant that what is seen – if seen at all – is wraiths of the departed, and not from elsewhere. The very waterspouts outside are said to be demonstrations of that belief. Third and last, another question: What purpose could call so small a sprinkling of them back – a few grains of sand out of the wilderness, unless, it may be, some festering grievance; or hunger for the living, sir; or duty left undone? In which case, mark you, which of any of us is safe?' (*Strangers and Pilgrims*)

> 'My dream was only – *after*; the state after death, as they call it. . . .' Mr. Eaves leaned forward, and all but whispered the curious tidings into her ear. 'It's – it's just the same,' he said. (*The Three Friends*)

There is no space in an essay of this length to study the technique which does occasionally creak with other than the tread of visitants; nor to dwell on the minor defects – the occasional archness, whimsicality, playfulness, especially when Mr. de la Mare is unwise enough to dress his narrator up in women's clothes (as he did in *The Memoirs of a Midget*). Perhaps we could surrender without too much regret one third of his short stories, but what a volume would be left. *The Almond Tree, Seaton's Aunt, The Three Friends, The Count's Courtship, Miss Duveen, A Recluse, Willows, Crewe, An Ideal Craftsman, A Froward Child, A Revenant, The Trumpet, Strangers and Pilgrims, Mr. Kempe, Missing, Disillusioned, All Hallows* – here is one man's choice of what he could not, under any circumstances, spare.

In all these stories we have a prose unequalled in its richness since the death of James, or dare one, at this date, say Robert Louis Stevenson. Stevenson comes particularly to mind because he played with so wide a vocabulary – the colloquial and the literary phrase, incorporating even the dialect word and naturalizing it. So Mr. de la Mare will play consciously with clichés (hemmed like James's between inverted commas), turning them underside as it were to the reader, and showing what other meanings lie there hidden: he will suddenly enrich a colloquial conversation with a literary phrase out of the common tongue, or enrich on the contrary a conscious literary description with a turn of country phrase – 'destiny was spudding at his tap root'.

With these resources at his command no one can bring the natural visible world more sharply to the eye: from the railway carriage window we watch the landscape unfold, the sparkle of frost and rain, the glare of summer sunlight, the lights in evening windows; we are wooed and lulled sometimes to the verge of sleep by the beauty of the prose, until suddenly without warning a sentence breaks in mid-breath and we look up and see the terrified eyes of our fellow-passenger, appealing, hungry, scared, as he watches what we cannot see – 'the sediment of an unspeakable obsession', and a certain glibness would seem to surround our easy conscious Christian answers to all that wild speculation, if we could ever trust ourselves to urge that cold comfort upon this stranger travelling 'our way'.

THE SARATOGA TRUNK

THE LONG trainload* draws by our platform, passes us with an inimical flash of female eyes, and proceeds on into how many more dry and gritty years. It set out in 1915 with some acclamation, carrying its embarrassing cargo – the stream of consciousness – saluted by many prominent bystanders – Miss West and Mrs. Woolf, Mr. Wells, Mr. Beresford, Mr. Swinnerton and Mr. Hugh Walpole:

> Miriam left the gaslit hall and went slowly upstairs. The March twilight lay upon the landings, but the staircase was almost dark. The top landing was quite dark and silent. There was no one about. It would be quiet in her room. She could sit by the fire and be quiet and think things over until Eve and Harriett came back with the parcels. She would have time to think about the journey and decide what she was going to say to the Fraulein. Her new Saratoga trunk stood solid and gleaming in the firelight.

Who could have foreseen in those first ordinary phrases this gigantic work which has now reached its two thousandth page, without any indication of a close? The Saratoga trunk becomes progressively more worn and labelled. There is no reason why the pilgrimage should ever end, except with the author's life, for she is attempting to represent the whole effect of every experience – friendship, politics, tea-parties, books, weather, what you will – on a woman's sensibility.

I am uncertain of my dates, but I should imagine Miss Richardson in her ponderous unwitty way has had an immense influence on such writers as Mrs. Woolf and Miss Stein, and through them on their disciples. Her novel, therefore, has something in common with Bowles's Sonnets. She herself became influenced about halfway through these four volumes (comprising twelve novels or instalments) by the later novels of Henry James – the result, though it increased the obscurity of her sensibility, was to the good, for she began to shed the adjectives which in the first volume disguise any muscles her prose may possess – 'large soft fresh pink full-blown roses' is only one phrase in a paragraph containing 41 adjectives qualifying 15 nouns. Or was it simply that Miriam became a little older, unhappier, less lyrical? In the monstrous subjectivity of this novel the author is absorbed into her character. There is no longer a Miss

* *Pilgrimage.* By Dorothy M. Richardson.

Richardson: only Miriam – Miriam off to teach English in a German school, off again to be a teacher in North London, a governess in the country, a dental secretary in Wimpole Street: a flotsam of female friendships piling up, descriptions of clothes, lodgings, encounters at the Fabian Society: Miriam taking to reviewing, among the first bicyclists, Miriam enlightened about socialism and women's rights, reading Zola from Mudie's (surely this is inaccurate) and later Ibsen, losing her virginity tardily and ineffectually on page 218 of volume 4. When the book pauses we have not yet reached the war.

There are passages of admirable description, characters do sometimes emerge clearly from the stream of consciousness – the Russian Jew, Mr. Shatov, waiting at the end of the street with a rose, patronizing the British Museum, an embarrassing and pathetic companion, and the ex-nurse Eleanor Dear, the lower middle-class consumptive clawing her unscrupulous pretty acquisitive way through other people's lives. There are passages, too, where Miriam's thought, in its Jacobean dress, takes on her master's wide impressionist poetry among the dental surroundings, as in this description of the frightened peer who has cancelled all his appointments:

> Through his staccato incoherencies – as he stood shamed and suppliant, and sociable down to the very movement of his eyelashes, and looking so much as if he had come straight from a racecourse that her mind's eye saw the diagonal from shoulder to hip of the strap of his binoculars and upon his head the grey topper that would complete his dress, and the gay rose in his buttonhole – she saw his pleasant life, saw its coming weeks, the best and brightest of the spring season, broken up by appointments to sit every few days for an indefinite time enduring discomfort and sometimes acute pain, and facing the intimate reminder that the body doesn't last, facing and feeling the certainty of death.

But the final effect, I fear, is one of weariness (that may be a tribute to Miss Richardson's integrity), the weariness of the best years of life shared with an earnest, rather sentimental and complacent woman. For one of the drawbacks of Miss Richardson's unironic and undetached method is that the compliments paid so frequently to the wit or intellect of Miriam seem addressed to the author herself. (We are reminded of those American women who remark to strangers, 'They simply worshipped me.') And as for the method – it must have seemed in 1915 a revivifying change from the tyranny of the 'plot'. But time has taken its revenge: after twenty years of subjectivity, we are turning back with relief to the old dictatorship, to the detached and objective treatment, while this novel, ignoring all signals, just ploughs on and on, the Saratoga trunk, labelled this time for Switzerland, for Austria, shaking on the rack, and Miriam still sensitively on the alert, reading far too much significance into a cup of coffee, a flower in a vase, a fog or a sunset.

THE POKER-FACE

ONE HAS seen that face over a hundred bar counters – the lick of hair over the broad white brow, the heavy moustache with pointed ends, the firm, good-humoured eyes, the man who is a cause of conviviality in other men but knows exactly when the fun should cease. He is wearing a dark suit (the jacket has four buttons) and well-polished boots. Could Sherlock Holmes have deduced from this magnificently open appearance anything at all resembling the bizarre truth?

Mr. Hesketh Pearson tells this far from ordinary story* with his admirable and accustomed forthrightness: Mr. Pearson as a biographer has some of the qualities of Dr. Johnson – a plainness, an honesty, a sense of ordinary life going on all the time. A dull biographer would never have got behind that poker-face; an excited biographer would have made us disbelieve the story, which wanders from whaling in the Arctic to fever on the West Coast of Africa, a practice in Portsea to ghost-hunting in Sussex. But from Mr. Pearson we are able to accept it. Conan Doyle has too often been compared with Dr. Watson: in this biography it is Mr. Pearson who plays Watson to the odd enigmatic product of a Jesuit education, the Sherlock-hearted Doyle.

It is an exciting story admirably told, and it is one of Mr. Pearson's virtues that he drives us to champion the subject against his biographer (Johnson has the same effect on the reader). For example, this reviewer would like to put in a word which Mr. Pearson omits for the poetic quality in Doyle, the quality which gives life to his work far more surely than does his wit. Think of the sense of horror which hangs over the laurelled drive of Upper Norwood and behind the curtains of Lower Camberwell: the dead body of Bartholomew Sholto swinging to and fro in Pondicherri Lodge, the 'bristle of red hair', 'the ghastly inscrutable smile', and in contrast Watson and Miss Mortsan hand in hand like children among the strange rubbish heaps: he made Plumstead Marshes and the Barking Level as vivid and unfamiliar as a lesser writer would have made the mangrove swamps of the West Coast which he had also known and of which he did not bother to write.

* *Conan Doyle: His Life and Art.* By Hesketh Pearson.

And, unlike most great writers, he remained so honest and pleasant a man. The child who wrote with careful necessary economy to his mother from Stonyhurst: 'I have been to the Taylor, and I showed him your letter, explaining to him that you wanted something that would wear well and at the same time look well. He told me that the blue cloth he had was meant especially for Coats, but that none of it would suit well as Fresson. He showed me a dark sort of cloth which he said would suit a coat better than any other cloth he has and would wear well as trousers. On his recommendation I took this cloth. I think you will like it; it does not show dirt and looks very well; it is a sort of black and white very dark cloth'; this child had obviously the same character as the middle-aged man who wrote chivalrously and violently against Shaw in defence of the *Titanic* officers (he was probably wrong, but, as Mr. Pearson nearly says, most of us would have preferred to be wrong with Doyle than right with Shaw).

It isn't easy for an author to remain a pleasant human being: both success and failure are usually of a crippling kind. There are so many opportunities for histrionics, hysterics, waywardness, self-importance; within such very wide limits a writer can do what he likes and go where he likes, and a human being has seldom stood up so well to such a test of freedom as Doyle did. The eccentric figure of his partner, Dr. Budd, may stride like a giant through the early pages of his biography, but in memory he dwindles into the far distance, and in the foreground we see the large, sturdy, working shoulders, a face so commonplace that it has the effect of a time-worn sculpture representing some abstract quality like Kindness or Patience, but never, one would mistakenly have said, Imagination or Poetry.

FORD MADOX FORD

THE DEATH of Ford Madox Ford was like the obscure death of a veteran – an impossibly Napoleonic veteran, say, whose immense memory spanned the period from Jena to Sedan: he belonged to the heroic age of English fiction and outlived it – yet he was only sixty-six. In one of his many volumes of reminiscence – those magnificent books where in an atmosphere of casual talk outrageous story jostles outrageous story – he quoted Mr. Wells as saying some years ago that in the southern counties a number of foreigners were conspiring against the form of the English novel. There was James at Lamb House, Crane at Brede Manor, Conrad at The Pent, and he might have added his own name, Hueffer at Aldington, for he was a quarter German (and just before the first world war made an odd extravagant effort to naturalize himself as a citizen of his grandfather's country). The conspiracy, of course, failed: the big loose middlebrow novel goes on its happy way unconscious of James's 'point of view': Conrad is regarded again as the writer of romantic sea stories and purple passages: nobody reads Crane, and Ford – well, an anonymous writer in *The Times Literary Supplement* remarked in an obituary notice that his novels began to date twenty years ago. Conservatism among English critics is extraordinarily tenacious, and they hasten, on a man's death, to wipe out any disturbance he has caused.

The son of Francis Hueffer, the musical critic of *The Times*, and grandson, on his mother's side, of Ford Madox Brown, 'Fordie' Hueffer emerges into history at the age of three offering a chair to Turgenev, and again, a little later, dressed in a suit of yellow velveteen with gold buttons, wearing one red stocking and one green one, and with long golden hair, having his chair stolen from him at a concert by the Abbé Liszt. I say emerges into history, but it is never possible to say where history ends and the hilarious imagination begins. He was always an atmospheric writer, whether he was describing the confused Armistice night when Tietjens found himself back with his mistress, Valentine Wannop, among a horde of grotesque and inexplicable strangers, or just recounting a literary anecdote of dubious origin – the drunk writer who thought himself a Bengal tiger trying to tear out the throat of the blind poet Marston, or Henry James getting hopelessly entangled in the long lead of his

dachshund Maximilian. Nobody ever wrote more about himself than
Ford, but the figure he presented was just as dubious as his anecdotes –
the figure of a Tory country gentleman who liked to grow his own food
and had sturdy independent views on politics: it all seems a long way
from the yellow velveteen. He even, at the end of his life, a little plump
and a little pink, looked the part – and all the while he had been turning
out the immense number of books which stand to his name: memoirs,
criticism, poetry, sociology, novels. And in between, if one can so put it,
he found time to be the best literary editor England has ever had: what
Masefield, Hudson, Conrad, even Hardy, owed to the *English Review* is
well known, and after the war in *the transatlantic review* he bridged the
great gap, publishing the early Hemingway, Cocteau, Stein, Pound, the
music of Antheil and the drawings of Braque.

He had the advantage – or the disadvantage – of being brought up
in pre-Raphaelite circles, and although he made a tentative effort to break
away into the Indian Civil Service, he was pushed steadily by his family
towards art – any kind of art was better than any kind of profession. He
published his first book at the age of sixteen, and his first novel, *The
Shifting of the Fire*, in 1892, when he was only nineteen – three years
before Conrad had published anything and only two years after the serial
appearance of *The Tragic Muse*, long before James had matured his
method and his style. It wasn't, of course, a good book, but neither was
it an 'arty' book – there was nothing of the 'nineties about it except its
elegant period binding, and it already bore the unmistakable Hueffer stamp –
the outrageous fancy, the pessimistic high spirits, and an abominable
hero called Kasker-Ryves. Human nature in his books was usually
phosphorescent – varying from the daemonic malice of Sylvia Tietjens to
the painstaking, rather hopeless will-to-be-good of Captain Ashburnham,
'the good soldier'. The little virtue that existed only attracted evil. But
to Mr. Ford, a Catholic in theory though not for long in practice, this was
neither surprising nor depressing: it was just what one expected.

The long roll of novels ended with *Vive le Roy* in 1937. A few deserve
to be forgotten, but I doubt whether the accusation of dating can be
brought against even such minor work as *Mr. Apollo, The Marsden Case,
When the Wicked Man*: there were the historical novels, too, with their
enormous vigour and authenticity – *The Fifth Queen* and its sequels: but
the novels which stand as high as any fiction written since the death of
James are *The Good Soldier* with its magnificent claim in the first line,
'This is the saddest story I have ever heard' – the study of an averagely

good man of a conventional class driven, divided and destroyed by un-conventional passion – and the Tietjens series, that appalling examina-tion of how private malice goes on during public disaster – no escape even in the trenches from the secret gossip and the lawyers' papers. It is dangerous in this country to talk about technique or a long essay could be written on his method in these later books, the method Conrad followed more stiffly and less skilfully, having learnt it perhaps from Ford when they collaborated on *Romance*: James's point of view was carried a step further, so that a book took place not only from the point of view but in the brain of a character and events were remembered not in chronological order, but as free association brought them to mind.

When Ford died he had passed through a period of neglect and was re-emerging. His latest books were not his best, but they were hailed as if they were. The first war had ruined him. He had volunteered, though he was over military age and was fighting a country he loved: his health was broken, and he came back to a new literary world which had carefully eliminated him. For some of his later work he could not even find a publisher in England. No wonder he preferred to live abroad – in Provence or New York. But I don't suppose failure disturbed him much: he had never really believed in human happiness, his middle life had been made miserable by passion, and he had come through – with his humour intact, his stock of unreliable anecdotes, the kind of enemies a man ought to have, and a half-belief in a posterity which would care for good writing.

FREDERICK ROLFE

EDWARDIAN INFERNO

THE OBSCURITY and what we curiously believe to be the crudity and
violence of the distant past make a suitable background to the Soul.
Temptation, one feels, is seldom today so heroically resisted or so
devastatingly succumbed to as in the days of Dante or of Milton; Satan
as well as sanctity demands an apron stage. It is, therefore, with a shock
of startled incredulity that we become aware on occasion even today of
eternal issues, of the struggle between good and evil, between vice that
really demands to be called satanic and virtue of a kind which can only
be called heavenly.

How much less are we prepared for it in the Edwardian age; in the age
of bicycles and German bands and gold chamber ware, of Norfolk jackets
and deerstalker caps. How distressingly bizarre seems the whole angelic
conflict which centred round Frederick Rolfe, self-styled Baron Corvo,
the spoilt priest, who was expelled from the Scots College at Rome, the
waster who lived on a multitude of generous friends, the writer of genius,
author of *Hadrian VII* and *Don Tarquinio* and *The History of the Borgias*.
When Rolfe's fictional self prayed in his Hampstead lodging:

> 'God, if ever You loved me, hear me, hear me. De Profundis ad Te, ad
> Te clamavi. Don't I want to be good and clean and happy? What desire have
> I cherished since my boyhood save to serve in the number of Your mystics?
> What but that have I asked of You Who made me? Not a chance do You
> give me – ever – ever –'

it is disquieting to remember how in the outside world Mr. Wells was
writing *Love on Wheels*, the Empire builders after tiffin at the club were
reading 'The Song of the Banjo', and up the crowded stairway of Grosvenor House Henry James was bearing his massive brow; disquieting too
to believe that Miss Marie Corelli was only palely limping after truth when
she brought the devil to London. For if ever there was a case of demoniac
possession it was Rolfe's: the hopeless piety, the screams of malevolence,
the sense of despair which to a man of his faith was the sin against the
Holy Ghost. 'All men are too vile for words to tell.'

The greatest saints have been men with more than a normal capacity for evil, and the most vicious men have sometimes narrowly evaded sanctity. Frederick Rolfe in his novel *Hadrian VII* expressed a sincere, if sinister, devotion to the Church that had very wisely rejected him; all the good of which he was capable went into that book, as all the evil went into the strange series of letters which Mr. Symons has described for the first time,* written at the end of his life, when he was starving in Venice, to a rich acquaintance.

He had become a habitual corrupter of youth, a seducer of innocence, and he asked his wealthy accomplice for money, first that he might use it as a temptation, to buy bait for the boys whom he misled, and secondly, so that he might efficiently act as pander when his friend revisited Venice. Neither scruple nor remorse was expressed or implied in these long accounts of his sexual exploits or enjoyments, which were so definite in their descriptions that he was forced, in sending them by post, so to fold them that only blank paper showed through the thin foreign envelopes.

These were the astonishing bounds of Corvo: the starving pander on the Lido and the man of whom Mr. Vincent O'Sullivan wrote to his biographer: 'He was born for the Church: that was his main interest.' Between these bounds, between the Paradise and the Inferno, lay the weary purgatorial years through which Mr. Symons has been the first to track him with any closeness. Mr. Symons's method, unchronological, following the story as he discovered it from witness to witness, lends Rolfe's vacillating footprints a painful drama. Continually, with the stamp of an obstinate courage, they turn back towards Paradise: from the rim of the Inferno they turn and go back: but on the threshold of Paradise they turn again because of the devilish pride which would not accept even Heaven, except on his own terms; this way and that, like the steps of a man pacing a room in agony of mind. It is odd to realize that all the time common-or-garden life is going on within hailing distance, publishers are making harsh bargains, readers are reporting adversely on his work, friends are forming hopeless plans of literary collaboration. Mr. Grant Richards and Monsignor Benson and Mr. Pirie Gordon and the partners of Chatto and Windus beckon and speak like figures on the other side of a distorting glass pane. They have quite a different reality, a much thinner reality, they are not concerned with eternal damnation. And their memories of Rolfe are puzzled, a little amused, a little exasperated, as if

* *The Quest for Corvo.* By A. J. A. Symons.

they cannot understand the eccentricity of a man who chooses to go abou
sheathed in flame in the heyday of the Entente Cordiale, of Sir Ernes
Cassel and Lily Langtry.

Mr. O'Sullivan wrote of Rolfe to Mr. Symons as a man 'who had only
the vaguest sense of realities', but the phrase seems a little inaccurate. His
realities were less material than spiritual. It would be easy to emphasize
his shady financial transactions, his pose as the Kaiser's godson, his complete inability to earn a living. It is terrible to think what a figure of crue
fun a less imaginative writer than Mr. Symons might have made of Rolfe
turned out of an Aberdeen boarding house in his pyjamas, painting pictures with the help of magic-lantern slides, forced to find employmen
as a gondolier, begging from strangers, addressing to the Pope a long in-
dictment of living Catholics. But against this material reality Mr. Symons
with admirable justice sets another: the reality of *Hadrian VII*, a novel o:
genius, which stands in relation to the other novels of its day, much as
The Hound of Heaven stands in relation to the verse. Rolfe's vice was
spiritual more than it was carnal: it might be said that he was a pander
and a swindler, because he cared for nothing but his faith. He would be
a priest or nothing, so nothing it had to be and he was not ashamed to live
on his friends; if he could not have Heaven, he would have Hell, and the
last footprints seem to point unmistakably towards the Inferno.

FROM THE DEVIL'S SIDE

'He was his own worst enemy': the little trite memorial phrase which
in the case of so many English exiles disposes discreetly and with a tasteful
agnosticism of the long purgatories in foreign *pensions*, the counted cop-
pers, the keeping up of appearances, sounds more than usually unconvincing when applied to Frederick Rolfe. It is the measure of the man's
vividness that his life always seems to move on a religious plane: his
violent hatreds, his extreme ingratitude, even his appearance as he described it himself, 'offensive, disdainful, slightly sardonic, utterly un-
approachable', have about them the air of demoniac possession. *The
Desire and Pursuit of the Whole*, the long autobiographical novel of the
last dreadful years in Venice, the manuscript of which was rediscovered
by Mr. A. J. A. Symons, has the quality of a mediaeval mystery play, but
with this difference, that the play is written from the devil's side. The
many excellent men and women, who did their best, sometimes an un-
imaginative best, to help Rolfe, here caper like demons beside the long

Venetian water-fronts: the Rev. Bobugo Bonsen (known on the angels' side, as Monsignor Benson), Harry Peary-Buthlaw, Professor Macpawkins, Lady Pash. It is instructive and entertaining to see the great and the good for once from the devil's point of view.

And the devil has been fair. Anyone who has read Mr. Symons's biography of Corvo will recognize how very fair. The facts (the correspondence with Bonsen and Peary-Buthlaw, for example) appear to be quite truthfully stated; it is Rolfe's interpretation which is odd. Offer the starving man a dinner or the homeless man a bed and instantaneously the good deed is unrecognizably distorted. The strangest motives begin obscurely to be discerned. Is it that one is seeing good from the devil's side: 'The lovely, clever, good, ugly, silly wicked faces of this world, all anxious, all selfish, all mean, all unsatisfied and unsatisfying': or is it possibly only a horribly deep insight into human nature?

The difficulty always is to distinguish between possession by a devil and possession by a holy spirit. Saints have starved like Rolfe, and no saint had a more firm belief in his spiritual vocation. He loathed the flesh (making an unnecessary oath to remain twenty years unmarried that he might demonstrate to unbelieving ecclesiastics his vocation for the priesthood) and he loved the spirit. One says that he writes from the devil's side, because his shrill rage has the same lack of dignity as Marlowe's cracker-throwing demons, because he had no humility ('he came as one to whom Mystery has a meaning and a method, as one of the intimate, and fortunate, as one who belonged, as a son of the Father'), and because, of course, he had a Monsignor among his enemies. But the devil, too, is spiritual, and when Rolfe wrote of the spirit (without the silly rage against his enemies or the sillier decorated style in which he tried to make the best of a world he had not been allowed to renounce) he wrote like an angel; our appreciation is hardly concerned in the question whether or not it was a fallen angel:

> He slowly paced along cypress-avenues, between the graves of little children with blue or white standards and the graves of adults marked by more sombre memorials. All around him were patricians bringing sheaves of painted candles and gorgeous garlands of orchids and everlastings, or plebeians on their knees grubbing up weeds and tracing pathetic designs with cheap chrysanthemums and farthing night-lights. Here, were a baker's boy and a telegraph-messenger, repainting their father's grave-post with a tin of black and a bottle of gold. There, were half a dozen ribald venal dishonest licentious young gondoliers; quiet and alone on their wicked knees round the grave of a comrade.

It was Saturday. The little triptych on the altar lay open – Sedes Sapientiæ, ora pro nobis. – How altogether lovely these byzantine eikons are! That is because they have Christian tradition – they alone, in religious art. Undoubtedly that council of the Church was inspired divinely which uttered the canon prohibiting painters from producing any ideals save those ecclesiastically dictated. Whoever dreams of praying (with expectation of response) for the prayer of a Tintoretto or a Titian, or a Bellini, or a Botticelli? But who can refrain from crying 'O Mother!' to these unruffleable wan dolls in indigo on gold?

Literature is deep in Mr. Symons's debt, and in debt, too, to all the libelled philanthropists without whose permission this book could hardly have been published.

A SPOILED PRIEST

Hubert's Arthur, the latest work of Frederick Rolfe to be brought into print by Mr. Symons, is a laborious experiment in imaginary history. The assumption is that Arthur was not murdered by King John but escaped and, after recovering a treasure left him by Richard Lion-Heart, won the crown of Jerusalem and finally, with the help of Hubert de Burgh, the chronicler of his deeds, gained the throne of England. Originally Rolfe collaborated with Mr. Pirie-Gordon, but after the inevitable quarrel he rewrote the story during the last months of his life. The style, we are told, 'was meant to be an enriched variant upon that of the *Itinerarium Regis Ricardi* and of William of Tyre, with an admixture of Maurice Hewlett.' Hewlett, alas, in this appallingly long and elaborate fantasy is too much in evidence, and perhaps only a knowledge of the circumstances in which it was written, to be gained from Mr. Symons's biography, gives it interest.

For if Rolfe is to be believed (a very big assumption) he brought this book to its leisurely decorative close at the very time when he claimed to be starving in his gondola on the Venetian lagoons.

The moment I cease moving, I am invaded by swarms of swimming rats, who in the winter are so voracious that they attack even man who is motionless. I have tried it. And have been bitten. Oh my dear man you can't think how artful fearless ferocious they are. I rigged up two bits of chain, lying loose on my prow and poop with a string by which I could shake them when attacked. For two nights the dodge acted. The swarms came (up the anchor rope) and nuzzled me: I shook the chains: the beasts plopped overboard. Then they got used to the noise and sneered. Then they bit the strings. Then they bit my toes and woke me shrieking and shaking with fear.

The very same day that he was writing this letter (whether truth or fiction doesn't really matter: one cannot doubt the imaginative vividness of the experience) he was penning, as if he had the whole of a well-fed life before him, some such slow decorative sentimental description as this of the dead St. Hugh singing before King Arthur:

> The pretty eyes were closed, the eyes of the innocent perfectly-satisfied happy face of the little red-gleaming head which reposed on the pillow of scarlet samite: but the smiling mouth was a little open, the rosy lips rhythmically moving, letting glimpses of little white teeth be seen. . . .

That to me is the real dramatic interest of *Hubert's Arthur*.

For on the whole it is a dull book of small literary merit, though it will be of interest to those already interested in the man, who can catch the moments when he drops the Hewlett mask and reveals more indirectly than in *The Desire and Pursuit of the Whole* his painfully divided personality. Reading his description of St. Hugh, 'the sweet and inerrable canorous voice of the dead', one has to believe in the genuineness of his nostalgia – for the Catholic Church, for innocence. But at the same time one cannot fail to notice the homosexual and the sadistic element in the lushness and tenderness of his epithets.

When he writes in the person of Hubert de Burgh: 'They would not let me have my will (which was for the life of a quiet clergyman). . . . So once every day since that time, I have cursed those monks out of a full heart,' one pities the spoiled priest; when he describes Arthur,

> the proud gait of the stainless pure secure in himself, wholly perfect in himself, severe with himself as with all, strong in disgust of ill, utterly careless save to keep high, clean, cold, armed, intact, apart, glistening with candid candour both of heart and of aspect, like a flower, like a maid, like a star,

one recognizes the potential sanctity of the man, just as one recognizes the really devilish mind which gives the formula for a throat-cutting with the same relish as in his book on the Borgias he had translated a recipe for cooking a goose alive. He is an obvious example to illustrate Mr. T. S. Eliot's remark in his study of the demoniac influence:

> Most people are only a very little alive; and to awaken them to the spiritual is a very great responsibility: it is only when they are so awakened that they are capable of real Good, but that at the same time they become first capable of Evil.

REMEMBERING MR. JONES

THIS BOOK* is as much a memorial to Edward Garnett as to Conrad: a memorial to the greatest of all publishers' readers, the man behind the scenes to whom we owe Conrad's works. A publisher's claim to the discovery of an author is suspect: it is the author who usually discovers the publisher, and the publisher's part is simply to pay a reliable man to recognize merit when it is brought to him by parcel-post. But we have Conrad's own testimony that had it not been for Edward Garnett's tactfully subdued encouragement he might never have written another book after *Almayer's Folly*, and one suspects it was Garnett who organized critical opinion so that Conrad had the support of his peers during the years of popular neglect. As for Garnett himself nothing could be more illuminating than his son's biographical note. Edward Garnett was brought up by parents who blended 'Victorian respectability with complete liberality of opinion. The children were undisciplined and completely untidy; only when they exhibited anything like worldliness or self-seeking were their parents surprised and shocked.'

Conrad's prefaces are not like James's, an elaborate reconstruction of technical aims. They are not prefaces to which novelists will turn so frequently as readers: they are about life as much as about art, about the words or the actions which for one reason or another were excluded from the novels – Almayer suddenly breaking out at breakfast on the subject of the ambiguous Willems, then on an expedition up-river with some Arabs, 'One thing's certain; if he finds anything worth having up there they will poison him like a dog'; about the prototype of Mr. Jones of *Victory*:

> Mr. Jones (or whatever his name was) did not drift away from me. He turned his back on me and walked out of the room. It was in a little hotel in the Island of St. Thomas in the West Indies (in the year '75) where we found him one hot afternoon extended on three chairs, all alone in the loud buzzing of flies to which his immobility and his cadaverous aspect gave a most gruesome significance. Our invasion must have displeased him because he got off the chairs brusquely and walked out, leaving with me an indelibly weird impression of his thin shanks. One of the men with me said that the fellow was the most desperate gambler he had ever come across. I said: 'A

* *Conrad's Prefaces to his Works*. With an essay by Edward Garnett.

98

professional sharper?' and got for answer: 'He's a terror; but I must say that up to a certain point he will play fair . . .' I wonder what the point was. I never saw him again because I believe he went straight on board a mail-boat which left within the hour for other ports of call in the direction of Aspinall.

They make an amusing comparison, these germs of stories, anecdotes remarkable as a rule for their anarchy (an appalling negro in Haiti) or their ambiguity (as when Lord Jim passed across Conrad's vision – 'One sunny morning in the commonplace surroundings of an eastern roadstead, I saw his form pass by – appealing – significant – under a cloud – perfectly silent') – they make an amusing comparison with those neat little dinner-table stories which set James off constructing his more intricate and deeper fictions, holding up his hand in deprecation to prevent the whole story coming out ('clumsy Life again at her stupid work'), just as the settings are socially widely dissimilar; Conrad on a small and dirty schooner in the Gulf of Mexico listening to the ferocious Ricardo's low communings 'with his familiar devil', while the old Spanish gentleman to whom he served as confidant and retainer lay dying 'in the dark and unspeakable cudd'; and James on Christmas Eve, before the table 'that glowed safe and fair through the brown London night', listening to the anecdote of his 'amiable friend'. It was a strange fate which brought these two to settle within a few miles of each other and produce from material gained at such odd extremes of life two of the great English novels of the last fifty years: *The Spoils of Poynton* and *Victory*.

The thought would have pleased Conrad. It would have satisfied what was left of his religious sense, and that was little more than a distant memory of the Sanctus bell and the incense. James spent his life working towards and round the Catholic Church, fascinated and repelled and absorbent; Conrad was born a Catholic and ended – formally – in consecrated ground, but all he retained of Catholicism was the ironic sense of an omniscience and of the final unimportance of human life under the watching eyes. Edward Garnett brings up again the old legend of Slavic influence which Conrad expressly denied. The Polish people are not Slavs and Conrad's similarity is to the French, once a Catholic nation: to the author for example of *La Condition Humaine*: the rhetoric of an abandoned faith. 'The mental degradation to which a man's intelligence is exposed on its way through life': 'the passions of men shortsighted in good and evil': in scattered phrases you get the memories of a creed working like poetry through the agnostic prose.

THE DOMESTIC BACKGROUND

THE DOMESTIC background *is* of interest: to know how a writer with the peculiar sensitivity we call genius compromises with family life. There is usually some compromise; few writers have had the ruthless egotism of Joseph Conrad who, at the birth of his first child, delayed the doctor whom he had been sent to fetch by sitting down with him and eating a second breakfast. The trouble is that a writer's home, just as much as the world outside, is his raw material. His wife's or a child's sickness: Conrad couldn't help unconsciously regarding them, as Henry James regarded the germinal anecdote at the dinner table, as something to cut short when he had had enough human pain for his purpose. 'Something human,' he put as epigraph to one of his novels, quoting Grimm 'is dearer to me than the wealth of all the world.' But no quotation more misrepresented him in his home, if Mrs. Conrad's memory is accurate.* Out of a long marriage she has remembered nothing tender, nothing considerate. On her own part, yes; she is the heroine of every anecdote.

It makes rather repellent reading, this long record of slights, grievances, verbal brutalities. Is it a true portrait? We are dealing with a mind curiously naïve (on one occasion she refers to Edward Thomas in uniform, wearing his khaki 'without ostentation, but correct in every detail'), unable to realize imaginatively her husband's devotion to his art, a mind peculiarly retentive of injuries. The triviality of her attacks on Ford Madox Ford, for example, is astonishing. For how many years has the grievance over a laundry bill fermented in this not very generous brain? After a quarter of a century the fact that Henry James served Mrs. Hueffer first at tea has not been forgotten.

She writes of Ford that he has reviled Conrad 'when he is beyond the power of defending himself'. The truth is that no one did more than Ford to preserve Conrad's fame, and no one has done more than Mrs. Conrad to injure it in this portrait she has drawn of a man monstrously selfish, who grudged the money he gave his children, who avoided responsibilities by taking to his bed, who was unfaithful to her in his old age. Of this last story we should have known nothing if it were not for Mrs.

* *Joseph Conrad and his Circle.* By Jessie Conrad.

Conrad's dark hints and evasions here. 'I made no comment': this is the phrase with which the story of his slights so often ends. But I do not think she is conscious of its complacency any more than she is conscious that the phrase with which she describes herself at the end of her book, one who has 'the privilege and the immense satisfaction of being regarded as the guardian of his memory', must seem to her readers either heartless or hypocritical.

It would be easy to cast doubt upon these ungrammatical revelations (on one occasion her memory fails her completely in the course of a paragraph). But there is obviously no conscious dishonesty in the one-sided record; the writer does not realize how damaging it is. 'The dear form', 'the dear fellow', 'the beloved face', one need not believe that these are meaningless endearments; it is simply that her mind is of a kind which harbours slights more easily than acts of kindness. She suffered – you cannot help believing that – suffered bitterly in this marriage, but it has never once occurred to her that Conrad suffered too:

> From the sound next door (we have three rooms) I know that the pain has roused Borys from his feverish doze. I won't go to him. It's no use. Presently I shall give him his salicylate, take his temperature and then go and elaborate a little more of the conversation of Mr. Verloc with his wife. It is very important that the conversation of Mr. Verloc and his wife should be elaborated – made more effective – more *true* to the character and the situation of these people.
>
> By Jove! I've got to hold myself with both hands not to burst into a laugh which would scare wife, baby and the other invalid – let alone the lady whose room is on the other side of the corridor. To-day completes the round dozen years since I finished *Almayer's Folly*.

'His own picturesque language' is Mrs. Conrad's phrase for this tortured irony.

One break comes every year in my quiet life. Then I go to Dresden, and there I am met by my dear friend and companion, Fritz von Tarlenheim. Last time, his pretty wife Helga came, and a lusty crowing baby with her. And for a week Fritz and I are together, and I hear all of what falls out in Strelsau; and in the evenings, as we walk and smoke together, we talk of Sapt, and of the King, and often of young Rupert; and, as the hours grow small, at last we speak of Flavia. For every year Fritz carries with him to Dresden a little box; in it lies a red rose, and round the stalk of the rose is a slip of paper with the words written: 'Rudolf – Flavia – always'.

So *The Prisoner of Zenda* ended. How one swallowed it all at the age of fourteen; the clever, brittle sentiment of a novel that has been made a schoolbook in Egypt, has been serialized in Japan, which has been filmed and staged time and again. Now it begins to fade out, like the ghost 'with a melodious twang'.

There is a true Edwardian air about *The Prisoner of Zenda*, *Phroso* and *The Dolly Dialogues*; and they may still survive awhile as period pieces. If one had tried, without Sir Charles Mallet's help,[*] to imagine the author, surely one would have hit on this frontispiece: the long, well-bred nose, the pointed legal face, the top hat gleaming in the late summer sun, the silver-headed cane and the chair beside the Row. Ladies with large picture hats slant off under the trees towards Hyde Park Corner. The author is amused; he has just come up to town from Lady Battersea's; he is composing a light whimsical letter on the latest political move and his own idleness to the Duchess of Sutherland, whom he knows affectionately as Griss. It is the atmosphere of Sargent, of Fabergé jewels, but one is not sorry that to this author, who enjoyed with such naïve relish the great houses, the little political crises, the vulgarity was hidden.

> Rich Jews at Court, in London and at Baden;
> Italian slang and golden chamberware;
> Adultery and racing; for the garden
> Muslin and picture hats and a blank stare.

He was a thoroughly Balliol best-seller: a double first, a President of the Union, he took his popularity (£70,000 earned in the first ten years

* *Anthony Hope and His Books.* By Sir Charles Mallet.

of writing) with admirable suavity. He was never really a professional writer: it is mainly the respectable underworld of literature that is represented in the letters of which Sir Charles Mallet's book is more or less a *précis*: he turned his novels off in a couple of months. Sometimes there were as many as three manuscripts awaiting publication. He managed in his delicate dealings with tragic or even blackguardly themes to retain the Union air of not being wholly serious. You could forgive his sentimentality because it struck so artificial an attitude. He was a Balliol man: he wasn't easily impressed by his great contemporaries. It seemed to him that Hardy was rather limited in his opinions, and when Henry James died, he wrote: 'a dear old fellow, a great gentleman . . . The critics call him a "great novelist": I can't think that.' His own work was highly praised by Sir James Barrie and Sir Gilbert Parker, but he was not conceited. 'Have you read my *Phroso*? I wrote it in seven weeks laughing, and now I have to be solemnly judged as though it were the effort of a life. It's really like explaining a kiss in the Divorce Court. . . .' An Isis Idol knows that next week he must inevitably be dethroned, and he was quite prepared to see himself superseded by another generation of popular writers who would appeal to a taste which was already beginning to reject the sentimental badinage of *The Dolly Dialogues*.

> 'I should describe you, Lady Mickleham,' I replied discreetly, 'as being a little lower than the angels.'
> Dolly's smile was almost a laugh as she asked:
> 'How much lower, please, Mr. Carter?'
> 'Just by the depth of your dimples,' I said thoughtlessly.

He always said that a run of about fifteen years would be his limit, and he wrote towards the end of his time: 'If I live to advanced age, I shall, I think, be dead while I yet live in the body. I don't complain. It is just . . . I've had a pretty good run.' It was the sporting, the thoroughly Isis manner, and one is rather sorry that he did live long enough to see his sales decline, that he didn't die, like Mr. Rassendyll, still king in Ruritania. His heart ought to have given way in his own fragile, romantic, rather bogus style at the highest leap – of his carefully recorded statistics.

THE LAST BUCHAN

MORE THAN a quarter of a century has passed since Richard Hannay found the dead man in his flat and started that long flight and pursuit – across the Yorkshire and the Scottish moors, down Mayfair streets, along the passages of Government buildings, in and out of Cabinet rooms and country houses, towards the cold Essex jetty with the thirty-nine steps, that were to be a pattern for adventure-writers ever since. John Buchan was the first to realize the enormous dramatic value of adventure in familiar surroundings happening to unadventurous men, members of Parliament and members of the Athenaeum, lawyers and barristers, business men and minor peers: murder in 'the atmosphere of breeding and simplicity and stability'. Richard Hannay, Sir Edward Leithen, Mr. Blenkiron, Archie Roylance and Lord Lamancha; these were his adventurers, not Dr. Nikola or the Master of Ballantrae, and who will forget that first thrill in 1916 as the hunted Leithen – the future Solicitor-General – ran 'like a thief in a London thoroughfare on a June afternoon'.

Now I saw how thin is the protection of civilization. An accident and a bogus ambulance – a false charge and a bogus arrest – there were a dozen ways of spiriting one out of this gay and bustling world.

Now Leithen, who survived the perils of the Green Park and the mews near Belgrave Square, has died in what must seem to those who remember *The Power House* a rather humdrum way, doing good to depressed and starving Indians in Northern Canada, anticipating by only a few months his creator's death.*

What is remarkable about these adventure-stories is the completeness of the world they describe. The backgrounds to many of us may not be sympathetic, but they are elaborately worked in: each character carries round with him his school, his regiment, his religious beliefs, often touched with Calvinism: memories of grouse-shooting and deer-stalking, of sport at Eton, debates in the House. For men who live so dangerously they are oddly conventional – or perhaps, remembering men like Scott and Oates, we can regard that, too, as a realistic touch. They judge men by their war-record: even the priest in *Sick Heart River*, fighting in the

---

* *Sick Heart River*. By John Buchan. 1940.

desolate northern waste for the Indians' salvation, is accepted by Leithen because 'he had served in a French battalion which had been on the right of the Guards at Loos'. Toc H and the British Legion lurk in the background.

In the early books, fascinated by the new imaginative form, the hairbreadth escapes in a real world, participating whole-heartedly in the struggle between a member of the Athenaeum and the man who could hood his eyes like a hawk, we didn't notice the curious personal ideals, the vast importance Buchan attributed to success, the materialism . . . *Sick Heart River*, the last adventure of the dying Leithen seeking – at Blenkiron's request – the missing business man, Francis Galliard, who had left his wife and returned to his ancestral North, has all the old admirable dry ease of style – it is the intellectual content which repels us now, the Scotch admiration of success. 'Harold has a hard life. He's head of the Fremont Banking Corporation and a St. Sebastian for everyone to shoot arrows at.' Even a nation is judged by the same standard: 'They ought to have made a rather bigger show in the world, than they have.' Individuals are of enormous importance. Just as the sinister Mr. Andrew Lumley in *The Power House* was capable of crumbling the whole Western world into anarchy, so Francis Galliard – 'one of Simon Ravelston's partners' – must be found for the sake of America. 'He's too valuable a man to lose, and in our present state of precarious balance we just can't afford it.'

But though *Sick Heart River* appears at the moment least favourable to these ideas (for it is not, after all, the great men – the bankers and the divisional commanders and the Ambassadors, who have been holding our world together this winter, and if we survive, it is by 'the wandering, wavering grace of humble men' in Bow and Coventry, Bristol and Birmingham), let us gratefully admit that, in one way at any rate, Buchan prepared us in his thrillers better than he knew for the death that may come to any of us, as it nearly came to Leithen, by the railings of the Park or the doorway of the mews. For certainly we can all see now 'how thin is the protection of civilization'.

BEATRIX POTTER

'IT IS said that the effect of eating too much lettuce is soporific.' It is with some such precise informative sentence that one might have expected the great Potter saga to open, for the obvious characteristic of Beatrix Potter's style is a selective realism, which takes emotion for granted and puts aside love and death with a gentle detachment reminiscent of Mr. E. M. Forster's. Her stories contain plenty of dramatic action, but it is described from the outside by an acute and unromantic observer, who never sacrifices truth for an effective gesture. As an example of Miss Potter's empiricism, her rigid adherence to what can be seen and heard, consider the climax of her masterpiece *The Roly-Poly Pudding*, Tom Kitten's capture by the rats in the attic:

> 'Anna Maria,' said the old man rat (whose name was Samuel Whiskers), 'Anna Maria, make me a kitten dumpling roly-poly pudding for my dinner.'
> 'It requires dough and a pat of butter, and a rolling pin,' said Anna Maria, considering Tom Kitten with her head on one side.
> 'No,' said Samuel Whiskers, 'Make it properly, Anna Maria, with breadcrumbs.'

But in 1908 *The Roly-Poly Pudding* was published, Miss Potter was at the height of her power. She was not a born realist, and her first story was not only romantic, it was historical. *The Tailor of Gloucester* opens:

> In the time of swords and periwigs and full-skirted lappets – when gentlemen wore ruffles, and gold-laced waistcoats of paduasoy and taffeta – there lived a tailor in Gloucester.

In the sharp details of this sentence, in the flowered lappets, there is a hint of the future Potter, but her first book is not only hampered by its period setting but by the presence of a human character. Miss Potter is seldom at her best with human beings (the only flaw in *The Roly-Poly Pudding* is the introduction in the final pages of the authoress in person), though with one human character she succeeded triumphantly. I refer, of course, to Mr. MacGregor, who made an elusive appearance in 1904 in *The Tale of Benjamin Bunny*, ran his crabbed earth-mould way through *Peter Rabbit* and met his final ignominious defeat in *The Flopsy Bunnies* in 1909. But the tailor of Gloucester cannot be compared with Mr. MacGregor. He is too ineffective and too virtuous, and the atmosphere of the story – snow, and Christmas bells and poverty – is too Dickensian. Incidentally in Simpkin Miss Potter drew her only unsympathetic portrait of a cat. The ancestors of Tom Thumb and Hunca-Munca play a humanitarian part. Their kind hearts are a little oppressive.

In the same year Miss Potter published *Squirrel Nutkin*. It is an unsatisfactory book, less interesting than her first, which was a good example of a bad *genre*. But in 1904, with the publication of *Two Bad Mice*, Miss Potter opened the series of her great comedies. In this story of Tom Thumb and Hunca-Munca and their wanton havoc of a doll's house, the unmistakable Potter style first appears.

It is an elusive style, difficult to analyse. It owes something to alliteration:

> Hunca Munca stood up in her chair and chopped at the ham with another lead knife.
> 'It's as hard as the hams at the cheesemonger's,' said Hunca Munca.

Something too it owes to the short paragraphs, which are fashioned with a delicate irony, not to complete a movement, but mutely to criticize the action by arresting it. The imperceptive pause allows the mind to take in the picture: the mice are stilled in their enraged attitudes for a moment, before the action sweeps forward:

> Then there was no end to the rage and disappointment of Tom Thumb and Hunca Munca. They broke up the pudding, the lobsters, the pears and the oranges.
> As the fish would not come off the plate, they put it into the red-hot crinkly paper fire in the kitchen; but it would not burn either.

It is curious that Beatrix Potter's method of paragraphing has never been imitated.

The last quotation shows another element of her later style, her love of a precise catalogue, her creation of atmosphere with still-life. One remembers Mr. MacGregor's rubbish heap:

> There were jam pots and paper bags and mountains of chopped grass from the mowing machine (which always tasted oily), and some rotten vegetable marrows and an old boot or two.

The only indication in *Two Bad Mice* of a prentice hand is the sparsity of dialogue; her characters had not yet begun to utter those brief pregnant sentences, which have slipped, like proverbs, into common speech. Nothing in the early book equals Mr. Jackson's, 'No teeth. No teeth. No teeth.'

In 1904 too *The Tale of Peter Rabbit*, the second of the great comedies, was published, closely followed by its sequel, *Benjamin Bunny*. In Peter and his cousin Benjamin Miss Potter created two epic personalities. The great characters of fiction are often paired: Quixote and Sancho, Pantagruel and Panurge, Pickwick and Weller, Benjamin and Peter. Peter was a neurotic, Benjamin worldly and imperturbable. Peter was warned by his mother, 'Don't go into Mr. MacGregor's garden; your father had an accident there; he was put in a pie by Mrs. MacGregor.' But Peter went from stupidity rather than for adventure. He escaped from Mr. MacGregor by leaving his clothes behind, and the sequel, the story of how his clothes were recovered, introduces Benjamin, whose coolness and practicality are a foil to the nerves and clumsiness of his cousin. It was Benjamin who knew the way to enter a garden: 'It spoils peoples' clothes to squeeze under a gate; the proper way to get in is to climb down a pear tree.' It was Peter who fell down head first.

From 1904 to 1908 were vintage years in comedy; to these years belong *The Pie and the Patty Pan*, *The Tale of Tom Kitten*, *The Tale of Mrs. Tiggy Winkle*, and only one failure, *Mr. Jeremy Fisher*. Miss Potter had found her right vein and her right scene. The novels were now set in Cumberland; the farms, the village shops, the stone walls, the green slope of Catbells became the background of her pictures and her prose. She was peopling a countryside. Her dialogue had become memorable because aphoristic:

> 'I disapprove of tin articles in puddings and pies. It is most undesirable – (especially when people swallow in lumps).'

She could draw a portrait in a sentence:

> 'My name is Mrs. Tiggy Winkle; oh yes if you please'm, I'm an excellent clear-starcher.'

And with what beautiful economy she sketched the first smiling villain of her gallery! Tom Kitten had dropped his clothes off the garden wall as the Puddle-Duck family passed:

> 'Come! Mr. Drake Puddle-Duck,' said Moppet. 'Come and help us to dress him! Come and button up Tom!'
> Mr. Drake Puddle-Duck advanced in a slow sideways manner, and picked up the various articles.
> But he put them on himself. They fitted him even worse than Tom Kitten.
> 'It's a very fine morning,' said Mr. Drake Puddle-Duck.

Looking backward over the thirty years of Miss Potter's literary career, we see that the creation of Mr. Puddle-Duck marked the beginning of a new period. At some time between 1907 and 1909 Miss Potter must have passed through an emotional ordeal which changed the character of her genius. It would be impertinent to inquire into the nature of the ordeal. Her case is curiously similar to that of Henry James. Something happened which shook their faith in appearances. From *The Portrait of a Lady* onwards, innocence deceived, the treachery of friends, became the theme of James's greatest stories. Mme Merle, Kate Croy, Mme de Vionnet, Charlotte Stant, these tortuous treacherous women are paralleled through the dark period of Miss Potter's art. 'A man can smile and smile and be a villain,' that, a little altered, was her recurrent message, expressed by her gallery of scoundrels: Mr. Drake Puddle-Duck, the first and slightest, Mr. Jackson, the least harmful with his passion for honey and his re-iterated, 'No teeth. No teeth. No teeth,' Samuel Whiskers, gross and brutal, and the 'gentleman with sandy whiskers' who may be identified with Mr. Tod. With the publication of *Mr. Tod* in 1912, Miss Potter's pessimism reached its climax. But for the nature of her audience *Mr. Tod* would certainly have ended tragically. In *Jemina Puddle-Duck* the gentle-man with sandy whiskers had at least a debonair impudence when he addressed his victims:

'Before you commence your tedious sitting, I intend to give you a treat. Let us have a dinner party all to ourselves!
'May I ask you to bring up some herbs from the farm garden to make a savoury omelette? Sage and thyme, and mint and two onions, and some parsley. I will provide lard for the stuff – lard for the omelette,' said the hospitable gentleman with sandy whiskers.

But no charm softens the brutality of Mr. Tod and his enemy, the repulsive Tommy Brock. In her comedies Miss Potter had gracefully eliminated the emotions of love and death; it is the measure of her genius that when, in *The Tale of Mr. Tod*, they broke the barrier, the form of her book, her ironic style, remained unshattered. When she could not keep death out she stretched her technique to include it. Benjamin and Peter had grown up and married, and Benjamin's babies were stolen by Brock; the immortal pair, one still neurotic, the other knowing and imperturb-able, set off to the rescue, but the rescue, conducted in darkness, from a house, 'something between a cave, a prison, and a tumbledown pig-stye', compares grimly with an earlier rescue from Mr. MacGregor's sunny vegetable garden:

The sun had set; an owl began to hoot in the wood. There were many unpleasant things lying about, that had much better have been buried; rabbit bones and skulls, and chicken's legs and other horrors. It was a shocking place and very dark.

But *Mr. Tod*, for all the horror of its atmosphere, is indispensable. There are few fights in literature which can compare in excitement with the duel between Mr. Tod and Tommy Brock (it was echoed by H. G. Wells in *Mr. Polly*):

> Everything was upset except the kitchen table.
> And everything was broken, except the mantelpiece and the kitchen fender. The crockery was smashed to atoms.
> The chairs were broken, and the window, and the clock fell with a crash, and there were handfuls of Mr. Tod's sandy whiskers.
> The vases fell off the mantelpiece, the canisters fell off the shelf; the kettle fell off the hob. Tommy Brock put his foot in a jar of raspberry jam.

Mr. Tod marked the distance which Miss Potter had travelled since the ingenuous romanticism of *The Tailor of Gloucester*. The next year with *The Tale of Pigling Bland*, the period of the great near-tragedies came to an end. There was something of the same squalor, and the villain, Mr. Thomas Piperson, was not less terrible than Mr. Tod, but the book ended on a lyrical note, as Pigling Bland escaped with Pig-Wig:

> They ran, and they ran, and they ran down the hill, and across a short cut on level green turf at the bottom, between pebble-beds and rushes. They came to the river, they came to the bridge – they crossed it hand in hand –

It was the nearest Miss Potter had approached to a conventional love story. The last sentence seemed a promise that the cloud had lifted, that there was to be a return to the style of the earlier comedies. But *Pigling Bland* was published in 1913. Through the years of war the author was silent, and for many years after it was over, only a few books of rhyme appeared. These showed that Miss Potter had lost none of her skill as an artist, but left the great question of whither her genius was tending unanswered. Then, after seventeen years, at the end of 1930, *Little Pig Robinson* was published.

The scene was no longer Cumberland but Devonshire and the sea. The story, more than twice as long as *Mr. Tod*, was diffuse and undramatic. The smooth smiling villain had disappeared and taken with him the pungent dialogue, the sharp detail, the light of common day. Miss Potter had not returned to the great comedies. She had gone on beyond the great near-tragedies to her *Tempest*. No tortured Lear nor strutting Antony could live on Prospero's island, among the sounds and sweet airs and cloud-capt towers. Miss Potter too had reached her island, the escape from tragedy, the final surrender of imagination to safe serene fancy:

> A stream of boiling water flowed down the silvery strand. The shore was covered with oysters. Acid-drops and sweets grew upon the trees. Yams, which are a sort of sweet potato, abounded ready cooked. The breadfruit tree grew iced cakes and muffins ready baked.

It was all very satisfying for a pig Robinson, but in that rarified air no bawdy Tommy Brock could creep to burrow, no Benjamin pursued his feud between the vegetable-frames, no Puddle-Duck could search in wide-eyed innocence for a 'convenient dry nesting-place'.

Note. On the publication of this essay I received a somewhat acid letter from Miss Potter correcting certain details. *Little Pig Robinson*, although the last published of her books, was in fact the first written. She denied that there had been any emotional disturbance at the time she was writing *Mr. Tod*: she was suffering however from the after-effects of 'flu. In conclusion she deprecated sharply 'the Freudian school' of criticism.

M Y FATHER used to have hanging on his bathroom wall a photo-
graphic group of young men in evening dress with bright blue
waistcoats. They were, I think, the officials of an Oxford undergraduate wining club, but with their side-whiskers and heavy moustaches
they had more the appearance of Liberal Ministers. Earnest and well-
informed, they hardly seemed to be members of the same world as Jack
Harkaway, whose adventures at Oxford were published in twopenny
numbers – or bound together in two volumes at 6*d.* apiece – by the 'Boys
of England' office some time in the early eighties. They seemed, sitting there
on hard dining-room chairs, squarely facing the camera, to hark back more
naturally to that much earlier Oxford described by Newman, when *Letters
on the Church by an Episcopalian* was a book to make the blood boil – 'One
of our common friends told me, that, after reading it, he could not keep
still, but went on walking up and down his room.' But unless we are to
disbelieve the literary evidence of *Jack Harkaway at Oxford,* the earnest
moustache is deceptive: it is the bright blue waistcoat which is the opera-
tive image, and I like to imagine that my father's photograph contains the
whole galaxy – Tom Carden, Sir Sydney Dawson, Fabian Hall, Harvey
and the Duke of Woodstock – of what must have been known universally
as a Harkaway year, for in 188– Harkaway succeeded in the then unpre-
cedented feat of winning his Blue for rowing, cricket and football and
ending the academic year with a double-first. All this too in spite of the
many attempts upon his life and honour engineered by Davis of Singapore
whom he had baffled while still a schoolboy in the East. Their reunion at
Sir Sydney Dawson's 'wine' is an impressive scene – impressive too in its
setting:

> 'A variety of wines were upon the table with all sorts of biscuits and
> preserved fruits. Olives, however, seemed to be the most popular. A box of
> cigars, which cost four guineas, invited the attention of smokers. . . . Jack
> walked over to a tall, effeminate looking young man, with a pale complexion,
> and having his hair parted in the middle.
> 'How do, Kemp?' he said.
> 'Ah, how do?' replied Kemp, with a peculiar smile. 'Allow me to introduce
> you to my friend, Mr. Frank Davis of Singapore.'
> Jack stared in amazement. Before him was his sworn and determined

enemy. Davis had told him that he was going to England to complete his education at a University. He had added that wherever Jack was, he would still hate him, and seek for his revenge. . . . That it was Davis of Singapore he had no doubt. He had lost one ear.

Making a cold and distant bow, Davis replied – 'Mr. Harkaway and I have met before.'

'Really!' exclaimed Kemp. 'I'm glad of that. It's such a nuisance helping fellows to talk. Davis is not in our college. He's a Merton man.'

It was unwise of Harkaway towards the end of this same 'wine' to transfix Kemp's hand to the table with a fork when he detected him cheating at cards. The incident led directly to the corruption of Sir Sydney with drink so that he could not ride in the steeplechase against the Duke of Woodstock's horse, Kemp up; to Jack's imprisonment for debt on the eve of the Boat Race (but the Jew's beautiful daughter Hilda, whom he had saved from drowning in the Cher, foiled *that* plot); to the kidnapping of Hilda and Emily, Jack's betrothed, by Davis and the Duke of Woodstock ("Let's have – aw – one kiss before we part," said the Duke, with an amorous glance in Hilda's direction. "Dash my – aw – buttons, but one kiss." "); to the foul attempt on Jack's life in a railway train, and to Kemp setting Emily alight – a rather bizarre episode:

He approached Emily, who was standing with her back to him in her muslin ball dress, looking very gauzy and fairylike.

Drawing a wax match from his pocket, he struck it gently, and held it under her skirt lighting the inflammable material in three places.

Then he retired with the same snakelike, gliding manner.

The story is, of course, a sensational one (it isn't often that an undergraduate arrives in Oxford with so teeming a past, and with a private tutor – Mr. Mole – who had been secretly married to a black woman in the east), but its chief value, I think, lies in its incidentals: the still-life of an Oxford breakfast – 'At ten o'clock a very decent breakfast stood on the table, consisting of cold game, hot fish, Strasbourg patties, honey in the comb, tea and coffee, with other trifles'; in the delightful turns of phrase:

'Do you dine in Hall?'
'No, we have ordered our mutton at the Mitre';

and the local manners:

'What shall we do?'
'Go and screw Scraper up,' said an undergraduate in his second year.
'Splendid!' replied Sir Sydney Dawson. 'Get a hammer and gimlet and some screws.'

H

Mr. Scraper was an unpopular tutor, and they did not care for consequences. . . . The Dean heard the noise, and summoning two tutors, wen
with the porter carrying a lantern to the scene of the disturbance.
'What is the matter, Mr. Scraper?' said the Dean.
'I am screwed up, sir,' said Mr. Scraper.

One notices in this wild scene outside Mr. Scraper's window an od
change in the character of one college: 'A friend of Dawson's who was
Brasenose man sank on his knees overcome by wine, and began to recit
a portion of Demosthenes' oration on the crown.'

But above all I value the book for its picture of Sir Sydney Dawson
imprudent, good-hearted, arrogant, the apotheosis of the wining club
With his aristocratic brutality and his spendthrift kindliness, he mus
have been every inch a blue waistcoat. Take, for example, the incident o
the explosive cigars in Sir Sydney's room: ' "I keep them for my tradesmen. The fellows come here worrying for orders and I give them a cigar
which soon starts them," replied the baronet laughing,' but when he ha
blown up Mr. Mole, scorched his face and tumbled him in a bowl of gold-
fish, he feels for the tutor – 'By Jove, this is not right. I must write a lette
of apology.' In the theatre 'as if to show his contempt for Oxford society
Sir Sydney Dawson took out his handsome cigar-case, and lighted up
though he knew it was against the rules', but his treatment of Franklir
who does lines for commoners in return for a consideration (' "I am one
of the servitors of the college. Perhaps you do not know what that is," he
added with a sad smile') shows he has a kind heart. ' "I wonder what
poor man at Oxford is like. I should like to see him. Perhaps an hour o
two with a poor man would do me good, always supposing he's a gentleman. I can't stand a cad." '

It may be argued, of course, that, because the author, Edwin J. Brett
had never been to Oxford, this whole setting is imaginary, an Oxford o
the heart, but I do not see why the well-known argument in favour o
immortality should not apply here too – that 'an instinct does not exist
unless there is a possibility of its being satisfied', and certainly the instinc
exists in this confused uncertain age – a will to return to Sir Sydney's
reckless self-assurance and his breakfasts, to 'a mutton at the Mitre', a dog-
cart 'spanking along the Iffley Road', to screwing Scraper up.

THE UNKNOWN WAR

THERE are legendary figures in this war* of whom most of us know nothing. Secretly, week by week, they fight against the evil things: against Vultz, the mad German inventor, against Poyner, preparing to unleash plague-stricken rats on India, and the sneering sarcastic Group-Captain Jarvis, who was really Agent 17 at Air Base B. Billy the Penman; Nick Ward, heroic son of an heroic father; Steelfinger Stark, the greatest lock expert in the world, who broke open the headquarters of the German Command in Norway; Worrals of the W.A.A.F.s; Flight-Lieutenant Falconer, with a price of 20,000 marks on his head, 'framed' as a spy; Captain Zoom, the Bird Man of the R.A.F. – these are the heroes (and heroines) of the unknown war. This can never at any time have been a 'phoney' war: from the word go, these famous individuals were on the job.

It is not surprising in some of these cases that we know little or nothing about it: even his fellow schoolboys are still unaware of the identity of Billy Baker. His biography records one occasion when he was rebuked in class for an untidy piece of dictation. 'The Headmaster would have got a shock if he had known he was scolding the boy who was known as "Billy the Penman", the hand-writing genius of the British Secret Service. That was a secret shared by very few people indeed.' (It was a fine piece of work which enabled Billy the Penman to substitute 500 'lines' – 'I must do my best handwriting' – for the details of a new anti-aircraft gun before the Nazi plane swooped down to hook the package from a clothes-line.)

On the other hand only the extreme discretion of his school-fellows can have prevented news of Nick Ward's activities reaching the general ear. Nick Ward, because of a certain birth-mark on his body, is considered sacred by Indian hillmen, and periodically he visits the Temple of Snakes in the Himalayas to gather information of Nazi intrigues. (To Ward we owe it that a plot to enable German bombers to cut off Northern India failed.) Unfortunately on one of these journeys he was spotted by enemy agents. 'It was because he had been recognized and because the Headmaster wished to protect him that all the boys at Sohan College had been ordered to wear hoods over their heads. It had thus become impossible

* Written in 1940.

for the Nazi agents to pick out Nick from the others. Later, Nick discovered that the local Nazi leader was Dr. Poyner the school medical officer.' Only a school medical officer was capable of conceiving the dastardly stratagem that nearly betrayed Ward into enemy hands. Hillmen crept up to the dormitory with pegs on their noses and blew sneezing powder into the room, so that the boys were forced to take off their hoods. (The pegs on their noses prevented the Indians being affected.)

Perhaps the spirit of these heroes is best exemplified by a heroine – Worrals, who shot down the mysterious 'twin-engined high-wing monoplane with tapered wings, painted grey, with no markings' in area 21-C-2. Her real name is Pilot-Officer Joan Worralson, W.A.A.F., and we hear of her first as she sat moody and bored on an empty oil drum, complaining of the monotony of life. 'The fact is, Frecks, there is a limit to the number of times one can take up a light plane and fly it to the same place without getting bored . . .' Boredom is never allowed to become a serious danger to these lone wolves: one cannot picture any of them ensconced in a Maginot line.

But the man who inspires one with the greatest admiration is Captain Zoom, the lone flyer who beats away on his individualistic flights borne up on long black condor wings, with a small dynamo ticking on his breast. Even his mad enemy Vultz couldn't withhold admiration. 'For a pig-dog of a Briton, he must have brains! This is a good invention. By the time I have improved it, it will be fit to use. Ja!' Vultz, it should be explained, was engaged in building a tunnel from Guernsey to Britain. 'The Nazis, since their occupation of the Channel Islands, had thought out a new scheme for invading Britain. They were tunnelling from Guernsey to Cornwall, using an entirely new type of boring-machine invented by a brilliant engineer named Vultz. This machine made tunnelling almost as quick as walking. Vultz, a fiend in human form, had a fixed hatred of R.A.F. men, and for this reason employed them as slaves in the tunnel.' No wonder Nick Ward on another occasion exclaimed that 'the Nazis stopped at nothing. They did not mind how foul were the tricks they tried or how many helpless victims died.' Listen to Vultz himself:

'It is here we must finish our tunnel,' he croaked. 'Portland Bill is the place. I don't care what the High Command says. If they want me to help them they must listen to me. It is the shortest distance across Channel from here.'

'Ja, that is right, Herr Vultz, but they say –' began a red-faced colonel.

'Bah, I will hear no more of it,' screeched the greatest engineer in Germany. 'I don't care what they say. You can tell them I will build my tunnel to Portland Bill or nowhere. It will be finished one week from today – if only they send me some more prisoners of war to work for me.'

The second man spoke up.

'We have hundreds of thousands of prisoners of all kinds, British, French and Polish. We can send you thousands of them but you demand R.A.F. men. Not enough R.A.F. men are being captured to supply you, Herr Vultz. Why will you not use someone else?'

The face of the mad engineer became twisted like that of a demon. He thumped the table.

'Because my boring-machine kills those who work in it. It shakes them to pieces, and I like to see R.A.F. men shaken to pieces. I have reason to hate them. I will have R.A.F. men or none. If they cannot capture enough, they must do so in some other way. I want five hundred R.A.F. men.'

In fact, Vultz lost even the men he had: they were rescued by Zoom, and the Guernsey tunnelling camp was pounded to pieces by the R.A.F. 'The Birdman had succeeded in his biggest job, the saving of Britain.'

But Vultz, one assumes, escaped. None of the leaders in this war ever dies, on either side. There are impossible escapes, impossible rescues, but one impossibility never happens – neither good nor evil is ever finally beaten. The war goes on; Vultz changes his ground – perhaps in happier days he may become again only a Pirate captain sniggering as his lesser victims walk the plank: Falconer, the air ace, is condemned to the firing squad, but the bullets have not been moulded that will finish his career. We are all of us seeing a bit of death these days, but we shall not see their deaths. They will go on living week after week in the pages of the *Rover*, the *Skipper*, the *Hotspur*, the *B.O.P.*, and the *Girls' Own Paper*; in the brain of the boy who brings the parcels, of the evacuee child scowling from the railway compartment on his way to ignominious safety, of the shelter nuisance of whom we say: 'How can anyone live with a child like that?' The answer, of course, is that he doesn't, except at mealtimes, live with *us*. He has other companions: he is part of a war that will never come to an end.

Part Three

SOME CHARACTERS

FRANCIS PARKMAN

My 23rd Birthday. Nooned at a mud puddle.' So Parkman noted in his journal* in 1846 and we shall look far for any comparable passage in the diaries of a creative artist. Certainly the wind has never played quite so freely at a historian's birth. The smell of documents, the hard feel of the desk chair, are singularly absent. Parkman had already ridden for three weeks on the arduous and dangerous Oregon trail, and in an earlier passage, a week or two back, he had let his imagination dwell on that vast range of experience already crossed between the ages of eighteen and twenty-two.

> Shaw and Henry went off for buffaloes. H. killed two bulls. The Capt. very nervous and old-womanish at nooning – he did not like the look of the hills, which were at least half a mile off – there might be Inds. there, ready to pounce on the horses. In the afternoon, rode among the hills – plenty of antelope – lay on the barren ridge of one of them, and contrasted my present situation with my situation in the convent at Rome.

Surely no other historian has planned his life work so young nor learned to write so hard a way. At the age of eighteen the whole scheme of his great work *France and England in North America* had captured his consciousness; there remained only to gather his material and to begin. One remembers the immense importance that Gibbon's biographers have attributed to his gentlemanly service in the Hampshire Militia, but what are we to think of a young historian who before starting to write his first volume, *The Conspiracy of Pontiac*, finds it necessary to make the long journey to Europe and Rome, there to stay in a Passionist monastery so that he may attain some imaginative sympathy with the Catholic missionaries who are the heroes of his second volume (published twenty-four years later) and after that to undertake his journey along the Oregon trail in quest of Indian lore, thus ruining his health for a lifetime in the mere gathering of background material?

Parkman was an uncertain stylist (as the admirable editor of these journals writes: 'There seems to have been a natural instinct for the phrase that is just a shade too high, just as his ear was naturally faulty'), but his

* *The Journals of Francis Parkman.* Edited by Mason Wade.

errors of taste are carried away on the great drive of his narrative, much as they are in the case of Motley and in our own day Mr. Churchill. He had ridden off through the dangerous wilderness with a single companion, like one of the heroes of his epic or a character in Fenimore Cooper, who had woken his genius, he had eaten dog with the Indians and stayed in their moving villages, he had watched the tribes gather for war and heard the news of traders' deaths brought in. He had listened to Big Crow's own account of his savagery – 'he has killed 14 men; and dwells with great satisfaction on the capture of a Utah, whom he took personally; and, with the other Sioux, scalped alive, cut the tendons of his wrist, and flung, still alive, into a great fire.' Since the seventeenth century no historian had so lived and suffered for his art. Like Prescott he all but lost his sight, so that he was forced to use a wire grid to guide his pencil, he suffered from misanthropy and a melancholia that snaps out like a dog even from his early journals ('the little contemptible faces – the thin, weak tottering figures – that one meets here on Broadway, are disgusting. One feels savage with human nature'). The work planned at eighteen, begun at twenty-eight, was only finished at fifty-nine, in the year before his death, by working against time and his own health. This was a poet's vocation, followed with a desperate intensity careless of consequences, and the journals are as important in tracing the course of the creative impulse as the journals of Henry James. And how closely we are reminded of the James family and their strange melancholia when we read in one of Parkman's letters:

Between 1852 and 1860 this cerebral rebellion passed through great and seemingly capricious fluctuations. It had its ebbs and floods. Slight and sometimes imperceptible causes would produce an access which sometimes lasted with little respite for months. When it was in its milder moods, I used the opportunity to collect material and prepare ground for the future work, should work ever become practicable. When it was at its worst, the condition was not enviable. I could neither listen to reading nor engage in conversation, even of the lightest. Sleep was difficult, and was often banished entirely for one or two nights during which the brain was apt to be in a state of abnormal activity which had to be repressed at any cost, since thought produced the intensest torture. The effort required to keep the irritated organ quiet was so fatiguing that I occasionally rose and spent hours in the open air, where I found distraction and relief watching the policemen and the tramps on the Malls of Boston Common, at the risk of passing for a tramp myself. Towards the end of the night this cerebral excitation would seem to tire itself out, and give place to a condition of weight and oppression much easier to bear.

Mr. Mason Wade is an impeccable editor, sensitive to the qualities of Parkman's style, its merits as well as its demerits, learned in his subject, passionately industrious in tracing the most transient character. His notes are often as fascinating as the text – on 'Old Dick' for example, an odd job man on Lake George, who collected rattlesnakes and exhibited them in a box inscribed: 'In this box a Rattell Snaick Hoo was Kecht on Black mountaing. He is seven years old last July. Admittance sixpence site. Children half price, or notten,' or on that strange character, Joseph Brant, alias Thayendanegea, Mohawk chief and freemason, who on one occasion saved from the stake a fellow mason who gave him the right sign. Brant was entertained by Boswell and painted by Romney. What a long way such a character seems from the murderers of the Jesuit Brébeuf (they baptized him with boiling water, cut strips of flesh from his living body and ate them, and opened his breast and drank his blood before he died).

Mr. Wade himself discovered these journals, with the romantic and paradoxical simplicity of a Chesterton detective story, in Parkman's old Boston home on Chestnut Street.

> Parkman's Indian trophies still hung on the walls; the bookcases still held the well-worn editions of Byron, Cooper, and Scott which were his life-long favourites; and in the centre of the room, covered with a dust sheet, stood the desk on which the great histories had been written. This desk was two-sided; the drawers on one side had obviously been inspected and emptied of most of their contents . . . the drawers on the other side had been over-looked; they contained the missing journals and a great mass of correspond-ence, including some of the most important letters Parkman wrote and received.

For the general reader the most interesting of Mr. Wade's discoveries is Parkman's journal of the Oregon Trail which Mr. Wade rightly prefers to the work based on it – Parkman's first and most popular book, popular perhaps because of the way in which it was adulterated to suit the fashion of the time by his friend Charles Eliot Norton, 'carefully bowdlerized of much anthropological data and many insights into Western life which seemed too crude to his delicate taste'. Mr. Wade quotes several examples of these changes from the vivid fluid journal to the stilted literary tones – the false Cooperisms – of the book. These Cooperisms, still evident in *The Conspiracy of Pontiac*, Parkman gradually shed. Life and literature at the beginning lay uneasily with a sword between them, so that nothing in the early books has the same sense of individual speech and character that we find in the journals. Here from the journals is a certain Mr. Smith of Palermo:

'Don't tell me about your Tarpeian rock. I've seen it, and what's more, the feller wanted I should give him half a dollar for taking me there. "Now look here!" says I, "do you s'pose I'm going to pay you for showing me this old pile of stones? I can see better rocks than this any day, for nothing; so clear out!" I'll tell you the way I do,' continued Mr. Smith, 'I don't go and *look* and *stare* as some people do when I get inside of a church, but I pace off the length and breadth, and then set it down on paper. Then, you see, I've got something that will keep!'

And here is an old soldier near the Canadian Border:

On entering the bar-room, an old man with a sun-burnt wrinkled face and no teeth, a little straw hat set on one side of his grey head – and who was sitting on a chair leaning his elbows on his knees and straddling his legs apart – thus addressed me: 'Hullo! hullo! What's agoin' on, now? Ye ain't off to the wars already, be ye? Ther' ain't no war now as I knows on, though there's agoin' to be one afore long, as damned bloody as ever was fit this side o' hell!' . . . He then began to speak of some of his neighbours, one of whom he mentioned as 'that G – d damnedest, sneakingest, nastiest puppy that ever went this side of hell!' Another he likened to a 'sheep's cod dried'; another was 'not fit to carry guts to a bear'.

Only with his third book – *The Jesuits in North America* – did the marriage satisfactorily take place. In the deeply moving *Relations* of the Jesuits that form the greater part of his material he found again the power of characteristic speech: the tortured priest Bressani who wrote with bitter humour to his Superior, 'I could not have believed that a man was so hard to kill,' and in another letter of ironic apology to the Jesuit General in safe Rome: 'I don't know if your Paternity will recognize the handwriting of one whom you once knew very well. The letter is soiled and ill-written; because the writer had only one finger of his right hand left entire, and cannot prevent the blood from his wounds, which are still open, from staining the paper. His ink is gunpowder mixed with water and his table is the earth.'

By this time, too, Parkman had learned the value of bald narrative:

Noel Chabanel came later to the mission; for he did not reach the Huron country until 1643. He detested the Indian life – the smoke, the vermin, the filthy food, the impossibility of privacy. He could not study by the smoky lodge-fire, among the noisy crowd of men and squaws, with their dogs, and their restless, screeching children. He had a natural inaptitude to learning the language, and laboured at it for five years with scarcely a sign of progress. The Devil whispered a suggestion into his ear: Let him procure his release from these barren and revolting toils, and return to France, where congenial and useful employments awaited him. Chabanel refused to listen; and when the temptation still beset him he bound himself by a solemn vow to remain in Canada to the day of his death.

And to complete the marriage Parkman had learned to control on occasion his poetic prose with fine effect as in this picture of Indian immortality:

In the general belief, however, there was but one land of shades for all alike. The spirits, in form and feature as they had been in life, wended their way through dark forests to the villages of the dead, subsisting on bark and rotten wood. On arriving they sat all day in the crouching posture of the sick, and when night came, hunted the shades of animals, with the shades of bows and arrows, among the shades of trees and rocks; for all things, animate and inanimate, were alike immortal, and all passed together to the gloomy country of the dead.

The last notebook Parkman kept contains an account of his desperate final battle against insomnia – the amount of sleeping draught, the hours of sleep gained. One column, *A Half-Century of Conflict*, had to be finished and inserted in its place to complete the great scheme. The hours of sleeping dropped as low as three and a half and only once in the three-year record rose above eight. In that bare mathematical catalogue there is something of the spirit of Chabanel. The historian had made his vow forty years before and it was kept.

SAMUEL BUTLER

ONE KNOWS the man well in his suit of scrubby black, his stained greenish felt, with his umbrella, his boots, the odour of tobacco on his clothes: he leans over the bookstall fingering the ugly cheap reprints of the Rationalist Press or remains for a long while absorbed by the Kensit literature in a small dingy shop near St. Paul's. Greeting him one is embarrassed by his inability to tell polite untruths. 'Good morning.' 'The morning is nothing of the kind.' He will not stoop to the mediaeval superstition of 'Good-bye'. He is an Honest Man and rather conscious of the fact, but he has gained little stature from his emancipation. One is instinctively aware in his past of an ugly, crippling childhood, attics and blackbeetles and some grim grammar school, and sadistic masters. His favourite author is Samuel Butler, and one remembers Butler's idea of immortality, the desiccated sentiment of:

> Yet meet we shall, and part, and meet again,
> Where dead men meet, on lips of living men.

Here, in the dry deformed aggressive spirit, is Samuel Butler's life everlasting. Few others will be found to swallow whole *The Fair Haven* and *Life and Habit*, *Evolution Old and New* and *God the Known and God the Unknown*, or even the note-books, of which this second selection has just appeared.* Out of the nineteen volumes of the collected works most people pick and choose, read *The Way of All Flesh* for the savour of hatred, *Erewhon* for the brilliant reporting of the opening chapters. But this would never have satisfied Butler who wanted to stuff himself neck and crop between the teeth of time.

These note-books witness it. He never overtly made clear quite why he copied and re-copied these random jottings into the carefully bound, dismally designed volumes 'in half black roan, with dark green pin-head cloth sides and shiny marbled end-papers'; it was not primarily as material for his books – 'I greatly question the use of making the notes at all. I find I next to never refer to them or use them'; if we are to believe him, 'they are not meant for publication', though a few lines later he writes, 'Many a

---

* *Further Extracts from the Note-Books of Samuel Butler*. Chosen and Edited by A. T. Bartholomew.

one of those who look over this book – for that it will be looked over by not a few I doubt not – will think me to have been a greater fool than I probably was'; but the motive is really obvious enough. These notes were to present to posterity the whole man in his wisdom, his wit, his hate, and even his triviality. There is something rather tryingly 'rough diamond' about the approach – 'You must take me just as you find me' – but alas, one finds him in these notes deep buried under the late Victorian rational dust. One digs and digs and is occasionally rewarded by the genuine gold glitter of a cuff-link.

The trouble is, he was not an artist. He remarks in one of the notes, 'I never knew a writer yet who took the smallest pains with his style and was at the same time readable.' To have thought twice about the words he used, to have tried to refine his language in order to express his meaning with greater exactitude, this would have been, in his view, to blaspheme against the essential Samuel ('You must take me just as you find me'). Better far to stick down everything as it came to mind, even when the note was as trivial as:

THE RIDICULOUS AND THE SUBLIME

As there is but one step from the sublime to the ridiculous, so also there is but one from the ridiculous to the sublime ;

as cheaply smart as:

CHRIST

Jesus! with all thy faults I love thee still ;

as meaningless as:

EVERYTHING

should be taken seriously, and nothing should be taken seriously.

There is a great deal of this kind of thing in the second selection from the note-books: a great many exhibitions of rather cocky conceit in his own smartness – 'So and so said to me . . . I said to him,' the smartness which makes *Erewhon* so insignificant beside *Gulliver*, many superficial half-truths in the form of paradoxes which have become aggravatingly familiar in the plays of his disciple; and always, in whatever subject he treats, the soreness of the unhealing wound. The perpetual need to generalize from a peculiar personal experience maimed his imagination. Even Christianity he could not consider dispassionately because it was the history of Father and Son. In *The Way of All Flesh* he avenged a little of his childhood's suffering, but he was not freed from the dead hand. His most serious criticism has the pettiness of personal hate, and how will posterity be able to take with respect attacks on Authority (whether it be the authority of God, Trinity College, or Darwin) when the mask it wears is always the cruel, smug, unimportant features of Theobald Pontifex?

THE UGLY ACT

THE WIDE and indiscriminating territory of literature, with all its range of human authorship from the Great Pashas to the D.P.'s, the criminals and the underground, surely contains few figures less agreeable than W. E. Henley. His reputation would hardly have survived into a centenary year on the strength of such poems as *Out of the Night* with his bombast and muddled thought (although Mr. Connell* finds them in all 'respectable anthologies' – odd epithet), and the fame of the editor must always be short lived. Only a biographer has time to look through the files of a dead review, listing the faded names of contributors that once, vivid with promise, seemed to cast a lustre over their leader – David Hannay, G. S. Street, Katherine Tynan, Marriott Watson, T. E. Brown and the like. And yet, in some strange way, this ill-tempered cripple does still live in literary history: we cannot quite forget him; he glares out at us from the shadows of the last century, breathing heavily through his big beard, his fist like Long John Silver's ready with his crutch, arousing our attention by the venom of his quarrels, by his ignobility and violence and the long-drawn-out malignity of his character, that elephantine quality which ensured his never forgetting what he considered an injury, although he was always ready to extend the warm hearty palm of forgiveness to a victim when the injury had been inflicted by himself.

The most famous of his quarrels was of course that with Stevenson, and the most long lived, for Henley nursed his memory of it nearly twenty years before at last he had his say about his dead friend in the famous *Pall Mall Magazine* review of Graham Balfour's biography. Of that review Henry James wrote, in a letter that Mr. Connell might have quoted if he had taken a more impartial view of Henley:

> It's really a rather striking and lurid – and so far interesting case – of long discomfortable jealousy and ranklement turned at last to posthumous (as it were!) malignity, and making the man do, *coram publico*, his ugly act, risking the dishonour for the assuagement . . . the whole business illustrates how life takes upon itself to give us more true and consistent examples of human unpleasantness than expectation could suggest – makes a given man, I mean, live up to his ugliness.

---

* *W. E. Henley.* By John Connell.

I

Mr. Connell, however, one must admit, is impartial enough for us to see Henley living up to his ugliness in a yet more extreme form. Wilde unaffected by the attacks on *Dorian Gray*, that had appeared under Henley's editorship, had written to him on the death of his daughter a letter of gentle and perceptive sympathy.

I am very sorry indeed to hear of your great loss – I hope you will let me come down quietly to you one evening and over our cigarettes we will talk of the bitter ways of fortune, and the hard ways of life. But, my dear Henley, to work – to work – that is your duty – that is what remains for natures like ours. Work never seems to me a reality, but as a way of getting rid of reality.

It is hard to uncover the source of Henley's rage against Wilde. Perhaps Wilde's very generosity – a quality in which Henley was deficient – called it out, in the same way that the money Henley regularly received from Stevenson, even after their friendship had ceased, made it all the more necessary to him to assert, however viciously, his independence. Perhaps it was simply the jealousy of a bad writer for his superior who had replied with such impervious wit and good humour to his critics in the *National Observer*. Wilde was not vulnerable to journalistic attack, and Henley seems to have felt a shabby delight at the thought that at least he was vulnerable to the law. And so again we have the sight of Henley exposing himself far more drastically than he exposed his victim in those ugly letters in which he kept Whibley in Paris posted on the news of the two trials.

Oscar at Bay was on the whole a pleasing sight . . . Holloway and Bow Street have taken his hair out of curl in more senses than one. And I am pretty sure that he is having a dam bad time . . .
As for Hosker, the news is that he lives with his brother, and is all day steeping, steeping himself in liquor, and moaning for Boasy! I am summoned to play the juryman next Monday (*je m'en fiche pas mal*), and it isn't impossible that I should have at least the occasion of sitting upon him. For, they say, he has lost all nerve, all pose, all everything; and is just now so much the Ordinary Drunkard that he has not even the energy to kill himself.

The depressing nature of the hero is emphasized by a certain drabness in his biographer. This is never at its best a well-written book, and Mr Connell shows little power of discrimination in his choice of material. The letters to Whibley are, for the most part, incredibly tedious – repeated complaints of overdue articles, news of his own books, bluff out-dated slang. Here is one typical paragraph to stand for hundreds: 'The book seems to be thriving no end. Nutt had ordered all the edition from the binder: and therewith the remainder of Ed. Sec. of *A.B. of V*. So the oof-bird may presently begin to flutter.'

Mr. Connell makes little attempt to place his subject critically – perhaps it is a pity that he makes any attempt at all. 'As a staff and talisman for a human being in the dark straits to which many are driven, *Out of the Night* has considerable virtue.' This, and the 'respectable anthologies', and the loose bandying of such a phrase as 'dark night of the soul' makes the reader wish that Mr. Connell's 'respectable' publishers had exercised a measure of editorial supervision. Nor do we have any more confidence in Mr. Connell as a judge of character than as a judge of literature. He hints darkly that the relationship between Stevenson and Henley was homo-sexual, but he produces no shred of evidence and he completely ignores the long series of letters from Stevenson to Henley in connexion with their collaboration – so far more interesting than the Whibley correspondence – that shows a detached professional relationship quite out of keeping with his picture of over-romantic friendship. It is doubtful whether Henley will interest future biographers and one therefore regrets that this biography is not more critical and more sensitive.

ERIC GILL

ROMAN CATHOLICISM in this country has been a great breeder of eccentrics – one cannot picture a man like Charles Waterton belonging to any other faith, and most of us treasure the memory of some strong individuality who combined a strict private integrity with a carefully arranged disregard of conformity to national ways of thought and behaviour. Eric Gill, with his beard and his biretta, his enormous outspokenness, his amorous gusto, trailing his family across the breadth of England with his chickens, cats, dogs, goats, ducks, and geese, belonged only distantly to this untraditional tradition; he was an intruder – a disturbing intruder among the eccentrics. He had not behind him the baroque internationalism of a great Catholic school, or the little primnesses of a convent childhood, to separate him from his fellow-countrymen along well-prepared lines, with the help of scraps of bizarre worldliness or the tag-end of peasant beliefs picked up in saints' lives.

Gill's father was a curate in the Countess of Huntingdon's Connexion in Brighton, who later conformed to the Anglican Church and became a different sort of curate in Chichester, doomed to bring up eleven children on £150 a year. 'He was from a "highbrow", intellectual, agnostic point of view, a complete nonentity; but he loved the Lord his God with all his sentimental mind and all his sentimental soul.' What Gill gained from his parents was a sense of vocation; money was never the standard by which values were gauged. 'They never complained about poverty as though it was an injustice. And they never put the pursuit of riches before us as an occupation worthy of good people.' There were tradesmen in the family, and there were missionaries in the South Seas. There was even in a sense art, for Gill's mother had been a singer in an opera company and his father read Kingsley and Carlyle and Tennyson's poems, and called his son after Dean Farrar's hero. It was all kindling-wood waiting for a fire – the grim Brighton railway viaduct with the huddled mean houses of Preston Park inserted between the railway lines, the small boy drawing engines and the father writing sermons, and the advertising sign of a machine-made bread against the sky, and a Mrs. Hart whispering dreadfully, 'There was a black-beetle in it' – and yet a sense of infinite possibility: 'My favourite author at that time was G. A. Henty, and the only prize I ever got at school was

Through the Sikh War. I remember walking home in the moonlight with my father and mother after the prize-giving and school concert in a daze of exaltation and pride.' The kindling-wood is always there if only a flame be found. In Gill's case Catholicism supplied the flame.

What followed in one sense is anti-climax, the progress of an artist not of the first rank – the railway engines giving place to architectural plans and those to letter-cutting and monumental masonry. The artist impressing himself on the face of London in W. H. Smith signs, in self-conscious Stations of the Cross; is it for this – and the little albums of dimly daring nudes – that the father painfully taught the love of God? As an artist Gill gained nothing from his faith, but the flame had been lit none the less; and perhaps it was the inability to express his vision that drove him into eccentricity – to the community life at Ditchling, from which again he fled when it became advertised by his Dominican friends – the disciplined Catholic private life advertised like the machine-made bread. His beard and his biretta were the expressions of fury against his environment. He hated commercial civilization, and everything he did was touched by it – a new kind of repository art grew up under his influence; above all, he hated his fellow-Catholics because he felt that they had betrayed their Catholicism, and of them he hated the priesthood most. It seemed to him that they had compromised too easily with capitalism, like that Bishop of San Luis Potosi, who hid the Papal Encyclical, *De Rerum Novarum,* in the cellars of the Palace because he believed it would encourage Communism.

> The clergy seem to regard it as their job to support a social order which as far as possible forces us to commit all the sins they denounce. . . . A man can be a very good Catholic in a factory, our parish priest used to be fond of saying. And he was very annoyed and called us bolshevists when we retorted: yes, but it requires heroic virtue and you have no right to demand heroic virtue from anyone, and certainly not from men and women in thousands and millions.

And again he wrote: 'Persons whom you would have thought could hardly exist, Catholic bank clerks and stockbrokers for instance, are the choice flower of our great Catholic schools.'

There, of course, he went wrong; Waterton is a much more likely product of Stonyhurst than a bank clerk, but he was right on the main issue – that in this country Catholicism which should produce revolutionaries produces only eccentrics (eccentricity thrives on an unequal social system), and that Conservatism and Catholicism should be as impossible

bedfellows as Catholicism and National-Socialism. Out of his gritty child
hood and his discovered faith a rebel should have been born; he wrot
like a rebel with a magnificent disregard for grammar, but something wen
wrong. Perhaps he made too much money, perhaps he was half-tamed by
his Dominican friends; whatever the reason his rebellion never amounted
to much – an article in a quarterly suppressed by the episcopate, addresse
to a working men's college, fervent little articles on sex. That overpower
ing tradition of eccentricity simply absorbed him until even his mos
outrageous anti-clerical utterances caused only a knowing smile on the
face of the faithful. The beard and the biretta won – he was an eccentri
too.

INVINCIBLE IGNORANCE

I N A book* which is at times crude and conceited, at others perceptive and tender, Havelock Ellis tells the story of an 'advanced' marriage. That is really the whole subject – there are chapters on his family and his childhood, on his experiences in Australia as a young school-teacher buried in a bush station and first conceiving his career in sexology, but these are only introductory to his meeting with Edith Lees, the secretary of the New Fellowship, and their long unhappy theoretical marriage. The background is already period: an odd charm hangs around the Fabian Society, around anarchists, feminism, what Ellis himself calls in an admirable phrase, 'that high-strung ethical tension': it is necessary to be reminded that encased in those years were real people, muddled and earnest and tortured.

This is an extraordinarily intimate autobiography, far too intimate to be suitable for general reading. 'What can it matter when we are both dead? Who can be hurt if she and I, who might have been hurt, are now only a few handfuls of ashes flung over the grass and flowers? To do what I have done here has been an act of prolonged precision in cold blood, beyond anything else that I have ever written. For I know that, to a large extent, the world is inhabited by people to whom one does too much honour by calling them fools. . . . All mankind may now, if they will, conspire together to hurt us. We shall not feel it.'

But it was really they who conspired together to hurt themselves, talking it all out beforehand – economics, heredity, birth-control – strolling along a Cornish beach, an odd, earnest, pathetic pair of lovers, who had left out of account all natural un-eugenic feelings, of jealousy or possession. Members of the New Fellowship presented them with a complete set of Emerson's Works.

But even under those auspices the marriage went wrong. There was never much passionate love between them, and Ellis soon considered himself at liberty to take a mistress. Writing forty years later he remained convinced that his wife had no ground for objection. Objection in any case was swept away by theory: the wife had to be friends with the mistress, and Ellis could see no reason for her pain when she pleaded

*My Life, by Havelock Ellis.

against a meeting between the lovers in the Cornish village where she and Ellis had first loved. So it went on – the woman always more natural than the man and struggling to be reasonable in his way. The pain stabs out from letter after letter, but Ellis never saw it, chiding her tenderly for failure in sympathy or understanding.

After a time they ceased to live as man and wife, though a kind of passionate tenderness always remained like a buoy to mark the position of a wreck. In London, Ellis had a flat of his own, and in the country they lived in two adjoining cottages (the middle-aged man, when his wife was ill, lay with one ear glued to the intervening wall). All the while Mrs. Ellis was being driven to the last breakdown of health and sanity by the remorseless Moloch theories that love was free, jealousy ignoble, possession an indignity. She couldn't always keep it up. 'Oh: Havelock, don't feel you don't want me. I let myself drift into thinking you only want Amy and not me. . . . All I feel I want in the world is to get into your arms and be told you want me to live.' This towards the end of her life, for the miracle was that their love was never killed by the theory – it was only tortured. On his side he never relented: he would write coolly, tenderly back about the spring flowers, and his work was never interrupted: the sexological studies continued to appear, full of case histories and invincible ignorance. And yet, between this ageing man with his fake prophet's air – rather like a Santa Claus at Selfridge's – and the woman haunted by extending loneliness and suspicion, so much love remained that one mourns at the thought of what was lost to them because they had not been born into the Christian tradition. Years after her death he writes with a kind of exalted passion and a buried religious feeling: 'Whenever nowadays I go about London on my business or my recreation, I constantly come upon them [places where they had met]: here she stood; here we met; here we once sat together; just as, even in places where she never went, I come upon some object, however trifling, which leads, by a tenuous thread of suggestion, to her. So that it sometimes seems to me that at every step of my feet and at every movement of my thought I see before me something which speaks of her, and my heart grows suddenly tender and my lips murmur involuntarily: "My darling!" '

HERBERT READ

SOME YEARS ago Mr. Read published an account of his childhood under the title *The Innocent Eye*. It must have come as a surprise to many of his readers that the critic of *Art Now* was brought up on a Yorkshire farm: a whole world of the imagination seems to separate the vale, the orchard, the foldgarth, the mill and the stockyard – the fine simple stony architecture of his childhood – from what was to come, which one is tempted unfairly to picture as a long empty glossy gallery with one abstraction by Mr. Ben Nicholson on the farther wall, perhaps two Ideas and a Navel in clay by Mr. Hans Arp on a pedestal on the parquet, and a decoration of wires with little balls attached dangling from the ceiling.

'The basin at times was very wide, especially in the clearness of a summer's day; but as dusk fell it would suddenly contract, the misty hills would draw near, and with night they had clasped us close: the centre of the world had become a candle shining from the kitchen window. Inside, in the sitting-room where we spent most of our life, a lamp was lit, with a ground glass shade like a full yellow moon. There we were bathed before the fire, said our prayers kneeling on the hearthrug, and then disappeared up the steep stairs lighted by a candle to bed.'

Now Mr. Read has written a sequel to *The Innocent Eye*,* taking the account of his own life on out of the Yorkshire vale; a grim Spartan orphans' school with a strong religious tone and the young Read absorbed in Rider Haggard; a clerkship in a Leeds Savings Bank at £20 a year, and the slightly older Read becoming a Tory and reading Disraeli and Burke; then Leeds University and loss of faith, religious and political, and so the war, and after it the literary career – and the settled literary personality, the agnostic, the anarchist and the romantic, bearing rather heavily the load of new knowledge and new art, the theories of Freud blurring the clear innocent eye. The first book was one of the finest evocations of childhood in our language: the second – finely written as it often is – records a rather dusty pilgrimage towards a dubious and uninteresting conclusion: 'This book will attempt to show how I have come to believe that the highest manifestation of the immanent will of the universe is the

* *Annals of Innocence and Experience.*

137

work of art' – sight giving place to thought: to abstractions which have not been abstracted but found ready-made – and in an odd way it doesn't quite ring true. There's an absence of humility, and no one can adequately write of his own life without humility. When Mr. Read, writing of his youth, remarks that 'in a few years there was scarcely any poem of any worth in my own language which I had not read'; when he writes of religion in a few dogmatic sentences as the phantasy of an after-life conceived in the fear of dea h, we have travelled a long way with him – too far – from the objective light of childhood and the first 'kill'. 'I do not remember the blood, nor the joking huntsmen; only the plumed breath of the horses, the jingle of their harness, the beads of dew and the white gossamer on the tangled hedge beside us.'

We have travelled too far, but we should never have known without *The Innocent Eye* quite how far we had travelled. That is the astounding thing – Mr. Read was able to go back, back from the intellectual atmosphere personified in Freud, Bergson, Croce, Dewey, Vivante, Scheller . . . And if we examine his work there have always been phases when he has returned: the creative spirit has been more than usually separated in his case from the critical mind. (He admits himself in one essay that submitting to the creative impulse he has written poetry which owes nothing to his critical theories.) The critic, one feels, has sometimes been at pains to adopt the latest psychological theories before they have proved their validity – rather as certain Anglican churchmen leap for confirmation of their faith on the newest statement of an astronomer. But the creative spirit has remained tied to innocence. 'The only real experiences in life,' writes Mr. Read, 'being those lived with a virgin sensibility – so that we only hear a tone once, only see a colour once, see, hear, touch, taste and smell everything but once, the first time.' One of the differences between writers is this stock of innocence: the virgin sensibility in some cases lasts into middle age: in Mr. Read's case, we feel, as in so many of his generation, it died of the shock of war and personal loss. When the Armistice came: 'There were misty fields around us, and perhaps a pealing bell to celebrate our victory. But my heart was numb and my mind dismayed: I turned to the fields and walked away from all human contacts.' In future there was to be no future: as a critic he was to be sometimes pantingly contemporary, and when he was most an artist he was to be furthest removed from his time.

'When most an artist': we are not permanently interested in any other aspect of Mr. Read's work. Anarchism means more to him than it will ever mean to his readers (in spite of that vigorous and sometimes deeply moving book, *Poetry and Anarchism*) – sometimes we suspect that it means little more to him than an attempt to show his Marxist critics that he too is a political animal, to give a kind of practical everyday expression to the 'sense of glory' which has served him ever since youth in place of a religious faith; and I cannot share his belief that criticism with the help of Freud will become a science, and a critical opinion have the universality of a scientific law. As an artist he will be assessed, it seems to me, by *The Innocent Eye*, by his only novel, *The Green Child*, by a few poems – notably *The End of a War*, by his study of Wordsworth, informed as it is by so personal a passion that it is lifted out of the category of criticism ('we both spring from the same yeoman stock of the Yorkshire dales, and I think I have a certain "empathetic" understanding of his personality which gives a sense of betrayal to anything I write about him'), and some scattered essays in which, too, the note of 'betrayal' is evident – the essays on Froissart, Malory and Vauvenargues in particular.

It is that author with whom we wish to dwell – however much lip service we may pay to books like *Art and Society*, *Art Now*, *Art and Industry* and the rest – the author who describes himself: 'In spite of my intellectual pretensions, I am by birth and tradition a peasant.' Even his political thought at its most appealing comes back to that sense of soil, is tethered to the Yorkshire farm – 'real politics are local politics'. The result of separating Mr. Read's creative from his critical work has an odd effect – there is colour, warmth, glow, the passion which surrounds the 'sense of glory', and we seem far removed from the rather dry critic with his eyes fixed on the distinctions between the ego and the id. The mill where the hero of *The Green Child* rescues Siloën from the sullen bullying passion of Kneeshaw is his uncle's mill – just as the stream which had reversed its course is 'the mysterious water' which dived underground and re-emerged in his uncle's field. And it may not be too imaginative to trace the dreadful sight that met Olivero's eyes through the mill window as Kneeshaw tried to force the Green Child to drink the blood of a newly-killed lamb to that occasion in the foldgarth when the child crushed his finger in the machine for crushing oil-cake. 'I fainted with the pain, and the horror of that dim milk-white panic is as ineffaceable as the scar which my flesh still bears.'

'Milk-white panic': like the Green Child himself Mr. Read has a horror of violence – a horror which preceded the war and did not follow it. The conflict always present in his work is between the fear and the glory – between the 'milk-white panic' and the vision which was felt by 'the solitary little alien in the streets of Leeds', the uncontrollable ambition which 'threw into the cloudy future an infinite ray in which there could always be seen, like a silver knight on a white steed, this unreal figure which was myself, riding to quixotic combats, attaining a blinding and indefinable glory.' If art is the resolution of a combat, here surely is the source of Mr. Read's finest work. Very far back – further than the author can take us – the conflict originated: it was already established when the machine closed, when the small boy felt the excitement of *King Solomon's Mines* and *Montezuma's Daughter*. Both sides of the conflict are personified and expressed in his poem *The End of a War*, in which the sense of glory is put first into the mouth of a dying German officer and then into the dialogue between the soul and body of the girl whom the Germans had raped and murdered – the glory of surrender to nationality and to faith, and last the revulsion in the mouth of the English officer waking on the morning of peace and addressing his dead enemy – the revulsion of an ordinary man crushed by the machine who has no sense of glory in martial action or in positive faith, caught up in violence and patiently carrying out of the conflict only the empirical knowledge that he has at least survived.

> The bells of hell ring ting-a-ling-a-ling
> for you but not for me – for you
> whose gentian eyes stared from the cold
> impassive alp of death. You betrayed us
> at the last hour of the last day
> playing the game to the end,
> your smile the only comment
> on the well-done deed. What mind
> have you carried over the confines?
> Your fair face was noble of its kind,
> some visionary purpose cut the lines
> clearly on that countenance.
> But you are defeated: once again
> the meek inherit the kingdom of God.
> No might can win against this wandering
> wavering grace of humble men.
> You die, in all your power and pride:
> I live, in my meekness justified.

Because we have detected a conflict between the sense of glory and the fear of violence it mustn't be thought that we have mistaken the meaning Mr. Read has attached to glory: glory, he has written many times, is not merely martial glory, or ambition. 'Glory is the radiance in which virtues flourish. The love of glory is the sanction of great deeds; all greatness and magnanimity proceed not from calculation but from an instinctive desire for the quality of glory. Glory is distinguished from fortune, because fortune exacts care; you must connive with your fellows and compromise yourself in a thousand ways to make sure of its fickle favours. Glory is gained directly, if one has the genius to deserve it: glory is sudden.'

In that sense glory is always surrender – the English officer also experienced glory in the completeness of his surrender to the machine: the 'wavering grace' too is glory. But just as the meaning of glory extends far beyond great deeds, so the fear of violence extends to the same borders. Surrender of any kind seems a betrayal: the milk-white panic is felt at the idea of any self-revelation. The intellect strives to be impersonal, and the conflict becomes as extensive as life – life as the artist describes it today, 'empty of grace, of faith, of fervour and magnanimity'.

Glory in that sense cannot be attained by the artist, for glory is the cessation of conflict: it is private like death. The mystic, the soldier, even the politician can attain glory – the artist can only express his distant sense of it. In his novel, *The Green Child*, Mr. Read conveyed as he had never done before, even in *The End of a War*, that private sense of glory. We see it working inwards from political glory – from the ideal state which Olivero found in South America back to the source of inspiration, the home of the 'innocent eye', back through fantasy to the dream of complete glory – the absolute surrender. Alone in his crystalline grotto, somewhere below the earth's surface, to which the Green Child led him, sinking through the water at the mill-stream's source, Olivero awaits death and petrifaction – the sense of sin which came between Wordsworth and his glory has been smoothed out, passion, the fear of death, all the motives of conflict have been eliminated as they had been from the dying German. Desire is limited to the desire of the final surrender, of becoming first rock, then crystal, of reaching permanency – ambition could hardly go further.

'When the hated breath at last left the human body, that body was carried to special caves, and then laid out in troughs filled with the petrous water that dripped from roof and walls. There it remained until the body turned white and hard, until the eyes were glazed under the vitreous lids, and the hair of the head became like crisp snail-shells, the beard like a few jagged icicles . . .'

It is the same sense of glory that impelled Christian writers to picture the City of God – both are fantasies, both are only expressions of a sense unattained by the author, both, therefore, are escapes: the solution of conflict can come no other way. The difference, of course, is that the Christian artist believes that his fantasy is somewhere attainable: the agnostic knows that no Green Child will ever really show him the way to absolute glory.

The difference – though for the living suffering man it represents all the difference between hell and purgatory – is not to us important. Christian faith might have borne poorer fruits than this sense of unattainable glory lodged in the child's brain on a Yorkshire farm forty years ago. Mr. Read's creative production has been small, but I doubt whether any novel, poem or work of criticism, is more likely to survive the present anarchy than *The Green Child*, *The End of a War*, and *Wordsworth*. The critic who has hailed so many new fashions in painting and literature has himself supplied the standards of permanence by which these fashions will be condemned.

GEORGE DARLEY

Book yet remains to be written on the tragedy of those rare poets who have been ruined by their own lack of conceit. It is a curious psychological fact that men with interests almost entirely intellectual will suffer a sense of inferiority and shame from a purely physical defect, which will sometimes cancel their whole work. There are cases, naturally, where that shame has not been disastrous, but none the less it has been present. Byron was driven by his lame leg to a bitter isolation and to satire: from the calm, but somewhat too facile loveliness of 'She walks in beauty like the night' to the tortured medley of buffoonery and grandeur which he called *Don Juan*. Byron's shame was our gain. Stevenson, however much he might sound the brazen trumpet of his heroics, was ashamed of his consumptive body. 'Shall we never shed blood?' he asked, only half-humorously, and he hoped that in the swords' clash of *Kidnapped*, his readers would forget that one man, by no stretch of imagination, could ever put himself in the round house with Alan Breck. And yet, because he too was forced like Byron, though by more material circumstances, into isolation, we have gained a level controlled prose as likely to endure as that of Addison, and at least one great novel *Weir of Hermiston*.

George Darley's defect compared with that of Byron and that of Stevenson seems small and very ludicrous. He had a stutter, and perhaps its lack of any possibility of a romantic pose made it the harder to bear. He was a poet of infinite potentiality, and he spent his poetic life almost entirely on the writing of pretty songs and unactable plays. Now, more than a hundred years since his death, his work, and among most even his name, is forgotten. He is to be found occasionally in anthologies – Robert Bridges included a large number of extracts from his *Nepenthe* in *The Spirit of Man* – and to the general public he is known, if he is known at all, as the author of a charming song, a favourite of the Victorian drawing-room.

> I've been roaming! I've been roaming!
> Where the meadow dew is sweet,
> And like a queen I'm coming
> With its pearls upon my feet.

Darley was born in 1795 in Dublin of Irish parents, the eldest of a family of four sons and three daughters. His parents went from Ireland to the United States, when he was still a child, and left him at Springfield, Co. Dublin, in the care of his grandfather, with whom he remained until he was about ten years of age. The impediment in his speech was already with him and probably already exaggerated in a morbid and nervous mind. But past misery is easily transmuted into happiness, and later, looking back, he was very ready to find in those years, in what is known as the Garden of Ireland, joys which at the time he had not recognized.

> When a child [he wrote] I thought myself miserable, but now see that by comparison I was happy, at least all the 'sunshine of the breast' I now enjoy seems a reflection of that in the dawn of life. I have been to *La belle France* and to *bella Italia*, yet the brightest sun which ever shone upon me broke over Ballybetagh mountains.

Little of Darley's early youth is known to us. On his parents' return from America he joined them in Dublin, entered Trinity College there in 1815 and graduated in 1820. Science and mathematics had been his studies, and in his studies he had lived. Human intercourse then, as later, was less shut out from him by his stutter than by the morbid introspection into which it plunged him. It made him first shy and then bold with the exaggerated self-importance which is so often to be found in dwarfs. He recoiled and sprang. He was determined in those first days, when nothing had been tried and therefore nothing had yet failed, to make the world take notice of him and forget the stutter. And the world, in the person of passing acquaintances, would never have noticed the stutter without his own self-conscious underlining. He was beautiful in a delicate, somewhat Shelleian fashion, 'tall and slight with the stoop of the student; delicate features slightly aquiline; eyes not large but very earnest, with often a far away expression; hair dark brown and waving.' There were times in those days when he completely forgot his impediment in excited conversation.

He had not been pre-eminently successful at Trinity College. Although he had a great talent for mathematics, his stutter had impeded him in a least one examination. No high academical post was open to him, and in any case a career of teaching was impossible. It was therefore with some sense, as well as some courage, that he flung himself in 1822 upon literary London, with his first volume of verse *The Errors of Ecstasie*. He was twenty-seven years old, but the majority of the poems must have been written years before, for they are completely devoid of merit. The lyric are full of the conceits of roses and bees from which the future poet neve freed himself. They are tuneful but seldom musical. The title poem is a long and very wearisome blank verse dialogue between a poet contemplating suicide and the moon. It is of interest for a few clearly autobiographical lines:

> Didst thou not barter Science for a song?
> Thy gown of learning for a sorry mantle?

and for a very occasional line where Darley is caught in a youthful pride and defiance which he lost too soon:

> I would not change the temper of my blood
> For that which stagnates in an idiot's veins,
> To gain the sad salvation of a fool.

When he wrote that, poor and halting though the blank verse might be, there was hope for Darley. Vitality and pride, the two most necessary sources for poetry, were his 'and at the rainbow's foot lay surely gold'.

Literary London was not unkind to the new poet. A critic wrote of his book that it was

> a work as well of intellect as of temperament, although his fancy has been inadequately controlled. . . . His poetry is to be blamed for the wildness of imagination, not the weakness of sensuality

and the next year found him a regular contributor to the *London Magazine*. It was the time of the proprietorship of Taylor and Hessey, when the contributors were invited to meet one another at dinner once a month at the offices of the firm in Waterloo Place. Here he met De Quincey, Procter, Talfourd, Clare, Hazlitt, Hood, whose finest poems, the *Ode to Autumn* and the sonnets on *Silence* and *Death*, appeared this very year in the magazine, Henry Cary, the translator of Dante, and Lamb. The two latter he was soon able to number among his few friends. There are occasional references to him in Lamb's letters, and he seems to have been a regular visitor at Enfield, sometimes in the company of Cary, sometimes in that of Allan Cunningham.

But the shyness induced by the stutter stood in the way of his friendships. In a volume of tales, *The Labours of Idleness*, which he published in 1826 under the name of Guy Penseval, he gave a clear picture of his own self-consciousness. We can see him at Waterloo Place sitting in the background of the conversation feeling himself neglected with a growing and unjust resentment, suddenly plunging into the conversation with the same asperity as characterized the dramatic criticism which he was now writing for the *London* under the pseudonym of John Lacy:

K

I always found myself so embarrassed in the presence of others, and everyone so embarrassed in mine – I was so perpetually infringing the rule of politeness, saying or doing awkward things, telling unpalatable truths, or giving heterodox opinions on matters long since established as proper, agreeable, becoming, and the contrary, by the common creed of the world, there was so much to offend and so little to conciliate in my manners, arrogant at one time, puling at another; dull when I should have been entertaining; loquacious when I should have been silent . . . that I quickly perceived obscurity was the sphere in which Nature had destined me to shine. . . . At first indeed there were several persons who liked, or seemed to like me, from a certain novelty or freshness in my manner, but as soon as that wore off they liked me no longer. I was 'an odd being' or 'a young man of some genius but very singular': something to fill up the gaps of tea-time conversation when the fineness of the evening and the beauty of the prospect had already been discussed by the party.

This feeling of inferiority, the idea that people only 'seemed' to like him, was no doubt enhanced by the London dinners, where Lamb and Hood set the key to a conversation which chiefly consisted in a quick succession of bad puns. And yet Darley had met with undeserved good fortune. He had established himself in literary London with one book of very mediocre verse and a volume of short stories, interspersed with lyrics. And *Sylvia* was growing in his head, *Sylvia* which was to set him upon the pinnacle of fame. The idea that he was carrying a masterpiece in his mind must have made the alternately shy and aggressive poet almost insupportable. Beddoes wrote to Kelsall in 1824, after a visit to Mrs. Shelley's:

> Darley is a tallish, slender, pale, light-eyebrowed, gentle-looking bald pate, in a brown suit and with a duodecimo under his arm – stammering to a most provoking degree, so much so as to be almost inconversible – he is supposed to be writing a comedy or tragedy, or perhaps both in one.

The filibustering medical poet from the sea coast of Bohemia was not likely to find Darley attractive, and in 1826 he wrote to Procter from Hanover a little impatiently: 'Is Darley delivered yet? I hope he's not a mountain.'

The next year *Sylvia* appeared, a pretty fairy comedy – as Miss Mitford said – 'something between *A Midsummer Night's Dream* and *The Faithful Shepherdess*'. Miss Mitford was charmed by it. So was the future Mrs. Browning, who found it 'a beautiful pastoral'. Lamb thought it 'a very poetical poem' and was pleased with the stage directions in verse. Beddoes, if he ever read it, remained discreetly silent, as silent as the public. Yet the play is very readable, and at one point shows a little of the swing and power which Darley was later to display in *Nepenthe*. In the penultimate scene, the stage directions, which have been growing looser and looser in texture, are suddenly abandoned for a vivid comparison between Byron and Milton:

> One gloomy Thing indeed, who now
> Lays in the dust his lordly brow,
> Had might, a deep indignant sense,
> Proud thoughts, and moving eloquence;
> But oh! that high poetic strain
> Which makes the heart shriek out again
> With pleasure half mistook for pain;
> That clayless spirit that doth soar
> To some far empyrean shore
> Beyond the chartered flight of mind,
> Reckless, repressless, unconfined,
> Springing from off the roofèd sky
> Into unceiled Infinity . . .
> That strain, this spirit was not thine.

But the ears of the public were as firmly closed to the occasional beauty as to the rather imitative prettiness of the whole. The mountain had brought forth its mouse.

Darley was not a man with the courage to stand against silence. Attack might have made him aggressive, silence only made him question his own powers, the most fatal act an artist can commit. He published no other poetry for public circulation until 1840, when his long and tedious play *Thomas à Becket*, showing the influence of Sir Henry Taylor, appeared, followed the next year by a still duller play, *Ethelstan*. In writing to Procter about the former play, he gave rein to the doubt which had been haunting him:

> I am indeed suspicious, not of you but myself; most sceptical about my right to be called 'poet', and therefore it is I desire confirmation of it from others. Why have a score of years not established my title with the world? Why did not *Sylvia*, with all its faults, ten years since? It ranked me among the small poets. I had as soon be ranked among the piping bullfinches.

Sylvia's failure drove him back to science. In the next few years he published a series of volumes on elementary mathematics, *A System of Popular Geometry, A System of Popular Trigonometry, Familiar Astronomy*, and *The Geometrical Companion*, several of which became popular. Indeed from this time on he was linked finally with mathematics. Carlyle spoke of him as:

Darley (George) from Dublin, mathematician, considerable actually, and also poet; an amiable, modest, veracious and intelligent man – much loved here though he stammered dreadfully.

Sir F. H. Doyle wrote of him as 'a man of true genius, and not of poetical genius alone, for he distinguished himself also as a mathematician and a man of science', and Allan Cunningham in *The Athenaeum* called him 'a true poet and excellent mathematician'. Darley himself, in a letter to Cary, wrote:

> I did not mean Mathematics inspired poetry but only that the Science was absolutely necessary for such an extravagates as I am. Only for this cooling study I should be out of my reason probably – like poor Lee's hero 'knock out all the start' and die like a mad dog foaming.

But the lyrics that Darley was writing, and occasionally publishing in the *London* and *The Athenaeum* to which he began to contribute a series of letters from abroad on foreign art, and his usual truculent dramatic criticism, show little of the fevered turmoil of mind at which the letter to Cary hints. That turmoil was to burst out once, and once only, unforgettably in *Nepenthe*. Now, as though his grip upon himself grew, as he became more and more conscious of the repressed, thwarted instincts within himself, the best of his lyrics show a calm, though sometimes complaining, restraint:

> Oh nymph! release me from this rich attire
> Take off this crown thy artful fingers wove;
> And let the wild-rose linger on the brier
> Its last, sweet days, my love!
>
> For me shalt thou, with thy nice-handed care,
> Nought but the simplest wreath of myrtle twine,
> Such too, high-pouring Hebe's self must wear,
> Serving my bower with wine.

When his grip relaxed, it was not yet into ungoverned imagination, but into pretty and cloying fancies, which sometimes break into a faint beauty of metaphor, as in the opening to his conventional and uninspired sonnet to Gloriana:

> To thee, bright lady! whom all hearts confess
> Their queen, as thou dost highly pace along,
> Like the Night's pale and lovely sultaness
> Walking the wonder-silent stars among.

But though it was his loneliness which caused his failure, it was loneliness that inspired some of his best lyrics. No one can contend that these short poems approach very close to greatness, but they are at their best extremely charming minor poetry. *The Dove's Loneliness* has mastery of a music and rhythm which seem to lie just outside analysis, and its dying close might have been written by Mr. de la Mare:

> Smile thou and say farewell! The bird of Peace,
> Hope, Innocence and Love and Loveliness,
> Thy sweet Egeria's bird of birds doth pray
> By the name best-belov'd thou'lt wend thy way
> In pity of her pain. Though I know well
> Thou woulds't not harm me, I must tremble still;
> My heart's the home of fear; ah! turn thee then,
> And leave me to my loneliness again.

Here are many of Mr. de la Mare's technical artifices, the half rhymes – Peace and Loveliness, well and still – the fondness for the letter 'l' in conveying the sense of uncertain and undefined longing, the alliteration of words, as well as letters – Love and Loveliness. Mr. de la Mare has been compared with Keats and Blake and Christina Rossetti. It is strange that no one has noted the affinity with Darley. The resemblance does not lie in one solitary poem, but is continually recurring:

> O was it fair:
> Fair, kind or pitiful to one
> Quite heart-subdued – all bravery done,
> Coyness to deep devotion turned,
> Yet pure the flame with which she burned, –
> O was it fair that thou shoulds't come,
> Strong in this weakness, to my home,
> And at my most defenceless hour,
> Midnight, shoulds't steal into my bower,
> In thy triumphant beauty more
> Fatal that night than e'er before?

But it is with the extraordinary *Nepenthe* that George Darley will live or die. A few copies of the poem were printed for private circulation in 1835, as Miss Mitford wrote,

> with the most imperfect and broken types, upon a coarse, discoloured paper, like that in which a country shop-keeper puts up his tea, with two dusky leaves of a still dingier hue, at least a size too small, for cover, and garnished at top and bottom with a running margin in his own writing.

It was not reprinted until 1897.

Nepenthe is one of the most remarkable poems that the nineteenth century produced. It was no wonder that Miss Mitford before this wild

medley of Shelley, Milton and Keats, made a single whole by the feverish
personality of Darley himself, wrote that 'there is an intoxication about
it that turns one's brain'. Darley himself in a letter to Chorley gives a
much needed explanation of its theme:

> to show the folly of discontent with the natural tone of human life. Canto I
> attempts to paint the ill-effects of over-joy; Canto II those of excessive
> melancholy. Part of the latter object remains to be worked out in Canto III,
> which would likewise show – if I could ever find confidence, and health and
> leisure to finish it – that contentment with the mingled cup of humanity is
> the true 'Nepenthe'.

But Darley, perhaps because he never found that Nepenthe, left the poem
a fragment.

The poem opens with the same speed, the same magical rush of
wings, on which it takes its whole course of 1600 odd lines:

> Over a bloomier land, untrod
>   By heavier foot than bird or bee
> Lays on the grassy-bosomed sod,
>   I passed one day in reverie:
> High on his unpavilioned throne
> The heaven's hot tyrant sat alone,
> And like the fabled king of old
> Was turning all he touched to gold.

The poem cannot be followed as a detailed plot. It remains in the mind as a
succession of vivid images:

> Sudden above my head I heard
> The cliff-scream of the thunder-bird,
> The rushing of his forest wings,
> A hurricane when he swoops or springs,
> And saw upon the darkening glade
> Cloud-broad his sun-eclipsing shade.

of beautiful episodes – the death of the phoenix, with its lovely lyric
O Blest Unfabled Incense Tree, which has found a place in many anthologies, and the less known but no less lovely:

> O fast her amber blood doth flow
>   From the heart wounded Incense Tree
> Fast as earth's deep embosomed woe
>   In silent rivulets to the sea!
>
> Beauty may weep her fair first-born,
>   Perchance in as resplendent tears,

Such golden dewdrops bow the corn
When the stern sickleman appears.

But oh! such perfume to a bower
Never allured sweet-seeking bee,
As to sip fast that nectarous shower
A thirstier minstrel drew in me.

Then follow episodes drawn too closely from Keats, bands of bac-
chantes and nymphs, who dance with too self-conscious a flow of drapery.
But soon the reader is whirled again over a changing panorama of sea and
land, India, Petra, Palmyra, Lebanon, Ionia, the Dardanelles, sees from
above the broken body of Icarus tossed backwards and forwards upon the
reefs, sees Orpheus torn by the Furies and in a last moment of frenzy the
two deaths are mingled and made his own, in the sound of the waves that
beat upon Icarus, the sound of the Furies' voices calling to the hunt:

In the caves of the deep — Hollo! Hollo! —
Lost Youth! — o'er and o'er fleeting billows!
Hollo! Hollo! — without all ruth! —
In the foam's cold shroud! — Hollo! Hollo!
To his everlasting sleep! — Lost Youth!

The second canto is less varied in note and less varied in sense.
Darley falters a little on his long flight, but there is still much to admire:
the extraordinary dignity of wording, and the impressive use of proper
names:

From Ind to Egypt thou art one,
Pyramidal Memphis to Tanjore,
From Ipsambul to Babylon
Reddening the waste suburban o'er;
From sandlocked Thebes to old Ellore,
Her caverned roof on columns high
Pitched, like a Giant Breed that bore
Headlong the mountain to the sky.

When it is remembered that this poem was written after Shelley's death,
when the most noted poets, with the exception of Wordsworth and
Coleridge, were Hood, 'Barry Cornwall', Joanna Baillie, and Laetitia
Elizabeth Landon, it is easy to realize something of the consternation with
which it was greeted by Miss Mitford. None of Darley's friends, to whom
the poem was sent, seems to have suggested a public printing. They were
bewildered, a little stunned, perhaps inclined to laugh. Even Miss Mitford,
who gave the hungry poet some measured praise, failed to read his poem

to the end. Perhaps Darley himself was bewildered by this one great flash of genius, this loud and boisterous changeling of his loneliness. The last lines of the poem express a wish to leave 'this busy broil' for his own accustomed clime:

> There to lay me down at peace
> In my own first nothingness.

Certainly his genius seems to have died at the moment of its first complete expression. The body of the poet lived on for another ten years, produced the two monumental plays, wandered about the Continent, wrote charming and growlingly despondent letters, as the 'pains, aches and petty tortures' of his ill-health increased, to some pretty cousins in Ireland, and died at last from an unromantic decline in London on November 23rd, 1846, still uncertain and doubting of his own powers.

Am I really a poet? was the question which always haunted him.

> You may ask could I not sustain myself on the strength of my own appro-
> bation? But it might be only my vanity, not my genius, that was strong. . . .
> Have not I too, had some, however few, approvers? Why yes, but their
> chorus in my praise was as small as the voice of my conscience, and, like it,
> served for little else than to keep me uneasy.

'Seven long years', he had written to Miss Mitford, in a letter, 'startling to receive . . . and terrible to answer', 'have I lived on a saying of Coleridge's that he sometimes liked to take up *Sylvia*.' It is time now for posterity, if only for the sake of *Nepenthe*, to grant Darley the position which he had not the courage and self-confidence to claim for himself.

AN UNHEROIC DRAMATIST

ROGER BOYLE, Earl of Orrery, is one of the great bores of literature, and it can hardly have been a labour of love for Mr. Clark to edit for the first time eight ponderous heroic plays, hardly lightened by two attempts at comedy. Yet all admirers of the period will be grateful: there is a peculiar satisfaction in seeing one more gap in Restoration scholarship filled with such immense efficiency: no crack between the bricks. Not for them the rather hollow excuse that Orrery was the pioneer of heroic drama in England. They will read with gorged satisfaction that one of these plays, *The Tragedy of Zoroastes*, has never before been printed and that Orrery's first play (Mr. Clark leaves us in no doubt of this) *The Generall* has been previously printed only in a private edition of eighty copies. Another great booming bogus piece, *The Tragedy of King Saul*, is added to the Orrery canon for the first time. All this, with the really magnificent notes on Restoration stage-craft, is a not unworthy harvest of eight years' labour.*

Roger Boyle (let us extend praise as far as it will go) was not always a worse poet than was Lee in his earliest plays: there are a few charming lines to be unearthed in *The Generall* (Mr. Clark curiously prefers the duller, maturer, emptier *Henry the Fifth*):

> Death which mankind in such high awe does keep
> Can only hold us in eternal sleep,
> And if a life after this life remains,
> Sure to our loves belong those happier plains,
> There in blest fields I'll pass the endless hours,
> And him I crown with love, I'll crown with flowers.

It is very minor poetry, of course, but it does shine out among the heroic sentiments. Otherwise the chief pleasure in this his best play is in the period note. Surfeited with action on the screen, one finds a curious charm in the passivity and irrelevance of a scene which opens: 'Filadin: Lett us then of our mistresses discourse.'

Roger Boyle was not the man for heroic drama. Dryden with his inalterable belief in authority which took him logically by way of Cromwell

* *The Dramatic Works of Roger Boyle, Earl of Orrery.* Edited by William Smith Clark.

to the Catholic Church, yes: Lee with the turbulent generous mind tha
brought him to Bedlam, yes: but we are aware of too great a gap betwee
the man and his poetry when we get as low as Settle, and Boyle present
us with the same incongruity. Mr. Clark has written his life in greate
detail though with infinitely less charm than Eustace Budgell (to whose
eighteenth-century biography he might surely have paid the tribute of
footnote) and the portrait he rather stiffly draws is that of a very politi
man, a man who lived on the dubious borderline between patronage an
treachery. He played no part in the Civil War in England, being fortunat
enough to be occupied in Ireland against the Catholic rebels: on th
King's death he began to correspond with Charles II, but Cromwell go
possession of the letters and in a remarkable scene which Mr. Clark migh
well have given in detail presented him with the choice between th
Tower and a command in Ireland. Boyle, of course, took the command
and on Cromwell's death began again his politic moves. But he was fore
stalled by Monck: the patriot always moves faster than the politic. Never
theless he became a friend of the King, wrote plays at the Royal command
and when he had the gout, served in Ireland, intrigued against Ormonde
and died unlamented by Burnet at the age of fifty-nine.

A man quite remarkably free from the impediments of friendship, how
can he do else but write a little hollowly on that favourite heroic theme

> But that I may be better understood
> Knowe friendshipp is a greater tye than blood.
> A sister is a name must not contend
> With the more high and sacred name of friend.

Burnet, if not his chaplain Morrice, saw through his pretence to religion
and there is one moment in *The Generall* when a somewhat similar
dramatic situation allows a direct comparison with Dryden. It will be
remembered how Don Sebastiano dealt with the theme of suicide:

> Brutus and Cato might discharge their Souls,
> And give them furlo's for another world:
> But we like Centries are oblig'd to stand
> In starless nights, and wait th' appointed hour.

But hear the politic accents of Burnet's 'very fickle and false man' in the
character of Altemara:

> When I am forc'd of two ills one to choose,
> 'Tis virtue then the greatest to refuse.
> When in this straight I by the Gods am plac'd.
> I'll rather cease to Live than live unchaste.

Without religion and without friendship, Orrery tried to write heroic dramas: the succession of plays, one imitated from the other, soon palled, even on Pepys, and he tried his hand at comedy. *Guzman* is quite unreadable buffoonery, but of *Mr. Anthony* it is just possible to say that it is as good as the worst of D'Urfey. He was, if that is in his favour, a clean writer: but then he seems to have had as little passion as he had religion.

DR. OATES OF SALAMANCA

MISS LANE is to be congratulated on her courage in undertaking so grim and unrelieved a work as a biography of Titus Oates (a work that has deterred biographers for nearly two hundred and fifty years) as well as on her skill and scholarship. No biographer can ever have been able to claim with more likelihood of truth that his work is definitive.*

It is interesting sometimes to speculate on how our ideas of a period would be modified if one character or one episode were removed. A man like Titus Oates occurs like a slip of the tongue, disclosing the unconscious forces, the night side of an age we might otherwise have thought of in terms of Dryden discussing the art of dramatic poesy, while his Thames boatmen rested on their oars and the thunder of an indeterminate sea battle came up from the Medway no louder than the noise of swallows in a chimney. The reach of human nature in his day, if Oates had not enlightened us, would not have extended much lower than the amiable vices of the Court: Rochester acting Dr. Bendo, Sedley prancing naked on the Epsom balcony, sin fluttering with the unimportance of a fan through the delicate cadences of Etherege's prose, that played so charmingly with the same counters, the Park, the Mulberry Gardens, the game of ombre, and as night falls "tis now but high Mall, Madam, the most entertaining time of all the evening'. And reaching the other way, would our hand have extended, without the martyrs of the Plot, much further than the piety of Bunyan? Until Oates came on the scene, it seemed hardly a period for courage any more than for evil. The career of Oates ploughed up the age and exposed the awful unchanging potentialities of human nature.

If we wished to present a portrait of evil in human terms it would be hard to find a more absolute example than the Salamanca doctor. At no point in his career does he seem to have been touched by any form of idealism. At no point is it possible to say that he was led on by a false fanaticism, or that he did wrong with any idea that right might come. His career was one of unexampled squalor, from his snotty-nosed childhood. 'I thought that he would have been a natural,' his mother is said

* *Titus Oates*, by Jane Lane.

o have reported, 'for his Nose always run and he slabbered at the mouth, and his Father could not endure him; and when he came home at night he Boy would used to be in the Chimney corner, and my Husband would ry take away this snotty Fool, and jumble him about, which made me often weep, because you know he was my child.' Yet the early years are he lighter side of Oates's life. So long as he was unsuccessful we can be entertained by the grotesqueness of his career: expelled from school, sent down from Cambridge, turned out of his living, wanted for his first perjury (he had coveted a schoolmaster's post at Hastings and therefore brought against the poor man an accusation of committing an unnatural offence in the church porch), a chaplain in the Navy and expelled again. The shadows fall with his success – his 'conversion' to Catholicism, his stay at St. Omer's College, and last the Plot itself.

Miss Lane is careful to give only such details of the Plot and the trials as come directly within the scope of her subject. She does not concern herself, for example, in any detail with the unsolved murder of Sir Edmund Berry Godfrey, a wise austerity perhaps in a book so long and necessarily so unrelieved in its horror. Her judgment of Charles II is admirably balanced and her condemnation brief and pointed. Of Oates's final trial she writes: 'King James left Oates to the Law, which was precisely what King Charles had done in the case of Oates's victims; but whereas Charles knew those victims to be innocent, James was convinced that Oates was guilty.' We prefer this final sentence on the King to the sentimental championship of Mr. Arthur Bryant: 'Alone, vilified, driven on every side, Charles remained calm and patient, etc.' The King, it is true, was fighting for the survival of the House of Stuart, but those innocent men, cut down from the gallows while still alive to be drawn and quartered, may well have wondered whether the price the King paid was not too vicarious. 'Let the blood lie on them that condemned them,' Charles is reported to have said, 'for God knows I sign with tears in my eyes,' but even if an appeal is made to God, responsibility cannot be so easily shifted and tears are more becoming after a crime than at the moment of commission. Perhaps this was the chief horror in the career of Oates, the corruption he exercised through fear. If he had had one redeeming quality, physical or mental, if he had charmed as some dictators have done with bonhomie or inspired confidence with false oratory, the corruption would have seemed less extreme, but fear was his only weapon, and Charles II joins the poor ex-schoolmaster William Smith as one of those on whose cowardice Oates found he could rely.

A HOAX ON MR. HULTON

No ONE, I suppose, will ever discover the authors of the odd elaborate hoax played on Mr. Hulton, the elderly printseller of Pall Mall, in 1744; the story itself has been hidden all these years in an old vellum manuscript book I bought the other day from a London bookseller. With its vivid unimportance it brings alive the geography of eighteenth-century tradesman's London, the wine-merchants at Wapping, the clockmakers in Fleet Street, the carriers and printers and bust-makers, all the aggrieved respectable victims of an anarchic imagination, and in the background memories of Layer's conspiracy and the word 'Jacobite' and a vague uneasiness.

The story is told in letters and occasional passages of dialogue with notes in the margin on the behaviour of the characters. It might be fiction, if these people did not all belong to fact. Who copied it out? It is hard to believe that any innocent person could have known so much. Mr. Hulton suspected his apprentices, and the whole world; there was a young man called Mr. Poet Rowzel, who knew more than he should have done; and an auctioneer, for some reason of his own, spoke of an upholsterer.

It began quite childishly on January 21st, 1744, with a letter which purported to come from Mr. Scott, a carpenter of Swallow Street, who wrote that he had many frames to make for the Prussian Ambassador, that he was ill of the gout and his men were overworked, and would Mr. Hulton call on him. Mr. Hulton had the gout himself, but he limped to Mr. Scott's house, when 'finding the whole was an imposition upon him and Scott, he hobbled back again muttering horrible imprecations against the letter-writer all the way'. Two days later the hoax really got under way. A stream of unwanted people arrived at Mr. Hulton's shop; Mr. Hazard, a cabinet maker of the 'Hen and Chickens' in Lincoln's Inn, with a quantity of Indian paper; Mr. Dard, a toy maker from the 'King's Arms' in the Strand, who had received a letter from the pseudo-Hulton offering to sell him a curious frame; a surgeon to bleed him, and a doctor from Bedlam. It would take too long to describe the events of these crowded days; how a Mr. Boyd brought snuffboxes and Mrs. Hulton had to buy one to quiet him before her husband returned; how Mr. Scarlett, an optician, arrived loaded with optic glasses, and was so ill-used by Mr. Hulton that he threatened proceedings; how Mr. Rutter, a dentist of Fleet Street, came to operate on an impostume, and was turned away by Mrs.

Hulton, who pretended her husband had died of it. Three pounds of anchovies arrived, and the printer of the *Harlaian Miscellany*, who was pushed roughly out of doors, and Mr. Cock, an auctioneer in the Great Piazza, who 'muttered something of an Irish upholsterer', and a female optician called Deane – Mrs. Hulton bolted the door against her, and spoke to her through the pane, which Mrs. Deane broke. 'Mr. Hulton at the noise of breaking the glass came forth from his little parlour into the shop, and was saluted by a porter with a dozen of port wine.' By this time he was losing control, and when Mr. Rogers, a shoe maker of Maiden Lane, wanted to measure him, 'Mr. Hulton lost all temper . . . and cursing, stamping and swearing, in an outrageous manner, he so frightened Mr. Rogers that the poor man, who is a Presbyterian, ran home to Covent Garden without once looking behind him.' After that Mr. Hulton shut up his shop, and went to bed for three days, so the man who had been told he had a peruke-maker's shop to dispose of failed to get at him. Even when the shop reopened Mr. Hulton thought it safer to stay upstairs, and leave things to his son. His son too was choleric and what he did to a young oculist who thought his father needed spectacles is unprintable here.

On February 2nd there is a break in the record, twenty-seven pages missing; but when the story begins again on September 4th Mr. Hulton is still on the run. Three dozen bottles of pale ale arrived that day; Mr. Hulton was obliged to pay for them, and 'Mrs. Hulton and her maid were fuddled while it lasted'. We must pass over the incident of the silversmith's wife, who pulled off Mrs. Hulton's nightcap, and the venison-pasty man who saw through the deceit, and enclosed the pseudo-Hulton's letter in piecrust and sent it to Mr. Hulton (the crust was given to the dog Cobb as they suspected poison). A more subtle form of hoax was in train. It began with an illiterate letter to Mr. Pinchbeck (son of Edward Pinchbeck, inventor of the alloy), accusing Hulton of having abused him 'in a monstrous manner' at a tavern, but this plot misfired; the two victims got together over a four-shilling bowl of punch.

It was then that the Reverend Aaron Thompson, of Salisbury, came on the scene (he who had baptized the conspirator Layer's child and allowed the Pretender to be a godparent by proxy). Somebody using his name ordered a number of articles which he said his agent Hulton would pay for – four canes with pinchbeck heads, a bust of Mr. Pope, a set of *The Gentleman's Magazine*, 'the books (of which you know the titles) against Bishop Berkley's Tar-Water', a complete set of Brindley's Classics, and even a chariot. This persecution caused Mr. Hulton to write to Mr.

Thompson accusing him of being a Papist and a Jacobite and threatening
him with the pillory, and the amazed Mr. Thompson 'receiving this lette
kept himself three weeks in a dark room lest he should see a letter of any
kind: by the persuasion of his wife, he at length came forth; but wore a
thin handkerchief over his eyes for above a month'. A lot of people'
nerves were getting jumpy as the hoax enlarged its scope, taking in Bath
and such worthy local characters as Mr. Jeremy Peirce, author of an
interesting little book about a tumour, and Mr. Archibald Cleland, th
surgeon who, it may be remembered, was concerned with Smollett in
controversy over the Bath waters. They all received letters from th
pseudo-Hulton, Cleland being told that Thompson had libelled him an
Peirce that Thompson had ordered him a set of *The Rake's Progress*. Th
real Aaron Thompson was by now convinced that he was the victim of
mad printseller, just as Hulton believed he was the victim of a mad clergy
man, and they both – egged on by their pseudo-selves – appealed to
Mr. Pitt of Salisbury, who assumed they both were mad. The stor
becomes inextricably confused with counter-accusations, the pseudo
Hulton writing to the real Aaron Thompson:

> You write, you read, you muzz or muse as you call it, till you are fitter fo
> Bedlam than the Pulpit: poor man! poor Aaron Thompson. I remember yo
> in Piccadilly knocking at the great Gates and returning bow for bow to th
> bowing Dean, your lean face, your awkward bow, your supercilious nod c
> the head are still in my mind . . .

and the pseudo-Thompson would send the accusation flying back, regret
ting to hear that Hulton and all his family had gone mad, and recallin
his strange way of walking about his shop 'and turning his thumbs on
over another, a sure sign of madness'. And all the while goods continue
to pour in, particularly drink – three gallons of the best Jamaica rum from
Wapping New-Stairs, which Mrs. Hulton drank and paid for, a gallon c
canary, a gallon of sherry and a pint of Madeira.

We shall never know the end – the last pages are torn out with an
clue they might have contained to the hoaxer. It was an age of practica
jokes, and he may have been one of those who baited Pinchbeck becaus
he was a 'King's friend', mocking at his nocturnal remembrancers an
writing odes about his patent snuffer. Perhaps Hulton, by his carefu
prosperity, had aroused the same balked malice of men who sympathiz
with the defeated and despise the conqueror and dare do nothing bu
trivial mischief to assert their independence – as next year proved whe
Charles Stuart turned back from Derby.

DON IN MEXICO

THIS IS an account by a Cambridge professor of two trips to the tourist resorts of Mexico,* but it pretends to be rather more. The professor is a Spanish scholar – and that should have been an advantage; but he was handicapped by the unenterprising nature of his journey – the usual round-trip by way of Mexico City, Taxco, Cuernavaca, Puebla, Vera Cruz, Merida, Chichen-Itza, by his friendships with Spanish Republicans as strange to the country as himself, by his ignorance of and antipathy to the religion of the country, and by a whimsical prose style less successful in conveying the atmosphere of Mexico than that of Cambridge-jokes on the Trumpington Road, charades with undergraduates in red-brick villas, bicycles in the hall. His book is self-illustrated with little dark holiday snaps called 'Puebla: Tiled House', or 'Mexico: Aztec Calendar Stone'; and like letters home his account is either very personal or else very guide-book at second-hand: 'The remains at Chichen-Itza lie in three groups. Those so far described belong to North Chichen; the others are referred to as Middle Chichen and Old Chichen. Following the trail from North Chichen to Middle Chichen, the first building one comes to . . .' and so on. But one can go to more accurate and comprehensive guide-books, and it is for the portrait of the Cambridge don abroad that this book will be read by the irreverent: the self-portrait of a middle-aged professor, one of 'the cultured and civilized', with a liking for weak tea and 'amusing conversation' on 'the plane of ripe but frivolous scholarship' – the authorship of *The Young Visiters*, for example.

In spite of the unconscious humour of many of the scenes, the book would not be worth attention if it were not symptomatic – symptomatic of the inhumanity of the academic brain, and its unreliability. Professor Trend, touring round the beauty spots, saw no sign of religious persecution. He noticed, it is true, a few religious colleges turned into libraries, but that to the nineteenth-century progressive mind was all to the good; apparently he did not notice in Mexico City the garages and cinemas that had once been churches. Anyway, there were plenty without these – 'Mexico, like Spain, somewhat overbuilt itself in the way of churches.' A church to the professor was an 'interior', a style of architecture: he was appalled in Peubla at 'the religiosity of the place'; 'tracts thrust into your

* *Mexico: A New Spain With Old Friends.* Professor J. B. Trend.

hands, individuals standing at the church doors to take a collection ever
before you could look in to see whether the interior was worth looking
at'. (One is reminded of the Mr. Smith whom Parkman encountered a
Palermo.)

It would be funny – the whimsicality, the self-importance, the ignor
ance – if it were not so heartless. However strong the detestation of thi
Cambridge don for the Roman Catholic Faith, he might have remembered
that those who held it were human. Shoot them and they bleed as copiousl
as a Republican. Starve them . . . He may have observed in Mexico Cit
the number of priests exercising their religious duties; he made n
inquiries, or he would have learnt that in Mexico City, as in other touris
centres, the law is winked at, so that priests who are forbidden to say Mas
in their own States and are, therefore, without means, flock to the capita
to escape starvation. The professor visited Orizaba in 1939: the churche
were certainly open; he did not ask the reason or he would have learn
how only two years before a child had been murdered by police officer
on her way from a Mass house, and how the peasants in retaliation ha
broken the churches open throughout the State of Vera Cruz. He was i
Mexico in 1938 too, and flew over Tabasco on his way to Yucatan. He di
not alight from his plane at Villa Hermosa, or he might by some lucky
chance have been present when the police fired on a crowd of peasants
men, women and children, who were setting up an altar in the ruins of
church. But, of course, no one interested in ecclesiastical architectur
would have visited Tabasco, for there were no churches left in the State

Blithely, whimsically, from his Cambridge study the professor writes
'As to religious persecution, it is (so far as my experience goes, and as fa
as I have been able to find out by inquiry) mostly imaginary.' His inquirie
must have been as limited as his experience, and any writer who describe
conditions of which the professor prefers to remain in ignorance he style
a 'propagandist'. He has all the suspicion of a provincial holiday-make
afraid of being 'had', and I shall probably be suspected of all sorts o
dishonest motives if I assure him that in the very year he was in Mexic
he had only to travel a little farther afield to discover States where th
churches were either destroyed or locked, where priests were forbidde
to say Mass, and where the sacraments of their Faith could be taken by th
people only in secret. Propaganda? But I have attended these secret Masse
myself in Chiapas. I doubt if my assurance will carry conviction: for as th
professor writes, 'My Mexico is not like that', and on another page, 'I hav
always had a preference for legends rather than for more sober history.'

PORTRAIT OF A MAIDEN LADY

EADING *No Place Like Home* by Beverley Nichols I found myself thinking of Guy Walsingham, the author of *Obsessions*, in Henry James's *The Death of a Lion*. It will be remembered how Mr. Morrow, of *The Tatler*, interviewed her, for Guy Walsingham was a woman, just as Dora Forbes, author of *The Other Way Round*, was a man. 'A mere pseudonym' – that was how Mr. Morrow put it – 'convenient you know, for a lady who goes in for the larger latitude.'

A confusing literary habit, which led me to wonder a little about the author of *No Place Like Home*. For all I know Mr. Nichols may be another Mr. Walsingham, a middle-aged and maiden lady, so I picture the author, connected in some way with the Church: I would hazard a guess that she housekeeps for her brother, who may be a canon or perhaps a rural dean. In that connexion she may have met the distinguished ecclesiastics who have noticed a previous book so kindly. ('The chapter on Sex', writes a dean, 'is the best sermon on the subject I have ever read.') She is not married, that I am sure, for she finds the sight of men's sleeping apparel oddly disturbing: 'It was almost indecent, the way he took out pyjamas and shook them,' and on her foreign holiday, described in this book, she hints – quite innocently – at a Man. 'His knowledge was encyclopaedic. His name was Paul. He was about forty-five. We had better leave it at that.'

It is impossible not to grow a little fond of this sentimental, whimsical and poetic lady. She conforms so beautifully to type (I picture her in rather old-fashioned mauve with a whale-bone collar): Christian, but only in the broadest sense, emotional, uninstructed and a little absurd, as when she writes of the Garden of Gethsemane: 'Here I had the greatest shock of all. *For the Garden was not even weeded!*' She is serious about Art ('Try a little experiment. Hold up your hand in front of your eyes so that you bisect a picture horizontally'), a little playful ('Dürers so great that you felt you must walk up to them on tiptoe'). She loves dumb animals, and hates to see even a field mouse killed ('One mustn't let oneself wonder if perhaps the mice were building a house, which has now been wrecked, if perhaps Mrs. Field Mouse was going to have babies, which will be fatherless'), and in *their* cause she shows considerable courage. ('On more than one occasion I have created useless and undignified scenes at theatres in a vain protest against the cruelty of dragging terrified and bewildered animals to the footlights for the delectation of the crowd.') This almost masculine aggressiveness is quite admirable when you consider the author's natural timidity, how nervous she is in aeroplanes. ('It is with the greatest difficulty that I refrain from asking the pilot if he is sure about the tail. Is it on? Is it on *straight?* What will happen if it falls off?') and how on one occasion, climbing a pyramid, she very nearly had what she calls a 'swooning sickness'.

But what engaging company on these foreign cruises and excursions a maiden lady of her kind must have been, exhilarated as she was by her freedom from parish activities. ('All that matters is that we are alone and free, *free*. Nobody can telephone to us. Nobody can ask us to lecture on the Victorian novelists. It is beyond the realms of possibility that anybody, for at least twenty-four hours, will ask us to open a chrysanthemum exhibition'), and hilarious with the unaccustomed wine ('We are, beyond a shadow of a doubt, Abroad. And not only Abroad. At Large. And not only At Large but in a delirious haze of irresponsibility, and white wine'). Her emotions are so revealing: she weeps, literally weeps, over Athens. She disapproves of women who don't grow old gracefully ('I also thought how very much nicer and younger the average woman of forty-five would look, in this simple uniform, than in the stolen garments of her daughter'), she feels tenderly towards young people ('The silvery treble of youth that is sweeter because it is sexless'), her literary preferences are quite beautifully commonplace: 'What a grand play Galsworthy would have written round the theme of Naboth's Vineyard.' Excitable, sound at heart, genuinely attached to her brother and the vicarage. 'The old dear,' one exclaims with real affection, and I was overjoyed that she got safely home to her own garden before – but I mustn't spoil her closing paragraphs:

'There they were, dancing under the elm, exactly as I had planned them.

'I was in time for the daffodils.'

MR. COOK'S CENTURY

ALREADY they seem to belong to history – those tourists of the 30's; they have the dignity and the pathos of a period, as they gather, the older ones in extraordinary hats and veils, the younger a little awkward and coltish, on the Continental platform at Victoria. Their baggage is all labelled for the Swiss *pensions*, the Italian lakes: in their handbags they carry seasick remedies and some of them tiny bottles of brandy; their tickets are probably in the hands of the courier, who now kindly and dexterously, with an old-world manner, shepherds them towards the second-class (first on boat), towards adventure – the first view of Mont Blanc, the fancy-dress dance at Grindelwald, the falls of Schlaffhausen (seen through stained glass for a few francs extra). How sad it is that war prevents the one-hundredth anniversary of the first Cook's excursion being celebrated in a suitable atmosphere – with lots of eau-de-Cologne and steam and shiny picture-papers, and afterwards the smell of oil and sea-gulls and a sense of suppressed ladylike excitement, and the scramble along the corridor with the right coupons towards the first meal on the Basle express – everything paid for in advance, even the tips.

Of course there was so much more to Cook's than that: that little daily gathering on the Continental platform was rather like the unimportant flower a big business executive may wear in his button-hole for the sake of some early association. Thomas Cook and Son, who, in 1938, could have arranged you an independent tour to Central Africa as easily as to Ostend, had become a world-power which dealt with Prime Ministers: they transported Gordon up the Nile, and afterwards the relief expedition – 18,000 troops, 130,000 tons of stores, and 65,000 tons of coal; they reformed the pilgrim traffic to Mecca, deported 'undesirables' from South Africa during the Boer War, bought the railway up Vesuvius, and knocked a gap in the walls of Jerusalem to let the Kaiser in; before the end of the nineteenth-century, under the son, they had far outstripped the dream of the first Thomas Cook, the young wood-turner and teetotaller and Bible-reader of Market Harborough, who on July 5th, 1841, chartered a special train to carry his local temperance association from Leicester to Loughborough, where a meeting was to be held in Mr. Paget's park. (The distance was twelve miles, and the return fare 1*s*.: it could hardly be

less today.) The words of Mr. John Fox Bell, secretary to the Midland
Counties Railway, have the right historic ring: 'I know nothing of you
or your society, but you shall have the train,' and Mr. Thomas Cook was
quite aware that he was making history.'The whole thing came to me', he
said, 'by intuition and my spirit recoiled at the idea of imitation.' (This
refers to the shameful attempt of the Mechanics Institute of Birmingham,
who had run an excursion on June 29th to Cheltenham and Gloucester,
to question the originality of his inspiration.) The cheers that greeted the
thirsty teetotallers as they scrambled from their open scorching trucks,
the music of the Loughborough band, the congratulatory speeches in
Mr. Paget's park bore Mr. Cook on a great wave of local pride, inspecting
hotels as he went, interviewing railroad secretaries, noting points of
interest – the fourteenth-century cathedral, the abbey ruin, the majestic
waterfall, on out of England into Wales – 'From the heights of Snowdon
my thoughts took flight to Ben Lomond, and I determined to try to get
to Scotland.' And get to Scotland he did with 350 men and women – we
don't know whether they were teetotallers, and at Glasgow the guns were
fired in their honour.

But Europe was another matter: Europe, to the Bible-reader and
teetotaller, must have presented a knotty ethical problem, and it was not
until 1860, after a personal look-round, that Mr. Cook brought his
excursionists to the Continent. It is easy to mock nowadays at the carefully conducted tour, but there have been times and places when a guide
is of great comfort. 'In 1865, through many difficulties, I got my first
party to Rome and Naples, and for several years our way was through
brigand-infested districts, where military escorts protected us.'

By the end of the century – under the rule of the second Cook – the
firm had become the Cook's we know today. I have before me a copy of
a paper called Cook's Excursionist, for March 18th, 1899; and already there
were few places in the world to which an excursion had not been arranged
– from the Tea and Coffee Rooms of Bora Bimki to the Deansgate
Temperance Hotel in Manchester. The link with Mr. Paget's park is still
there, not only in the careful choice of hotel but in the advertisements –
for Dr. E. D. Moore's Cocoa and Milk, and the Compactum Tea Baskets.
I like to feel that this – the spring of 1899 – marks the serene height of
Mr. Cook's tours, for brigands have ceased to trouble, and there is no
suspicion that they may one day come again. Keating's Powder has taken
the place of the military escort; Mrs. Welsley Wigg is keeping 'an excellent
table' in Euston Square, and a young lady, 'who last year found them

perfectly efficacious', is cautiously recommending Roach's Sea-Sickness Draughts – perhaps this year won't be so lucky? At John Piggott's in Cheapside you can buy all the clothes you need for a conducted tour: the long black Chesterfield coat, the Norfolk suit, suitable for Switzerland, and the cap with a little button on top, the Prince Albert, the Leinster overcoat with velvet lapels, and with them, of course, the Gladstone bag strapped and double-strapped, secure against the dubious chambermaid and the foreign porter. What would they have thought – those serene men with black moustaches, and deer-stalkers for the crossing, if they could have seen in a vision the great familiar station-yard, dead and deserted as it was a few months back, without a cab, a porter or a police-man, just a notice, 'Unexploded Bomb', casually explaining what would have seemed to them the end of everything; no trains for France, no trains for Switzerland, none for Italy, and even the clock stopped? It is, when you come to think of it, a rather sad centenary year.*

* Written in 1941.

GREAT DOG OF WEIMAR

My TITLE is not, I must explain at once, a disrespectful reference to the great German poet, but to another inhabitant of Weimar, equally interesting but less well known. Perhaps I should have heard long ago of the unbearable Kurwenal, the companion (it would be inaccurate and flippant to call him the pet) of Mathilde, Baroness von Freytag-Loringhoven, but if I had not opened by chance a little book called *When Your Animal Dies*, written by Miss Sylvia Barbanell and recently published by the Psychic Press, I should have remained in ignorance that dogs had ever spoken – not only Kurwenal, the dachshund of Weimar, but Lola Kindermann, the airedale, and her father Rolph Meokel, of Mannheim. I have always suspected dogs: solid, well-meaning, reliable, they seem to possess all the least attractive human virtues. What bores, I have sometimes thought, if they could speak, and now my most appalling conjectures have been confirmed.

Miss Barbanell's is – let me emphasize it – a serious book: the unbearable Kurwenal could have no place in a humorous one. He is here a minor character: Miss Barbanell is mainly concerned with the after-life of animals towards which she gently leads us by her stories of animal intelligence – an after-life not only for the unbearable Kurwenal and his kind but also for cats, pet pigs and goats. We hear of two pet frogs materializing, and of Red Indian 'guides' who answer evasively – in language oddly unlike Fenimore Cooper's – embarrassing questions about bugs. (The lesser – undomesticated – creatures, it appears, join a group soul: there is a group soul for every species and sub-species, but nobody seems worried at the thought of how the group bug grows every time a Mexican crushes one with his toe: as for roast chicken, in future it will seem to me like eating a theosophist.)

But to return to the unbearable Kurwenal. Nobody can question *his* claim to immortality, with his strong moral sense, his rectitude and his little clean clerical jokes. Perhaps I should have explained that the Baroness von Freytag-Loringhoven (with a name like that she must have been a friend of Rilke) taught him to speak a language of barks, and the appalling dog was only too ready to learn. Five hundred investigators investigated him, including Professor Max Müller, but he seems on the whole to have endured them with exemplary patience. Only once did he rebel, and that momentarily, against a young neurologist of Berne University, exclaiming, 'I answer no doubters. Bother the asses.' It is the only recorded instance when this vile dog behaved other than well; there is no suggestion that he ever buried a bone, and the imagination boggles with embarrassment at the thought of the intimate scenes that must have taken place between Kurwenal and the Baroness when he was being house-trained. He would have done nothing to make the situation easier. 'To me,' he was in the habit of saying with priggish self-approval, 'learning is a great happiness,' and to a young scientist who visited him, he said, 'I like to have you here. You are more sincere than most people.' He was that kind of dog: one pictures the earnest melting brown gaze between the ears like ringlets.

Dachshunds, of course, are always serious and usually sentimental, but occasionally one has seen them shocked into abandon by a fleshy bone, a good smell or an amiable tree. Not so the unbearable Kurwenal. Miss Barbanell writes that he had an 'attractive personality and grand sense of humour', but those words one uses of a dean who does – sometimes – unbend. 'Kurwenal had a roguish sense of fun. The Baroness was given a very fine Roman rug for him on her birthday. Kurwenal said, "I find rug nice, will tear." Then he paused before he added with a sly look in his eye, "Not".'

If you accompanied Kurwenal on his walks you were more likely to be edified than amused. He was fond of discussing religion in a rather evangelical way. 'On one of these occasions he said to the Baroness, "I often pray." She asked, "What do you pray for?" Kurwenal answered, "For you." ' Once, during tea, Professor Max Müller discussed with his hostess the slaughter of dogs for food. 'He thought that the topic must be of particular interest to Kurwenal and asked the dog whether he had followed the conversation. "Yes," replied Kurwenal. "Do you wish to say something about it?" "Yes," answered the dog, and barked out the following: "The Christian religion prohibits killing." ' Sometimes when I remember that all this was spoken in the German language I feel sorry even for the unbearable Kurwenal: to think of those constructions – that awful drift of guttural words – expressed with a sort of slow pedantry in barks. For Conversations with Kurwenal were quite as protracted as Conversations with Eckermann. With the same neurologist from Berne who was the victim of Kurwenal's only breach of good manners the dachshund carried on a conversation lasting nearly an hour. One pictures him on a hard ornate chair facing the scientist across a salon table: I doubt if even the Baroness ever held Kurwenal on her knees (it would hardly have been proper and it certainly would not have been suitable). 'When the scientist was about to leave, he turned to the dachshund and said, "I nearly forgot to ask you what you think about a dog's soul." "It is eternal like the soul of man," replied Kurwenal.'

Earnest, thoughtful, full of familiar quotations (he knew his *Hamlet*), his manner lightened very rarely by a touch of diocesan humour, this dachshund possessed as well the awful faculty of always saying – and doing – the right thing. There was the message he sent with his photograph to the Animal Defence Society in London: there was the emotional scene with the military widower.

> The Baroness tells how she was visited by a friend, an army officer, who was very sad because his wife had recently passed on. Kurwenal said to his owner, 'We must cheer him up.' The dog approached the downcast man. 'Do you want to say something to him?' asked the Baroness. 'Yes,' replied Kurwenal.
> 'You can make up such nice little poems now,' she said. 'Make one for him.' Without much delay Kurwenal recited:
>
> > 'I love no one as much as you.
> > Love me too.
> > I should like you with me every day.
> > Of happiness a ray.'
>
> Touched by the intelligent dog's sympathy, the depressed man's spirits brightened considerably.

Kurwenal, I am heartlessly glad to say, has 'passed on'. Otherwise he would probably have become a refugee, for his Christian principles would never have allowed him to support the Nazi party; around Bloomsbury therefore we should have heard continually his admonitory barks, barks about the great Teutonic abstractions – eternity, the soul, barks of advice, reproof, consolation. Strangely enough there is no record in a book crammed with séances, apparitions, invisible pawings, of the great dog's return. Silence has taken him at last, but I for one feel no doubt at all that somewhere he awaits his mistress – no, that is not a word one can use in connexion with Kurwenal and the Baroness – his former companion, ready to lead the Baroness von Freytag-Loringhoven firmly among the group souls and the Red Indian 'guides', among the odd frequenters of the Kluski séances – the buzzard, the Eastern sage and his weasel, the Afghan with his maneless lion – into the heart of the vague theosophic eternity.

Part Four

PERSONAL POSTSCRIPT

THE REVOLVER IN THE CORNER CUPBOARD

I CAN remember very clearly the afternoon I found the revolver in the brown deal corner cupboard in the bedroom which I shared with my elder brother. It was the early autumn of 1922. I was seventeen and terribly bored and in love with my sister's governess – one of those miserable, hopeless, romantic loves of adolescence that set in many minds the idea that love and despair are inextricable and that successful love hardly deserves the name. At that age one may fall irrevocably in love with failure, and success of any kind loses half its savour before it is experienced. Such a love is surrendered once and for all to the singer at the pavement's edge, the bankrupt, the old school friend who wants to touch you for a dollar. Perhaps in many so conditioned it is the love for God that mainly survives, because in his eyes they can imagine themselves remaining always drab, seedy, unsuccessful, and therefore worthy of notice.

The revolver was a small genteel object with six chambers like a tiny egg stand, and there was a cardboard box of bullets. It has only recently occurred to me that they may have been blanks; I always assumed them to be live ammunition, and I never mentioned the discovery to my brother because I had realized the moment I saw the revolver the use I intended to make of it. (I don't to this day know why he possessed it; certainly he had no licence, and he was only three years older than myself. A large family is as departmental as a Ministry.)

My brother was away – probably climbing in the Lake District – and until he returned the revolver was to all intents mine. I knew what to do with it because I had been reading a book (the name Ossendowski comes to mind as the possible author) describing how the White Russian officers, condemned to inaction in South Russia at the tail-end of the counter-revolutionary war, used to invent hazards with which to escape boredom. One man would slip a charge into a revolver and turn the chambers at random, and his companion would put the revolver to his head and pull the trigger. The chance, of course, was six to one in favour of life.

How easily one forgets emotions. If I were dealing now with an imaginary character, I would feel it necessary for verisimilitude to make him hesitate, put the revolver back into the cupboard, return to it again after an interval, reluctantly and fearfully, when the burden of boredom became too great. But in fact I think there was no hesitation at all, for the next I can remember is crossing Berkhamsted Common, gashed here and there between the gorse bushes with the stray trenches of the first Great War, towards the Ashridge beeches. Perhaps before I had made the discovery, boredom had already reached an intolerable depth.

I think the boredom was far deeper than the love. It had always been a feature of childhood: it would set in on the second day of the school holidays. The first day was all happiness, and, after the horrible confinement and publicity of school, seemed to consist of light, space and silence. But a prison conditions its inhabitants. I never wanted to return to it (and finally expressed my rebellion by the simple act of running away), but yet I was so conditioned that freedom bored me unutterably.

The psycho-analysis that followed my act of rebellion had fixed the boredom as hypo fixes the image on the negative. I emerged from those delightful months in London spent at my analyst's house – perhaps the happiest months of my life – correctly orientated, able to take a proper extrovert interest in my fellows (the jargon rises to the lips), but wrung dry. For years, it seems to me, I could take no aesthetic interest in any visual thing at all: staring at a sight that others assured me was beautiful I would feel nothing. I was fixed in my boredom. (Writing this I come on a remark of Rilke: 'Psycho-analysis is too fundamental a help for me, i helps you once and for all, it clears you up, and to find myself finally cleared up one day might be even more helpless than this chaos.')

Now with the revolver in my pocket I was beginning to emerge. I had stumbled on the perfect cure. I was going to escape in one way or another and because escape was inseparably connected with the Common in my mind, it was there that I went.

The wilderness of gorse, old trenches, abandoned butts was the unchanging backcloth of most of the adventures of childhood. It was to the Common I had decamped for my act of rebellion some years before with the intention, expressed in a letter left after breakfast on the heavy black sideboard, that there I would stay, day and night, until either I had starved or my parents had given in; when I pictured war it was always in terms of this Common, and myself leading a guerilla campaign in th ragged waste, for no one, I was persuaded, knew its paths so intimately (how humiliating that in my own domestic campaign I was ambushed by my elder sister after a few hours).

Beyond the Common lay a wide grass ride known for some reason as Cold Harbour to which I would occasionally with some fear take a horse and beyond this again stretched Ashridge Park, the smooth olive skin of beech trees and the thick last year's quagmire of leaves, dark like old pennies. Deliberately I chose my ground, I believe without any real fear – perhaps because I was uncertain myself whether I was play-acting; perhaps because so many acts which my elders would have regarded as neurotic, but which I still consider to have been under the circumstances highly reasonable, lay in the background of this more dangerous venture.

There had been, for example, perhaps five or six years before, the disappointing morning in the dark room by the linen cupboard on the eve of term when I had patiently drunk a quantity of hypo under the impression that it was poisonous: on another occasion the blue glass bottle of hay fever lotion which as it contained a small quantity of cocaine had probably been good for my mood: the bunch of deadly nightshade that I had eaten with only a slight narcotic effect: the twenty aspirins I had taken before swimming in the empty out-of-term school baths (I can still remember the curious sensation of swimming through wool): these acts may have removed all sense of strangeness as I slipped a bullet into a chamber and, holding the revolver behind my back, spun the chambers round.

Had I romantic thoughts about the governess? Undoubtedly I must have had, but I think that at the most they simply eased the medicine down. Boredom, aridity, those were the main emotions. Unhappy love was, I suppose, sometimes driven boys to suicide, but this was not suicide, whatever a coroner's jury might have said of it: it was a gamble with six chances to one against an inquest. The romantic flavour – the autumn scene, the small heavy compact shape lying in the fingers – that perhaps was a tribute to adolescent love, but the discovery that it was possible to enjoy again the visible world by risking its total loss was one I was bound to make sooner or later.

I put the muzzle of the revolver in my right ear and pulled the trigger. There was a minute click, and looking down at the chamber I could see that the charge had moved into place. I was out by one. I remember an extraordinary sense of jubilation. It was as if a light had been turned on. My heart was knocking in its cage, and I felt that life contained an infinite number of possibilities. It was like a young man's first successful experience of sex – as if in that Ashridge glade one had passed a test of manhood. I went home and put the revolver back in the corner cupboard.

The odd thing about this experience was that it was repeated several times. At fairly long intervals I found myself craving for the drug. I took the revolver with me when I went up to Oxford and I would walk out from Headington towards Elsfield down what is now a wide arterial road, smooth and shiny like the walls of a public lavatory. Then it was a sodden unfrequented country lane. The revolver would be whipped behind my back, the chambers twisted, the muzzle quickly and surreptitiously inserted beneath the black and ugly winter tree, the trigger pulled.

Slowly the effect of the drug wore off – I lost the sense of jubilation, I began to gain from the experience only the crude kick of excitement. It was like the difference between love and lust. And as the quality of the experience deteriorated so my sense of responsibility grew and worried me. I wrote a very bad piece of free verse (free because it was easier in that way to express my meaning without literary equivocation) describing how, in order to give a fictitious sense of danger, I would 'press the trigger of a revolver I already know to be empty'. This piece of verse I would leave permanently on my desk, so that if I lost my gamble, there would be incontrovertible evidence of an accident, and my parents, I thought, would be less troubled than by an apparent suicide – or than by the rather bizarre truth.

But it was back at Berkhamsted that I paid a permanent farewell to the drug. As I took my fifth dose it occurred to me that I wasn't even excited: I was beginning to pull the trigger about as casually as I might take an aspirin tablet. I decided to give the revolver – which was six-chambered – a sixth and last chance. Twirling the chambers round, I put the muzzle to my ear for the last time and heard the familiar empty click as the chambers revolved. I was through with the drug, and walking back over the Common, down the new road by the ruined castle, past the private entrance to the gritty old railway station – reserved for the use of Lord Brownlow – my mind was already busy on other plans. One campaign was over, but the war against boredom had got to go on.

I put the revolver back in the corner cupboard, and going downstairs I lied gently and convincingly to my parents that a friend had invited me to join him in Paris.

VIVE LE ROI

'GODD SAIVE aour grechieuss Kinng. Longg laive aour nobeul Kinng. Godd saive zi Kinng.' That is *Paris-Soir* teaching Paris in phonetics to sing the National Anthem, and that, too, I like to think, is what happens when democracies entertain each other – something a little comic and a little moving as well – like the small boy dressed in a Guard's uniform out with his mother, the slightly inaccurate Union Jacks, the postcard sellers who offer you pictures of the Royal Family furtively: they can't change the habit of a lifetime. We are already familiar with the meetings of dictators – 'stone, bronze, stone, steel, stone, oak-leaves, horses' heels over the paving'. The monuments look made to last for ever, and the friendship is over at the railway station. Here in Paris the decorations are as transient as flowers, but the friendship – it is inconceivable that it can ever seriously be threatened, and so we can take the celebrations lightly between friends.

The flags, of course, are everywhere, little splashes of bright colour against the grey Paris stone. They hang in trophies on the lamp-posts and wave in pairs on the hoods of the little green 'buses: they are to be seen above the advertisements of Byrrh – 'recommandé aux femmes' – and in the shop windows, among the Chaussures Walk-Over, the Walk-Over Unics and the Walk-Over Seductas. And as one might expect, there is an elegant variation on our flag below Maggy Rouff's windows on the Champs Élysées – an impression of Union Jack rather than real Union Jacks.

A democracy doesn't have to be dignified all the time – there are the odd attractive monsters on the Seine, a whole school of them, grey and rocky and old, with gold teeth like all Latins and a brood of young like scorpions or whiting – though it can vie with the dictatorships when it chooses: the Place Vendôme, great royal red hangings, embroidered with golden crowns, falling down the front of the grey eighteenth-century stone, green laurel wound above the highest windows as if it had grown like moss with time. The façade of the Opera is not spoiled by elaborate decoration, only red hangings with gold loops below the tall windows. In the Champs the standards are a little faded by the long delay – it might be a charming French compliment – and obelisks of mirror glass, as sharp as icicles, reflect the banners and trophies as they stir in the grey air and the spray of the fountains, a crystalline triumph. And the little ugly Bois de Boulogne station has been transformed – or rather avoided, pushed aside by a small graceful pavilion with thin white pillars and a white canopy and a great fall of scarlet curtain and golden seal-like lions of unleonine intelligence who gaze sidelong at the golden statue of France on a white pediment across the way.

One is aware all the time that it is a Republic which is welcoming the King. There are, therefore, amusing contrasts – in the Place de la Concorde are giant plaques which light up at night: in one the axe which killed a king under the Sansculotte cap that reminds most Englishmen, I think, of the demned elusive Pimpernel and old women extras knitting under the guillotine and Sidney Carton saying: 'It is a far, far better thing . . .'; and next to it the Royal lion and unicorn – sleek and svelte with tiny vicious waists and little wicked decorative faces. One reads with interest in the Press about the King's chauffeur, M. Duthoit – 'C'est un excellent père de famille, il a une fille de douze ans qui fait de très brillantes études.'

It is a Republic too undoubtedly at night, when there are free performances of *Othello* at the Odéon in honour of the King, and people shout and push and the police get rough and shrill, and there are little flurries and fights and excitements – in honour of Shakespeare. And everywhere are street dances – bystreets marked off by paper streamers. 'It is very good', a French poet said, 'to dance in the street. It is a symbol,' and the motorcars and 'buses line up and wait for the dance to finish, while the fireworks play above the Seine and giant golden fountains rise and fall and the monsters sit like idols in green spray.

But at last comes Tuesday afternoon. The King's arrival is imminent – he must have left Boulogne. Workmen are still dodging about behind the great trophies, shifting ladders. It is often said that Paris is not France. That was not, on Tuesday, true. Old ladies in black veils from the Provinces stared at Paris over the tops of 'buses – like Judy, and let themselves heavily down on stools in the Champs – like blocks of Epstein stone. People got argumentative over the elaborate police precautions – no window boxes allowed along the route, special passports for apartment owners opposite the station and no guests allowed, police agents in place of concierges, armed chauffeurs. But, as a taxi-driver said to me, in that marbled prose which seems to come as naturally to Paris drivers as humour to London 'bus conductors: 'Today every Frenchman is a police agent.'

The Gardes Mobiles arrive: whippet tanks – camouflaged as in war –

line one side of the Place de la Concorde: soldiers distribute themselves among the shops and houses which overlook the route. It reminded me of the day of the General Strike – steel helmets down every side street: shift a stone and you disturb a soldier – but this is not a national crisis but a social call. It is the technique enforced by one assassination and the methods of dictatorships.

The Gardes Mobiles line the route in front of the police and troops are placed in front of *them*. Field-guns and Spahis make a circle round the Arc de Triomphe – small dark fanatical faces above the white robes: police officers are silhouetted on all the roofs, among the chimney pots. A plain-clothes man at the corner of the Rue de Tilsitt searches a working girl's attaché-case – one is suddenly granted an intimacy one doesn't want with a private life among the balls of wool – as when a bombed house discloses its interior.

Then the standards go by and the buglers twirl their bright brass instruments in the sun and the people clap. It is not too solemn. Black soldiers march side by side with white – and that too is republican, no racial nonsense, a fading dream of human equality. And there is a little good-humoured laughter as the President is whisked quickly past towards the station in a flurry of plumes and breast-plates. The sun has come blindingly out, and the mannequins lean decoratively down over Paris like gargoyles.

And when the King at last went by, preceded by Spahis and sur-rounded by the Republican Guard riding at a canter, so that all you saw was a cocked hat and some gold lace between the horses and plumes, and he had gone, what you chiefly felt was pity. It was very moving, of course, when a foreign band played 'God Save the King' and the cheers came rattling down past the Arc de Triomphe and the Spahi sabres flashed and a fierce old gentleman in a beard barked 'À bas les chapeaux' and French-men cried out 'Vive le Roi!' and then 'Vive la Reine!' (though they didn't sing 'Godd saive ze Kinng'), but it was a pity one felt most of all – pity for the human race who have made it impossible for a simple and kindly gentleman to visit another in the way of friendship without these elaborate precautions, just because he represents his country. The King is among friends, but that in these days is not enough – Paris must put herself in a state of siege to protect him. I shall remember for a long while the black Senegalese soldiers who lined the Avenue Marigny when the King drove to the Élysée to call on the President, and their gentle and destructive smile – this was not Africa, this was civilization.

FILM LUNCH

'IF EVER there was a Christ-like man in human form it was Marcus
Lowe.'

Under the huge Union Jack, the Stars and Stripes, the massed
chandeliers of the Savoy, the little level Jewish voice softly intones. It is
Mr. Louis B. Mayer, head of Metro-Goldwyn-Mayer, and the lunch is
being held to celebrate the American company's decision to produce films
in this country. Money, one can't help seeing it written on the literary
faces, money for jam; but Mr. Mayer's words fall on the mercenary
gathering with apostolic seriousness.

At the high table Sir Hugh Walpole leans back, a great bald forehead, a
rather softened and popular Henry James, like a bishop before the laying-
on of hands – but oddly with a long cigar. Miss Maureen O'Sullivan waits
under her halo hat . . . and Mr. Robert Taylor – is there, one wonders, a
woman underneath the table? Certainly there are few sitting anywhere
else; not many, at any rate, whom you would recognize as women among
the tough massed faces of the film-reviewers. As the voice drones remorse-
lessly on, these escape at intervals to catch early editions, bulging with
shorthand (Mr. Mayer's voice lifts: 'I must be honest to myself if I'm to
be honest to you . . . a 200,000,000-dollar corporation like the Rock of
Gibraltar . . . untimely death . . . tragedy'); they stoop low, slipping
between the tables, like soldiers making their way down the communica-
tion trenches to the rest billets in the rear, while a voice mourns for
Thalberg, untimely slain. The bright Very lights of Mr. Mayer's eloquence
soar up: 'Thank God, I say to you, that it's the greatest year of net results
and that's because I have men like Eddy Sankatz' (can that have been the
name? It sounded like it after the Chablis Supérieur, 1929, the Château
Pontet Canet (Pauillac), 1933, G. H. Mumm, Cordon Rouge, 1928, and
the Gautier Frères Fine Champagne 20 *ans*).

'No one falls in the service of M.G.M. but I hope and pray that someone else will take his place and carry on the battle. Man proposes and God
in his time disposes. . . .' All the speakers have been confined to five
minutes – Mr. Alexander Korda, Lord Sempill, Lord Lee of Fareham and
the rest, but of course that doesn't apply to the big shot. The rather small
eyes of Mr. Frank Swinnerton seem to be watching something on his

beard, Mr. Ivor Novello has his hand laid across his stomach – or is it his heart?

One can't help missing things, and when the mind comes back to the small dapper men under the massed banners Mr. Mayer is talking about his family, and God again. 'I've got another daughter and I hope to God . . .' But the hope fumes out of sight in the cigar smoke of the key-men. 'She thought she'd like a poet or a painter, but I held on until I landed Selznick. "No, Ireen," I'd say, "I'm watching and waiting." So David Selznick, he's performing independent now.'

The waiters stand at attention by the great glass doors. The air is full of aphorisms. 'I love to give flowers to the living before they pass on. . . . We must have entertainment like the flowers need sunshine. . . . A Boston bulldog hangs on till death. Like Jimmy Squires.' (Jimmy Squires means something to these tough men. They applaud wildly. The magic name is repeated – 'Jimmy Squires'.) 'I understand Britishers,' Mr. Mayer continues, 'I understand what's required of a man they respect and get under their hearts.'

There is more than a religious element in this odd, smoky and spirituous gathering; at moments it is rather like a boxing match. 'Miss O'Sullivan' – and Miss O'Sullivan bobs up to her feet and down again: a brown hat: a flower: one misses the rest. 'Robert Taylor' – and the world's darling is on his feet, not far from Sir Hugh Walpole, beyond the brandy glasses and Ivor Novello, a black triangle of hair, a modest smile.

'He comes of a lovely family,' Mr. Mayer says. 'If ever there was an American young man who could logically by culture and breeding be called a Britisher it's Robert Taylor.'

But already we are off and away, Robert Taylor abandoned to the flashlight men. It's exactly 3.30 and Mr. Mayer is working up for his peroration: 'It's midday. It's getting late. I shall pray silently that I shall be guided in the right channels. . . . I want to say what's in my heart. . . . In all these years of production, callous of adulation and praise . . . I hope the Lord will be kind to you. We are sending over a lovely cast.'

He has spoken for forty minutes: for forty minutes we have listened with fascination to the voice of American capital itself: a touch of religion, a touch of the family, the mixture goes smoothly down. Let the literary men sneer . . . the whip cracks . . . past the glass doors and the sentries, past the ashen-blonde sitting in the lounge out of earshot (only the word 'God' reached her ears three times), the great muted chromium studios wait . . . the novelist's Irish sweep: money for no thought, for the banal situation and the inhuman romance: money for forgetting how people live: money for 'Siddown, won't yer' and 'I love, I love, I love' endlessly repeated. Inside the voice goes on – 'God . . . I pray . . .' and the writers, a little stuffed and a little boozed, lean back and dream of the hundred pounds a week – and all that's asked in return the dried imagination and the dead pen.

BOOK MARKET

A SUNK railway track and a gin distillery flank the gritty street. There is something Victorian about the whole place – an air of ugly commercial endeavour mixed with odd idealisms and philanthropies. It isn't only the jumble of unattractive titles on the dusty spines, the huge weight of morality at sixpence a time; even the setting has an earnestness . . . The public-houses are like a lesson in temperance.

It isn't all books by any means in the book market: a dumb man presides over the first stall given up to paintbrushes and dividers; we pass wireless parts, rubber heels, old stony collections of nuts and bolts, gramophone records, cycle tyres, spectacles (hospital prescriptions made up on the spot under the shadow of the gin distillery), a case of broken (I was going to say moth-eaten) butterflies – privet-hawks and orange-tips and red admirals losing their antennae and powder, shabby like second-hand clothes. One stall doesn't display its wares at all: only labels advertising Smell Bombs, Itching Powder, Cigarette Bangs – Victorian, too, the painful physical humour, reminding us of Cruickshank on the poor and Gilbert on old age.

And then at last the books. It is a mistake to look for bargains here, or even to hope to find any books you really want – unless you happen to want Thackeray, Froude or Macaulay on the cheap. Those authors are ubiquitous. No, the book market is the place for picking up odd useless information. Here, for instance, is Dibdin's *Purification of Sewage and Water*, published by the Sanitary Publishing Company, next to *Spiritual Counsel for District Visitors*, *Submarine Cables* and *Chicago Police Problems*, published – it seems broadminded – by the Chicago University Press. Of course, there are lots of folios called *View of the Lakes* or of Italy, Switzerland, the Tyrol, as the case may be; and one can buy, in pale-blue paper parts, Bessemer on *Working Blast Furnaces*. *Doll Caudel in Paris* seems to be part of a series and looks a little coarse.

Somebody had left a book open on a stall, and I read with some amazement: 'George Moore had a great idea of duty. "If I have one thing," he says in his diary, "it is an imperative sense of duty." He was always possessed with the full sense of "doing his duty". He wished to do it; and he prayed to God to help him do it. But what duty?' What, indeed? Of

course, one remembers the scene in *Salve*, when Moore said a prayer with
Mr. Mahaffy and was presented with a prayer-book, but this emphasis on
duty seemed a little odd until I found the title-page and the author –
Samuel Smiles, LL.D. This George Moore was not a writer, but a whole-
sale merchant and a philanthropist, and here, perhaps, is the real delight
of the book market – nowhere else would one be likely to find the life of a
Victorian draper. And it is rewarding. Smiles deserved his popularity;
there is a bold impressionist vitality about his style; he roughs in very
well the atmosphere of commercial travelling: the astute offer of a
favourite snuff, the calculated jest, the encounters in hotel rooms – the
Union Hotel, Birmingham, and the Star at Manchester, the seedy atmosphere of benevolence – what he calls 'Mr. Moore's labours of love': the
hospital for incurables, the penny bank, the London Porters' Benevolent
Association, the Kensington Auxiliary Bible Society, the Pure Literature
Society (Mr. Moore's favourite book, unlike his namesake's, was *The
Memoirs and Remains of Dr. M'Cheyne*). His oddest philanthropy perhaps
was 'in marrying people who were not, but who ought to have been,
married' – or else his attempt to introduce copies of the Bible into the best
Paris hotels. But Dr. Smiles had more than vigour; he had a macabre if
ungrammatical imagination, as when he describes the end of the first Mrs.
Moore. 'Her remains were conveyed to Cumberland. On arrival at
Carlisle, Mr. Moore slept in the Station Hotel. It seemed strange to him
that while in his comfortable bed, his dead wife should be laying cold in
the railway truck outside, within sight of the hotel windows.'

Macabre – but not quite so macabre as this other book which had lost
half its title-page, but seems to be called *The Uncertainty of the Signs of
Death*. Published in 1746, and illustrated with some grim little copper-
plates, it contains 'a great variety of amusing and well-attested Instances of
Persons who have return'd to Life in their Coffins, in their Graves, under
the Hands of the Surgeons, and after they had remain'd apparently dead
for a considerable Time in the Water'. A scholarly little work, which
throws some doubt upon the story that Duns Scotus 'bit his own Hands
in his Grave', it carries in the musty pages some of the atmosphere of an
M. R. James story – there is an anecdote from Basingstoke too horrible to
set down here which might have pleased the author of *O Whistle and I'll
Come to You*. I was pleased to find a few more details of Ann Green, who
was executed at Oxford in 1650 and was revived by her friends – about
whose resurrection, it may be remembered, Anthony Wood wrote some
rather bad verses – and before laying the book back beside the battered

rown tin trunk which carried the salesman's stock, I noted this recipe for
eviving the apparently dead: 'We ought to irritate his Nostrils by intro-
ucing into them the Juice of Onions, Garlick, and Horse-radish, or the
eather'd End of a Quill, or the Point of a Pencil: stimulate his Organs of
Touch with Whips and Nettles; and if possible shock his Ears by hideous
shrieks and excessive Noises.'

Poor human body which must be clung to at all costs. There is very
ittle light relief in the book market – an old copy of *Three Men on the
Bummel,* that boisterous work, all sobs and horseplay, and a promising
olio out of my reach called simply *The Imperial Russian Dinner Service.*
The smell of mortality, morality, and thrown-out books go together –
nd the smell of the antiquated Metropolitan Line. Here is another
moralist. In *Posthuma Christiana* (1712, price 6*d.*) William Crouch, the
Quaker, laments the Restoration – 'The Roaring, Swearing, Drinking,
Revelling, Debauchery, and Extravagancy of that Time I cannot forget,'
nd a few lines, as I turned the pages, caught the imagination as Blind
Pew once did at the Benbow Inn. He is quoting an account of the Quakers,
hirty-seven men and eighteen women, who were banished to Jamaica.
The Ship was called *The Black Eagle,* and lay at anchor in *Bugby's Hole,*
he Master's name was *Fudge,* by some called *Lying Fudge.*' They lay in
he Thames seven weeks, and half of them died and were buried in the
marshes below Gravesend. 'Twenty-seven survived, and remained on
oard the Ship; and there was one other Person of whom no certain
account could be given.'

That is the kind of unexpected mystery left on one's hands by a morn-
ng in the book market. A storm was coming up behind the gin distillery,
nd the man with the Itching Powder was picking up his labels – trade isn't
ood these days for his kind of bomb. It was time to emerge again out of
he macabre past into the atrocious present.

BOMBING MANŒUVRE

I HAD been reading Halévy's Epilogue to his *History of the Englis*
People on the way to the aerodrome, bumping through the flat, salt
eastern county when the first labourers were going to work; yester
day's posters still up outside the little newsagents which sold odd antiqu
highly coloured sweets; the squat churches surrounded by the graves o
those who had had placid deaths. Halévy is depressing reading, 1895·
1905; the old power politics which have returned today: secret arrange
ments between politicians: words astutely spoken at social gatherings
agreements which were anything but gentlemen's: the sense of middle
aged men with big ideas in a shady racket. One always prefers the ruled t
the rulers, and the servants of a policy to its dictators: this hard-bitter
unbeautiful countryside, this aerodrome – belonging to Eastland – wher·
none of the officers flying the huge camouflaged Wellington bombers wa
over twenty-three.

Presumably the war between Eastland and Westland had the sam·
political background one found in Halévy – human nature does no
change; but the war was on and nothing mattered except careful naviga
tion, so that you descended from the clouds on the right target, and :
delicate hand and eye, so that you did not crash while hedge-hopping ove
a dozen counties at two hundred miles an hour. You could even enjoy
yourself now that the war was on. At tea time a bomber zoomed down and
up, almost brushing (so it seemed to the inaccurate eye) the mess-room
window, making everybody jump – you could shoot the mess up withou
a court martial because it gave practice to the machine-gunners round th
aerodrome in siting an enemy target.

I had not realized the amount of clothes one had to wear; one felt lik·
a deep-sea diver, in overalls, with the heavy shoulder-straps and stee
clamps of the parachute equipment and the inflated waistcoat for saving
one's life at sea, the helmet with the padded earphones and the microphon·
attachment dangling by the mouth with a long flex to be attached to :
point near one's chair. But then this is not the kind of war which entail
much walking; it is a sitting war from which it is impossible to run. Nor
knowing only passenger planes, had I realized the fragile look of the hug·
bombers inside, all glass and aluminium, tubes coiling everywhere, a long

mpty tunnel like a half-built Underground, leading to the rear gun; a
ttle cramped space in front behind the cockpit for the navigator at his
ıble and the wireless operator. In the cockpit you felt raised over the
‑hole world, even your own plane: space between your legs and glass
nder your feet and glass all round, encased in something like the trans-
‑arent bullet-nose of a chlorotone capsule.

Under the feet at first there was water as we drove for half an hour out
ver the North Sea, climbing to 12,000 feet, hands and toes chilling. We
‑ere the leading plane of four, and it was odd up there in the huge din (the
Vellington is the noisiest bomber these pilots have handled), in the
ımense waste of air, to see the pilot use the same trivial gestures through
side window as a man might make signalling to a car behind. Then as an
ıdication to the other pilots that he needed room, he wobbled his plane
nd the whole squadron turned, a lovely movement in the cold clear high
ltitude light: the great green-brown planes sweeping round in formation
ɔwards Westland and the distant inland target.

Then the Blackwater: Gravesend – with the oil tanks like white
ounters on the Tilbury side. Cloud obscured everything, and afterwards
: seemed no time at all before the engines were shut off and each plane in
ırn dived steeply down, cutting through the great summer castles of
loud, and it was Hampshire below. So far no fighter squadron had
ıtercepted us; whether we had been a mark for anti-aircraft guns we
ould not tell, but they had had their last chance. It was low flying from
ow on to the target in Berkshire – with a maximum height of about
oo feet at 200 m.p.h., too low for gunfire; nor could any fighter squadron
ı the upper air observe us as we bumped just above the hills and woods
he same colour as ourselves. Once, miles away, little black flies at perhaps
,000 feet, three fighters patrolled a parallel track and slowly dropped
ehind: we were unspotted. One felt a momentary horror at the exposure
f a whole quiet landscape to machine-gun fire – this was an area for
vacuation, of small villages and farms where children's camps might
ɔossibly be built, and it was completely open to the four aircraft which
wept undetected from behind the trees and between the hills. There was
oom for a hundred English Guernicas.

In an air-liner one does not recognize speed – a Hercules seems slower
han a cross-country train, objects below move so slowly across the
vindow pane at 3,000 feet, but at 200, and we were often at 100 and
ometimes as low as 50, the world really does flash by – county giving
ɔlace to county, one style of scenery to another, almost as quickly as you

would turn the pages of an atlas. We were out of Hampshire, climbing
down so close to the turf that it was like combing a head, up the fore
head and over, into Berkshire, above our target, wheeling round, or
great wing revolving like the sail of a windmill against the bright summe
sky, off again, and five minutes later cutting across a fighter aerodrom
with the planes lined up and the men idling and no chance of taking o
before we were away, driving a lone road home along the Thames, abov
the film studios of North London and back along the flat Dane-drenche
Eastern countries. It must be the most exciting sport in the world, lo
flying, but the bumps are hard on the stomach and I was not the only or
sick – the second pilot was sick, too, and the navigator passed me a
encouraging note – 'not feeling too good myself'.

Over the coast at 100 feet, the popular resort, people resting on th
beach after boarding-house luncheon or taking reluctant exercise on th
pier, and out to sea again, climbing into the comfortable upper air: the
the last turn, the pilot signalling to his squadron, and the four plane
closing up – the sense of racing home. Everybody began to smile, th
navigator packed up his maps and instruments and drawing pins in a bi
green canvas bag, and the Wellingtons drove back in close formation
260 miles an hour. It had been a good day: even if the war had been a re
one, it would still have been a good day – the six-hour flight over, sweep
ing along to the buttered toast and the egg with the tea, and the radi
playing in the mess. Whatever causes a future Halévy might unearth of th
war between Westland and Eastland these men would not be responsib
– action has a moral simplicity which thought lacks.

AT HOME

ONE GETS used to anything: that is what one hears on many lips these days,* though everybody, I suppose, remembers the sense of shock he felt at the first bombed house he saw. I think of one in Woburn Square neatly sliced in half. With its sideways exposure it looked like a Swiss chalet: there were a pair of skiing sticks hanging in the attic, and in another room a grand piano cocked one leg over the abyss. The combination of music and skiing made one think of the Sanger family and Constant Nymphs dying pathetically of private sorrow to popular applause. In the bathroom the geyser looked odd and twisted seen from the wrong side, and the kitchen impossibly crowded with furniture until one realized one had been given a kind of mouse-eye view from behind the stove and the dresser – all the space where people used to move about with toast and tea-pots was out of sight. But after quite a short time one ceased to look twice at the intimate exposure of interior furnishings, and waking on a cement floor among strangers, one no longer thinks what an odd life this is. 'One gets used to anything.'

But that, I think, is not really the explanation. There are things one never gets used to because they don't connect: sanctity and fidelity and the courage of human beings abandoned to free will: virtues like these belong with old college buildings and cathedrals, relics of a world with faith. Violence comes to us more easily because it was so long expected – not only by the political sense but by the moral sense. The world we lived in could not have ended any other way. The curious waste lands one sometimes saw from trains – the crated ground round Wolverhampton under a cindery sky with a few cottages grouped like stones among the rubbish: those acres of abandoned cars round Slough; the dingy fortune-teller's on the first-floor above the cheap permanent waves in a Brighton back street: they all demanded violence, like the rooms in a dream where one knows that something will presently happen – a door fly open or a window-catch give and let the end in.

I think it was a sense of impatience because the violence was delayed – rather than a masochistic enjoyment of discomfort – that made many writers of recent years go abroad to try to meet it halfway: some went to

* October, 1940.

189

Spain and others to China. Less ideological, perhaps less courageous, writers chose corners where the violence was more moderate; but the hint of it had to be there to satisfy that moral craving for the just and reasonable expression of human nature left without belief. The craving wasn't quite satisfied because we all bought two-way tickets. Like Henry James hearing a good story at a dinner-table, we could say, 'Stop. That's enough for our purpose,' and take a train or a boat home. The moral sense was tickled: that was all. One came home and wrote a book, leaving the condemned behind in the back rooms of hotels where the heating was permanently off or eking out a miserable living in little tropical towns. We were sometimes – God forgive us – amusing at their expense, even though we guessed all the time that we should be joining them soon for ever.

All the same – egotistical to the last – we can regard those journeys as a useful rehearsal. Scraps of experience remain with one under the pavement. Lying on one's stomach while a bomb whines across, one is aware of how they join this life to the other, in the same way that a favourite toy may help a child, by its secret appeal, to adapt himself to a strange home. There are figures in our lives which strike us as legendary even when they are with us, seem to be preparing us like parents for the sort of life ahead. I find myself remembering in my basement black Colonel Davis, the dictator of Grand Bassa, whose men, according to a British Consul's report, had burned women alive in native huts and skewered children on their bayonets. He was a Scoutmaster and he talked emotionally about his old mother and got rather drunk on my whisky. He was bizarre and gullible and unaccountable: his atmosphere was that of deep forest, extreme poverty and an injustice as wayward as generosity. He connected like a poem with ordinary life (he was other people's ordinary life): but it was ordinary life expressed with vividness. Then there was General Cedillo, the dictator of San Luis Potosi (all my dictators, unlike Sir Nevile Henderson's, have been little ones). I remember the bull-browed Indian rebel driving round his farm in the hills followed by his chief gunmen in another car, making plans for crops which he never saw grow because the federal troops hunted him down and finished him. He was loved by his peasants, who served him without pay and stole everything he owned, and hated by the townspeople whom he robbed of water for his land (so that you couldn't even get a bath). His atmosphere was stupidity and courage and kindliness and violence. Neither of these men were of vintage growth, but they belonged to the same diseased erratic world as the

ictators and the millionaires. They started things in a small way while
he world waited for the big event. I think of them sometimes under the
avement almost with a feeling of tenderness. They helped one to wait,
nd now they help one to feel at home. Everybody else in the shelter, I
magine, has memories of this kind, too: or why should they accept
iolence so happily, with so little surprise, impatience or resentment?
'erhaps a savage schoolmaster or the kind of female guardian the young
Kipling suffered from or some beast in himself has prepared each man for
his life.

That, I think, is why one feels at home in London – or in Liverpool or
Bristol, or any of the bombed cities – because life there is what it ought to
e. If a cracked cup is put in boiling water it breaks, and an old dog-
oothed civilization is breaking now. The nightly routine of sirens,
arrage, the probing raider, the unmistakable engine ('Where are you?
Where are you? Where are you?'), the bomb-bursts moving nearer and
hen moving away, hold one like a love-charm. We are not quite happy
vhen we take a few days off. There is something just a little unsavoury
bout a safe area – as if a corpse were to keep alive in some of its members,
he fingers fumbling or the tongue seeking to taste. So we go hurrying
ack to our shelter, to the nightly uneasiness and then the 'All Clear'
ounding happily like New Year's bells and the first dawn look at the
vorld to see what has gone: green glass strewn on the pavement (all
roken glass seems green) and sometimes flames like a sticky coloured
late from the *Boys' Own Paper* lapping at the early sky. As for the
ictims, if they have suffered pain it will be nearly over by this time. Life
as become just and poetic, and if we believe this is the right end to the
nuddled thought, the sentimentality and selfishness of generations, we
an also believe that justice doesn't end there. The innocent will be given
heir peace, and the unhappy will know more happiness than they have
ver dreamt about, and poor muddled people will be given an answer they
ave to accept. We needn't feel pity for any of the innocent, and as for the
guilty we know in our hearts that they will live just as long as we do and
o longer.

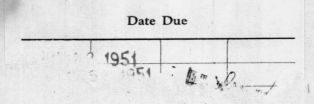